DREAMS OF APPALOOSAS

A LOVE STORY

BY DENNIS HIGMAN

To my wife, Lee, who never doubted we could do it, and her Appaloosa, Happy, who inspired us to see it through.

Cover design by Hiller Higman
Drawings and paintings by Lee Higman

AUTHOR'S NOTE

This is a work of fiction. Although there is a Wisdom, Montana, it bears no resemblance to the town or its people as depicted in this book and there is no Church of the Divine Light Reformed, 7/7 or Windhorse Ranch.

While The Battle of the Big Hole did take place, the real General Howard, known to the Nez Perce as "General Day-After-Tomorrow", was far to the rear and certainly did not die at the hands of Eagle from the Light. The character of Eagle, a legendary chief, like other Nez Perce warriors in this book, is not based on historical fact, only the author's imagination.

What is not fiction, however, is what an early morning walk through the ghostly bare tepee poles that stand along the meandering river at the Nez Perce Big Hole National Battlefield will confirm: this is a magical place, haunted by silent spirits of the Nez Perce women and children who were attacked here by U.S. troops without warning and murdered in the early morning hours of August 9, 1877. And the fact that their thousands of fine Appaloosa horses were stolen, shot, driven off and scattered to the wind, never to return to their ancestral homeland in this life.

"The Nez Perce possess lofty, elegantly formed active and durable horses, pied, with large spots of white irregularly scattered and intermixed with black brown bey or some other dark color."
Meriwether Lewis

"The generality of the Nez Perce horses are much finer than any Indian horses I have yet seen. Fine limbs, rising withers, sloping well back, uncommonly sinewy and sure-footed. I have seen thousands of these horses grazing on the mountain. In one place lodgings of common Indians calling themselves poor have six or seven hundred of them, running from common Cayuses to elegant chargers fit to mount a prince."
Henry Miller, The Oregonian, 1861

"Allison closed her eyes and once again smelled the sage, felt the sun on her back, the warmth of a horse, put her foot in the stirrup and stepped up into a better world, a world of grace and endless possibilities where Tom and Red Coyote were waiting."
Dreams of Appaloosas

PROLOGUE

Wisdom Montana Messenger

July 2, 2007 Special Edition

TOM HOWARD AND SONS LAID TO REST
4<u>TH</u> Generation Rancher and Sons Honored by Friends and Neighbors

Hundreds of mourners turned out yesterday afternoon for the funeral of rancher Tom Howard and his twin sons, Justin and JB Howard. Tom Howard, 52, owner of the Windhorse Ranch and his teenage sons died in a tragic trucking accident on Lost Trail Pass June 28th during a violent thunderstorm in which 14 of their prize winning Appaloosas also perished. The Howards were eulogized and fondly remembered by friends and neighbors as they were laid to rest in the family cemetery in a solemn ceremony presided over by the Reverend William Harper of Grace Episcopal Church in Palo Alto, California, Mr. Howard's friend and pastor of many years there.

The Howard boys were leaders at school and in the community. Justin, 17, was president-elect of his senior class at Wisdom High School and runner-up in the National Junior Rodeo Bull Riding Championships last year. His twin brother, JB, was Captain of the Wisdom High School football team, a starting forward on the basketball team and a National Merit Scholar.

Tom Howard was president of his senior class at Wisdom High in 1973, the valedictorian, and an All State football player. He quarterbacked the team that won a Montana AA football championship, went on to graduate from Stanford University and founded the highly successful micro technology company "Full House" in Palo Alto, California. He had recently retired and returned to Wisdom to start an Appaloosa breeding facility on his Windhorse Ranch after an absence of many years.

Mr. Howard is survived by his oldest brother, Ben Howard, of Wisdom, owner of the family's historic 7/7 Ranch, his wife Allison, a nationally known artist and teacher at Wisdom High School, and their three-year-old son Tristan. Mr. Howard's former wife, Priscilla Baconess, the mother of Justin and JB, remembered here as Queen of the Wisdom Roundup, was unable to attend. She is reportedly in poor health and living in California.

Pall bearers for Mr. Howard included: his brother Ben; Carlos Garcia, foreman of the Windhorse Ranch; his business partner from Palo Alto, California, Mr. Jim Webster; father-in-law, Mr. Fred Garnett, Padua Hills,

California; David Anderson, science teacher at Wisdom High School; and long time Custer County Sheriff, Jim Christian, who played on the championship Wisdom High football team with Mr. Howard. The Howard boys were carried to the family cemetery by members of the Wisdom High football team.

Other dignitaries in attendance included Montana State Senator Hiram Walker, a college classmate of Mr. Howard, and University of Montana President, Dr. Jon Manville, a long time friend.

Sheriff Christian gave the eulogy, remembering Mr. Howard as a friend who was always there when you needed him and a loyal companion in good times and bad. He lamented the loss of the Howard boys, student leaders and fine athletes.

Mrs. Allison Howard concluded the ceremony by reading a poem in tribute to her late husband, titled "On the Wings of Eagles." Halfway through her presentation, she was overcome with grief. The Reverend Harper finished the reading for her. As the caskets were lowered, bagpipers played "Amazing Grace", one of Mr. Howard's favorite tunes.

Mr. Howard and his sons were laid to rest beside his parents, the late Allen and Florence Howard, his grandparents, Ben Howard Senior and wife Melisa, and great grandfather General Zackery Howard, Civil War veteran and hero of the Battle of the Big Hole. General Howard's wife, Carrie, returned to her birth place in Blue

Hill, Maine in her later years and is interred there.

Friends of Mr. Howard and his sons have established a scholarship in their names to send deserving local boys and girls to college. Contributions may be made to the Howard Memorial Foundation c/o Mr. Bill Snipes, President, Wisdom Savings and Loan.

DREAMS OF APPALOOSAS
Chapter One: Montana Nights

The leather bound journal fell silently to the carpeted floor, the black and white Border Collie snuggled closer, a cold lonely wind moaned in the eves. "My Dear Tom, where are you?" was all she'd written. She couldn't keep her eyes open.   Pulling the down comforter tightly around her, Allison Howard drifted into a fitful sleep.

Tom was standing some distance away, staring out over the valley, dressed for travel in his laced high-top Georgia riding boots, long waterproof canvas drover's coat and black felt cowboy hat with a spray of raven feathers in its silver band. So handsome and self assured, it made her ache. Light of her life.

"Look over there," he said with urgency, pointing with one hand and extending the other in an invitation to join him.

"What? Where?" She hurried to him; sharp saw-toothed grass hurt her bare feet. The sun was setting, a

collapsing fiery orange balloon sinking behind the Beaverhead Mountains. Purple shadows gathered. A chill swept over her. How had it changed so quickly?

"Over there, riding the Appaloosa on the ridge."

She saw movement in the fading light, or thought she did; something that might have been. She huddled against him. You could freeze up here at night, even in summer.

"It's Eagle from the Light."

"I can't see him."

"He's there; I've got to talk to him."

She held his arm. "Take me with you."

"I'm sorry." He gently removed her hand. "This is something I have to do alone."

"Don't go. Stay with me."

"I can't, Allie." His intense blue eyes were already far away.

"Please." She hung on the tails of his long riding coat as he swung into the saddle. If she let him go now, he might never come back.

"Don't worry." Tom gave her a familiar pat on the shoulder. He'd made up his mind and was on his way. "I'll always be with you, honey, wherever you are. That's a promise."

"But what about Tristan?"

Allison sat bolt upright, threw off tangled covers and rushed to the adjoining bedroom. Tristan was sleeping peacefully on his side, surrounded by stuffed animals, favorite green fuzzy T Rex cradled in his arms. Relieved, she watched the steady rise and fall of his breathing, kissed him gently on a warm, pink cheek and went back to their bed. The digital clock/radio read 3 a.m., still time to bring Tom back.

They lay in a tangle of discarded blue jeans, underwear, shirts and boots in the hot sun on a thick carpet of meadow grass and wildflowers. He smelled of vanilla aftershave and Black Label. She straddled him; eyes closed, found his mouth with hers, and dug her fingernails into his bare back. "That's it, honey."

Even when they separated, the aftershocks continued to pulse through her body. Side by side, holding hands, breathing hard, slick with sweat, naked bodies streaked with red clay and crushed flowers--- Prairie Smoke, Scarlet Gilia, Bitterroot, Rock Penstemon, Lupine and Paintbrush. He knew them all by name.

A cool breeze washed across her body, soothing and gentle as her lover's touch, sending a delicious shiver of pleasure radiating out from between her legs. The faint jingle of tack from horses grazing nearby came on the breeze.

To her, the correct nomenclature of flowers was irrelevant; they were very different that way. What she cared about was color, shape and design: blue petals ribbed with intricate veins of yellow, orange and black; tiny rose colored leaves curving and twisting like shells on the beach; and her favorite, the delicate Prairie Smoke, pink feathery plumes sweeping across hillsides in the spring, dancing like low hanging smoke on the wind.

"Son of a bitch," he finally said, talking to the clear blue sky, "that wasn't so bad for an old man, was it?"

She laughed, rolling on her hip to face him, the light so intense she had to shade her eyes to see his face. A fly lazily circled over them, buzzing noisily in the high mountain air. Crickets whirred and clicked. "You set the bar pretty high with that one, big boy, and I won't forget it next time."

"What makes you think there'll be a next time?"

He ran a finger along her parted lips. She closed her mouth over the length of it. He kissed one nipple, then the other. The wild, raw smell of sex, blooming sagebrush and ripe musty earth engulfed them. Aroused, she lay back, closed her eyes, ready to give herself to him again and again.

Somewhere a bluebird sang his cheerful song.

Allison turned over in bed and buried her face in the pillow. It smelled of lilacs. "Oh, Tom," she murmured, "Please don't leave me."

————————

But he spurred his horse into a gallop. Desperately, she ran after him, stumbling, falling on the uneven ground, struggling to her feet, but he disappeared over the crest of the hill, and when she got there, he was gone. She fell on hands and knees and cried, rocking from side to side, mourning her loss.

In the valley below, the last rays of sun settled like a spotlight on the ghostly Indian village of bare tepee poles and tattered banners standing vigil over the silvery Big Hole River snaking silently in and out of aspen groves. Their leaves were already turning red and gold and beginning to fall. A cold winter about to descend.

Shivering violently, she got to her feet and turned back, desperately searching for the place where they'd made love. Lost in the gathering darkness. Alone, naked, vulnerable, wandering from unfamiliar place to unfamiliar place.

————————

"I can't let it end like this." Allison struggled against the heavy drag of sleep. The bluebird was silent, the room cold and dark. She had to get back to that peaceful sunny hilltop, recreate the flowers, the sky. But the pieces drifted away and she wandered after them, searching.

———————

"Tom? Where are you?"

No answer. Hooded floodlights glowed in the darkness behind neatly trimmed ivy. The brick quad at Scripps College; she'd crossed it many times.

Stone fountains, marble statuary. Acrid smog hung in the humid Mediterranean air. Palm trees rustling. A low persistent hum from the freeway, steadily pumping life in and out of Los Angeles, regular as a heart beat.

The stucco classrooms and vine covered dorms were dark and silent but lights shone in the art department. Her locker was there with paint clothes and sandals.

Naked, she ran toward the building. Racing up stone steps, trying to remember her locker combination; he came out the double wooden doors, blocking her path. She froze.

"Hello there, I've been looking all over for you."

"You've not supposed to be here." Cringing, sick to her stomach. How could she have been so stupid!

"Says who?" he replied pleasantly, eyes on her breasts. "Come on in. It's just you and me burning the

18

midnight oil like old times."

The same cable knit sweater with leather patches on the elbows, green corduroys and battered penny loafers with no socks. Long gray hair pulled back in a pony tail, peppery stubble on his acne scared face that everyone claimed had been quite handsome in his youth.

"Stay away from me, Lyn!" She struggled to run but couldn't move.

"Oh, that will never happen again." He laughed, flashing an ingratiating smile. "I made a mistake and I'm really sorry, okay?" He reached out to touch her breast.

"You're not allowed to come near me!" He smelled of wine, oil paint and sweet pipe tobacco.

"You haven't got any clothes on," he chuckled, running his eyes over her naked body. "Come on, let's go do it."

"No, Tom will kill you!" Heart pounding, she stepped back.

"Oh, I don't think so, Allison. Tom's dead."

"He's not dead!"

"Oh come on." Grabbing her roughly by the shoulder, he put a grasping hot hand on her thigh. "You still like me; I know you do."

"Stop, goddamn it!"

Fingers probed. She pushed him away. "I never loved you! I hate you! You disgust me!"

"Fucking cunt!" He hit her across the face.

Stunned, tasting blood, she ran across the deserted quad, out the gate, praying her horse would be there. Saved, Happy was waiting. "God, am I glad to see you."

She fumbled with the quick release knot, gathered the reins in one hand, grasped his mane and swung up onto his broad bare back.

"Okay, Happy, let's go." She wheeled the big grey and white spotted Appaloosa in a circle to face him, but Lyn wasn't there. "Coward!"

Riding up the deserted street lined with parked cars at a brisk trot, hooves echoing on the blacktop, past darkened Spanish style whitewashed houses gleaming in the moonlight.

After pausing for the scattered midnight traffic to clear, they galloped across Foothill Boulevard. Tangerine cars weaving around a fire breathing Appaloosa at the full gallop with a tall, long haired, naked, strawberry blond, fair skin and freckles, stretched out on his back.

Cool orange groves led to the mountains, tall wind machines on either side, silent sentinels. Happy's driving rhythm gave her a series of intense sexual climaxes. Giddy with pleasure. An engorged pink clitoris floated over them in a star studded sky.

Flattening her slender body, face on his neck as she'd done so many times as a girl, galloping through the groves, the ripple of hot muscles, his heart pounding between her legs, the sweet musk of horse sweat.

Lights of home and safety, the smell of jacaranda trees and peaceful cooing doves. The pleasure of a barefoot walk across cool red tiles.

A thundering explosion! A massive fire ball!

Happy reared, throwing her violently to the ground. Searing heat, the agonizing cries of men and horses, the smell of burning flesh. "Tom!" Thrashing, struggling, sick with fear, desperate to save them.

_____

"Oh please, God, help my boys."

Something stirred in the darkness beside her. Warm and alive. She turned and looked into the eyes of a red coyote.

_____

Brown eyes flecked with silver and gold. Extraordinarily beautiful, kind, all knowing eyes that understood suffering and death. He sat in silence, watching her in the low mist that rose from the warm soft earth where she lay.

"Oh, hello, Red Coyote." She knew he meant no harm; Tom called them "God's dogs".

He tipped his head inquisitively, ears up, alert. Was he smiling? Tom assured her coyotes didn't smile. She wasn't so sure.

"You'll have to excuse me; I've had an awful, awful night. I've got to get some sleep."

Red Coyote nodded with understanding.

Nightmares, Tom and the twins waving goodbye from the cab of their silver Kenworth, Lyn Barnett leading her into a motel, a sickening skid on the rain soaked highway. The explosion. Endless screams of men and horses.

"Please stay with me," she begged Red Coyote.

He turned and turned, rustling around in dry leaves and finally, with a sigh, plopped down, resting his head on her midriff. She put her hand on his stomach. She was safe.

"Allie, it's me. Wake up."

A hand touched her shoulder. She turned away, annoyed at having her dream interrupted.

"Allie, are you alright?"

She rolled over and looked into emerald green eyes. "Kat?" Intense morning sun streamed through the windows. "What are you doing here?"

Katherine Garnett laughed, throwing that long

mane of red hair back with a graceful gesture. "I was under the impression I had an open invitation, kiddo. I got in late last night."

"No, I mean here, now. What time is it?" She sat up, disoriented, nightgown damp with passion, jaw aching from the blow. Numbing shock, the taste of blood.

"About eight, eight ten to be exact." Stylishly dressed and always beautiful, her sister was ready to ride in Tony Lama snake skin boots, tight fitting Ralph Lauren jeans and a red silk, long sleeved blouse revealing cleavage.

"Where's Tristan?" Cold panic! All she had left in this world. Her only connection to Tom.

"He's okay, Allie. He's down in the kitchen with Afracela, playing with his dinosaurs."

"Sorry, I was afraid I lost him too." The dog, sleeping in the hollow of her stomach, looked up at her with unblinking devil-or-angel yellow eyes. Her Red Coyote. Stay with me.

Kat gave her an appraising look. "Nothing to be sorry about, we're all here, Allie."

"I know, I know." She stroked the dog's head. Soft, silky. "You're a good boy, Mackay." The twins bought him for her at a rodeo in a little Idaho town called Mackay. A squirming puppy, they knew she'd fall in love.

"How about some coffee, kiddo?"

"That would be great, thanks." She swung her legs over the edge of the bed and stood up slowly, weak, shaky.

"You okay?"

"I didn't sleep very well, just give me a minute." Tom leaving her naked and vulnerable; the screams of men and horses, the truck exploding in a fireball; Lyn forcing himself on her. Why had he come back so clearly after all these years?

Kat poured coffee from a silver carafe into the Spode cups with the beautiful pastel flowers Tom's grandmother brought from Chicago. "Let's sit over here by the window and enjoy the scenery."

"Sounds good." The rich smell of coffee filled the room. She retrieved her sheepskin slippers from under the bed where Mackay had dragged them.

Everything was where it should be. Tom's work boots in the corner, his computer and business papers on the roll-top desk, rifles and shotguns locked behind leaded glass doors, polished stocks gleaming in the morning sun. Books they shared and loved lined the walls, Bancroft's History of the West, John James Audubon's Birds of America.

Her nightgown with the red and blue running horses smelled of sex. Would her sister, the Los Angeles County prosecuting attorney, notice? Kat didn't miss much. Allison picked up her journal off the floor and carefully put in on the nightstand.

"Have a seat, kiddo." Kat motioned her toward one of the leather chairs facing the window, handing her a cup of steaming coffee.

This was where she and Tom started their day. From the second story window, the 5,000 acre Windhorse Ranch spread out to the north, Afracela's garden, the corrals, weathered grey barn, green pastures dotted with grazing Appaloosas, and beyond, towering mountain ranges surrounding the Big Hole Valley---the Anacondas, Bitterroots, Pioneers, Beaverheads.

"I never get tired of this view," Kat said.

"Neither do I." A light dusting of early September snow shimmered on the mountains under a fiery blue Montana sky, a color she could never get right. It was going to be an early winter.

Kat reached over and touched her arm. "I didn't mean to ruin your beauty sleep, kiddo, but I heard you thrashing around so I thought I'd better wake you."

"It's okay, I needed waking up." The touch of her big sister's hand steadied her, as it always had. Kat the leader. Captain of the basketball team. They'd won a state championship together in high school. "I was having bad dreams, nightmares."

"Anything you want to share?"

Where to start, how to tell her about the passion and loss? And Lyn. Not now, that would really set Kat off. Later when the time was right.

"Nightmares about the accident?"

"That and everything bad that's ever happened to me---all mixed up. Do you ever have dreams like that?"

Kat shook her head. "No, fortunately all I ever dream about are points of law, closing arguments, mundane stuff." She sampled the coffee. "You know this is really good, better than Starbucks."

"Hard to beat Afracela's coffee, isn't it?" A haze of orange dust rose from the corral. The familiar whistle and cry of the twins working horses. A wild surge of hope. Allison stood up, carefully putting her coffee cup on the window sill, not trusting herself to hold it steady. She'd watched them on so many mornings like this, when the light was pure and the intoxicating smell of sagebrush filled the air.

Kat looked at her intently. "What's going on out there?"

Allison closed her eyes and saw them clearly. Justin in a cutoff T shirt and chaps; JB in his yellow hooded "Wisdom High Football" sweatshirt, red hair flying.

Silence. Time stopped. And in the stillness, an aching love.

"Allie?"

She opened her eyes and blinked. Gone. "I just can't let them go, Kat, I can't."

"Oh, Allie, I'm so sorry." Kat got up and put an arm around her shoulder. "You have to give yourself some time, kiddo; it's only been two months. You've just lost the love of your life, your stepsons, your horses, everyone but Tristan. It'll gradually get better. I know it doesn't seem that way now, but it will."

"I hope you're right." She wanted to throw herself in her sister's arms and weep.

"Look, Allie, it's a beautiful day. Tom wouldn't want us moping around like this and neither would the twins. Why don't you get dressed and we'll go for a ride."

DREAMS OF APPALOOSAS
Chapter Two: Bluebird Days

Chilling screams of men and horses, always there, day and night, awake or asleep. Would they ever go away? Allison slowly hooked her bra and put on a faded pair of Levi boot jeans while Mackay, sitting on his haunches, looked up at her. "I'm glad you're here." She leaned down and gave him a hug, then pulled a navy turtleneck over her head, buttoning an old red plaid flannel shirt over it. Every move was heavy labor; her arms and legs threatening to drag her down. "Oh, God, I'm so tired."

Mackay tipped his head, ears up. "You don't have dreams like that do you? You chase rabbits; you're a lucky boy." She'd watched him, sound asleep, legs twitching, a coyote smile on his face. "Well, come on, we better get moving, Kat's waiting."

Her sister wouldn't accept any excuses, she never had, whether they were playing basketball or putting together Allison's first big art show in Pasadena. And this morning, they'd go riding whether she liked it or not. Allison went over to the vanity and sat down.

Mackay followed, tail wagging.

A mountain bluebird, perched on the window sill behind them, suddenly burst into song. She saw his reflection in the mirror, a startling, electric blue. A picture of happiness. "Nothing gets you down, does it?"

He responded with a renewed burst of trilling.

Allison pulled her strawberry blond hair into a ponytail and carefully fastened the tiny gold horse pendant around her neck that Tom had given her for their second anniversary on a beautiful morning, just like this one.

Her hand lingered on the pendant, turning it over and over in her fingers. "God, I wish you were here, honey. It's going to be one of your spectacular bluebird days."

They'd mounted special bird houses for them on fence posts all over the ranch, facing south to catch the sun. There might be a hundred by now. Who would help her clean them out this fall? They'd always done it together. Messy work, scrub brushes and ammonia that stung her nose, but at the end of the day, a quiet ride home through the glorious reds and yellows of fall in the stillness of a violet dusk.

Tristan was still too young to be of much help, although he'd be good company. Carlos would come with her, of course, but it wouldn't be the same. Tears rose. Loss of their small, everyday routines was what she missed the most. Looking back to catch sight of him, expecting him to be there, the crushing sense of emptiness and sorrow when he wasn't.

Allison wiped away her tears, appraising the face that stared back at her in the vanity, now older and worn. It took her by surprise. The beginning of crow's feet around steady hazel eyes. Smooth skin, pale and drawn, dotted with a spray of freckles across high cheek bones. Lips pressed together, she gingerly ran a hand along her jaw where Lyn Barnett, in that totally unexpected moment of fury and hatred, had shattered it years ago.

A fading memory until last night. Nothing visible, but the slight indentation would always remind her. Come on, let's do it. Goddamn you, stay away from me. Only a dream, but dreams mattered. Why had he come back to haunt her?

The bluebird stopped singing, cocked his head and fixed her with opaque black eyes. "I know, I'm working on it." She applied a tinted sunscreen to her face. "That's better, don't you think?"

Another song. "I take it that's a yes."

They'd been so happy. Two lucky people who somehow met each other in a crowded world of strangers and found they shared a dream. "I won't let it go," she murmured. "That's a promise."

The bird hopped restlessly back and forth across the window sill, making tiny scratching noises. "Okay, relax." What was he trying to tell her, or was he just being a bluebird? He lived in a world of incredible beauty, color and rich design impossible to duplicate. "If you'll sit still for me, I'll try to do a decent portrait of you, Mister, but not today."

A classic shape, color would be the problem. Turquoise or phthalo blue? She'd found a tiny bluebird feather once that looked dull grey but when turned to the sun, the leading edge became a shimmering blue fire. Could she somehow capture that?

Allison gave her face a final appraisal and stood up to pull on the tall black riding boots Tom had custom made for her on her 37th birthday. It felt good to have them on.

Mr. Bluebird watched and waited. "You better hit the road yourself, pal. In case you haven't noticed, it's time to head south." Or was it west? Tom would know. With a silent flick of wings, the bluebird launched off the window sill into his new day full of possibilities. Sadly, she watched him go, his tiny darting form quickly blending into the vast blue of the Montana morning sky.

She took one last look around the room they'd shared for five wonderful years, their romantic hideaway. Loath to leave its comfort, she hesitated, stopping at Tom's desk and, with her forefinger, traced the cross and each raised silver letter on his black granite paper weight reading "FAITH AND COURAGE", just as he had every morning. A gift from his good friend Reverend Harper after Priscilla left him with the twins. Tom said it saved his life. Maybe it would save hers.

"Come on, Mackay, let's find Kat and get this day started, shall we?"

The dog followed her down the quiet hallway, a reassuring presence at her heel. Narrow wooden stairs warped by a century of hot summers and freezing winters creaked under her boots. As they passed the cavernous living room, last remnant of the original homestead, she saw Kat looking at the painting she'd left on the fireplace mantel.

Mackay ran to greet her. Allison followed.

"Who is this anyway, Allie?"

"Eagle from the Light, a Nez Perce war chief."   Up on the ridge, riding the Appaloosa, see him?

"Wonderful name."

"Yes, it is." A blaze of basic colors---vivid blues, yellows, greens, and reds, thick and vital, like the man sitting straight and tall on his Appaloosa in a blood red blanket coat, bare legged, head shaved, face a mask of ochre and black, long feathered lance at the ready in one hand, war club dangling from the other.

"I'm serious, kiddo. This is great. I feel his power and intensity; it's remarkable."

"Thanks. I'm glad you like it." Kat had a good eye for art.

"So what's the story with this guy? Why does he look so hell bent on mayhem?"

"Because Tom's great grandfather killed his family, burned them alive in their tepees at the Battle of the Big Hole, along with a lot of other women and children."

The heirloom grandfather clock clanged out the hour like a fire bell. A jarring death knell that echoed the length of the long narrow room with its rough planked floors and brown cracked leather furniture.

"Jesus, Allie, I thought he was a hero. That's the old boy over there, isn't it?" Kat pointed to the full length photograph of the General that hung on darkened log walls among other grim, sepia toned Howard family photographs---long bearded men, wasp-waisted women, and stoic unsmiling children.

"That's him, General Zackary Howard. History may call him a hero, but he was a mass murderer, and he built this ranch right over the unmarked graves of his victims."

"You're kidding. I thought the battlefield was a monument next to your ranch."

"It used to be on the ranch, but Tom's father donated the site to the federal government. It's a National Monument now."

They went to take a closer look at the General in full dress uniform, curly, shoulder length hair, arms crossed, sheathed sword at his side. One knee-high booted foot on a raised dais, General Howard stared at them arrogantly.

Kat leaned closer. "My God, look at those eyes."

"What about them?"

"They remind me of a guy I'm prosecuting in LA, a drug dealer, a stone cold killer. He's got eyes just like that, blank, like a shark."

"Well, you've got that right."

"So why have you put these two together?" Kat asked.

"Because this is where Eagle killed him."

"The General? I thought he was killed during the fighting."

"No, it was long after the war was over. Eagle rode all the way from Canada where he was hiding and galloped in here on his Appaloosa and ran the old boy through with a lance while he was eating dinner with his wife. It's in the family history."

"Jesus, that must have been quite a scene. What happened to his wife?"

"He didn't touch her. Unlike the Army, Eagle had a sense of honor. He came back to kill the man responsible for murdering his family and that's exactly what he did."

Kat had turned and was examining the double doors at the back of the room.

"And in case you're wondering, yes, a horse will fit, Tom measured them."

Kat shook her head. "I knew there was something I never liked about this room."

"That's probably because everything that's wrong

with the Windhorse is in here." She pointed to the dusty heads of trophy animals gunned down over the years by the Howards. "It was built on a culture of violence and death." Glassy eyed mountain lions, Bighorn sheep, pronghorn antelope, deer, elk, buffalo and a gigantic moose head looked down on them. "Tom and I were going to get rid of a lot of this stuff but we never got around to it."

Kat went back to the painting. "Well, this is a good addition. You've done a great job of giving Eagle back his dignity---and a place of honor."

"I hope so, I did my best. I also wanted to put some color and life in this room."

"You've certainly done that. So whatever happened to him?"

"They hung him in the town square."

"Just like that?"

"The same day. A dentist cut off his head and put the skull on display in his office."

"That's barbaric."

"Yes, it is, but it's pretty typical of how we treated the Nez Perce. They were a proud independent people, breeders of fine horses who literally saved Lewis and Clark from starvation. We repaid them by breaking every treaty, forcing them off their ancestral lands and penning them up like cattle on reservations."

"So they rebelled." Kat put her hands on her hips and looked from the painting of Eagle to General

Howard.

"Some did, mostly small bands led by chiefs like Joseph, Looking Glass, White Bird and Eagle from the Light. There were only about 750 of them, a few hundred warriors at most, but the rest were women, children and old people. They fought the good fight against the army for 1,700 miles, trying to get to Canada."

"But they didn't make it."

"No, they fell fifty miles short of the Montana border north of the Big Paw Mountains. They were freezing and starving; it was hopeless. Joseph surrendered with his famous 'I will fight no more forever' speech. A few like Eagle escaped. General Howard promised Joseph they could go home, but instead herded them off to prison camps in Kansas where most died of disease and starvation. We basically tried to exterminate them. The injustice of it all breaks my heart."

"I know it does, Allie. It's one of the things I admire most about you, your passion for justice."

"You have that passion too, Kat."

"Had. I think I buried it somewhere along the way."

"That's not true. You're the most compassionate person I know. Come on, this is depressing me, let's get out of here." She took Kat's arm and led her into the warm hallway leading to the kitchen. "You know, sometimes I'd like to burn that horrible room to the ground, but unfortunately, it would take the rest of the house with it."

"You wouldn't want to do that, Allie, this is a marvelous place. You and Tom have transformed it into something wonderful."

The spacious remodeled kitchen with its skylights, commercial gas range, walk-in refrigerator and gleaming copper cookware, was a warm intimate space filled with light, love and fond memories, everything the living room was not.

Here amidst the smells of coffee, bacon and the clatter of pots and pans, Tom and the twins boisterously made pancakes every Sunday, watching NFL football on the big screen, cheering while they cooked. To overcome the haunting emptiness, Allison was lining the walls with paintings of their life together.

Kat went straight to them. "My God you've been turning out a lot of really good work in the last two weeks, Allie. These are fabulous."

"Do you think so?"

"Yes, I do. I'm very impressed, particularly under the circumstances. Where do you find the time?"

"At night when I can't sleep." Gripped by a creative fever beyond control. "It keeps them close and it gives me hope. Do you know what I mean?"

"Of course, I do. They're filled with love and joy."

"Yes, they are."

Tristan's faint laughter came drifting through the open window, pure and uplifting. She needed to hold him, feel his face against hers, drink in his smell. "Do you want something to eat before we go riding?"

"No, I'm fine; Afracela said she packed us a lunch. Hey, I really do love this one."

"So do I." Tristan in short pants and oversize Stanford T shirt on Tom's shoulders, clutching his favorite green dinosaur with Keith, Tom's Appaloosa, beside them. A crystal blue sky, warm sun, freshly cut hay, chirping birds, rattling crickets and the gentle sigh of wind roaming down the valley like a living thing.

"Father and son. A couple of handsome devils."

"They are, aren't they?" The crushing pain would be unbearable if she lost the ability to imagine them as they were, vibrant and alive.

"And these guys, the "Windhorse Gang", they look friendly enough."

Tom and the red-headed twins in cowboy shirts, blue jeans and boots in front of the ranch gate, six shooters strapped on for dramatic effect. Justin and JB in tall white Hoot Gibson cowboy hats and Tom in his trademark black hat with the spray of raven feathers in its silver band. Behind them, Buddhist prayer flags on gate posts framed the snow covered Beaverhead Mountains.

"Not a mean bone in any of them." Boys already as tall as their proud father, arms around each other in an eternal embrace.

"What are you going to do with all these, Allie? You're running out of space."

"I don't know." They'd brought the prayer flags back from their honeymoon in Nepal. A flapping blizzard of reds, greens and whites flying at the top of high mountain pass where howling winds tore them asunder, scattering prayers the length and breadth of the Himalaya. A powerful demonstration of man's indomitable spirit and faith. Such a memorable time. Numbing cold, light-headed, gasping for breath in thin air.

When she found remnants of the flags around the ranch, she saved them for Tristan in a metal box. Someday, when he was older, they would take them out and she would tell him about prayers that rode on the wind.

"I'll bet your gallery in Cambria would love to have some of these."

"Probably, but that's not why I paint them. They're not for sale." She turned away to hide her tears and went to the refrigerator.

"I'm sorry, Allie. I didn't mean the ones of Tom and the boys. I was thinking more about the landscapes, like this one, "Horse Heaven Hill"."

"Especially not that one." Ten black and brown Appaloosas grazing on a purple hill that curved with the earth under puffy green and white clouds marching across an aqua marine sky. Horses on a hill of dreams. The hill where Tristan was conceived.

"I've upset you. I didn't mean to do that; I'm only trying to help."

"I know you are, Kat, but I feel their presence when I paint and every time I look at the paintings. It's like they're with me and the accident never happened." She took out some carrots for Happy and began cutting them up on the side board, hot tears running down her cheeks.

"I understand. I didn't realize."

Allison wiped the tears away and turned to her sister. "It's alright. You know we could ride up there today if you'd like, it's a beautiful spot." Balanced on the knife edge between earth and sky where anything was possible.

"That would be great. I've upset you, haven't I? I wasn't thinking; I'm really sorry." Kat came over and hugged her.

"There's nothing to be sorry about, absolutely nothing. I'm just so grateful for every minute you're here."

"I'll always be here for you, Allie."

"Oh, Kat, that means more to me than you'll ever know. Come on, let's say hello to Tristan and go for that ride."

Allison led the way through the mud room and picked up Tom's canvas drover coat, smelling of hay, horses and his vanilla aftershave.

"Why are you taking a coat?"

"Because you never know about mountain weather this time of year. You better grab one too."

———————

Despite the hot sun, the morning air was chilly. A cottontail rabbit bolted across the lawn; Mackay gave chase. Allison looked to the corrals, hoping for a miracle, but they stood empty, silent. She stopped.

"Did you forget something, kiddo?"

"No, I was thinking about the twins and how much I miss them." Justin and JB, their voices so real.

"So do I; they were wonderful boys."

Tristan ran towards her, bowlegged in his Oshkosh overalls, Tom's old mixed breed sheep dog, Dotty Girl, right behind him, limping along.

"Mommy! Mommy!"

She picked him up as he charged into her open arms, twirled him around and kissed him on both cheeks. "Good morning, honey, it's so good to see you." Fresh and clean, her blond hair, Tom's sky blue eyes.

"So do I get a kiss too?" Kat stepped forward.

Dotty Girl growled protectively, hair up on the back of her neck.

"I don't think she likes me."

"It's not that, she's just doing her job. It's okay,

Dottie, she's family. Give Aunty Kat a good morning kiss, Tristan."

He did, then twisted in Allison's arms and shouted "pumpkins," pointing to Afracela in the garden.

"Wow, let's go see them." Heavier each time she picked him up; learning new words every day.

"I was a big help."

"I'll bet you were." Tom would be so proud.

"Mornin', Mrs."

"Good morning Afracela. Thanks for taking care of Tristan, I'm afraid I overslept." She put him down.

"We get up early and go to work so you can sleep."

"Well, I really appreciate it."

Afracela Garcia. Short, solid, reassuring, a deeply lined brown face that lit up when she smiled. Her shiny hair, tied back in a bun, ink black despite her age. A monumental little woman in a flowing yellow, green and purple peasant dress; red roses stitched on the cuffs and neck line, her Coat of Many Colors.

"Carlos he bring the horses around; lunch is there." She pointed to the saddle bags on the ground.

"Thanks. I don't know what I'd do without you two."

Permanent fixtures at the ranch since Tom's father picked them up hitch hiking on a bitterly cold night fifty years ago, heading south after picking apples in Washington State. Afracela was fifteen and pregnant. He brought them home, gave them work, built them a cottage, sent their five children to college and left the cottage and ten acres to them in his will. Allison regretted never knowing Tom's parents.

This fantastic garden was Afracela's creation, a riot of colors, smells and sounds, purple cabbages, tall green corn stalks with silky tassels, giant yellow sunflowers, the smell of mint mingled with sagebrush, a cacophony of twittering, chattering blackbirds, robins, magpies, and darting swallows. A painting for tonight.

Afracela in her Coat of Many Colors, rooted and entwined in vines, vegetables and flowers. An eternal garden flowing across the landscape.

Red headed Cassin's finches crowded Tom's "bird condo," a multilayered feeder on a high metal pole in the center of the garden. The barn cat, Tiger, crouched at the base, following the chirping birds with patient eyes.

The sound of trotting horses echoed on dry ground, hollow rhythmic thumps growing louder as they came around the corner of the barn. Carlos in the lead on her Appaloosa mare, Moon Woman, trailing her blind Happy Horse, and Tony, a bay American Saddlebred they kept for guests. Mackay was herding them along but broke off, rushing over to greet her.

"So did that little rabbit get away?" He leaned against her leg, panting hard, pink tongue hanging low. She gave him a pat.

The old Mexican wheeled the horses around smartly, brought them to a stop, swung one leg over the saddle horn and slid gracefully to the ground in one fluid motion. "Buenos dias, senoras, good day to ride."

"Yes, it certainly is." Allison gave him a traditional Mexican abrazo and a kiss on each unshaven, dusty cheek. He submitted, but this wiry little man, flowing white hair sprouting out from under a battered blue Dodger's baseball cap, was all hard edges, a man more in tune with horses than people. Without Tom, any chance they had of rebuilding their Appaloosa herd rode squarely on his shoulders.

"Good morning, Carlos." Kat extended her hand. "It's good to see you again."

"The pleasure is mine, senora." He put his calloused hand over hers in a rare gesture of intimacy.

Her fair skinned, red haired, six foot sister dressed to the nines and seventy-year-old Carlos Garcia, ageless Mayan face and obsidian eyes, faded denim shirt, tan work pants, and hand tooled vaquero boots decorated with red and green snakes. What a contrast.

Carlos on a pyramid under a blue velvet sky, naked to the waist, red and green snakes wrapped around his chest, a headdress of power feathers---eagle, parrot, flicker, American kestrel, raven, Merlin Falcon .

The old Mexican turned to Tristan. "You ready to ride, hijo?"

"On Happy Horse?"

"On the Happy Horse." He effortless hoisted the boy onto the gelding's bare back. "You hold tight," he said, showing him how to grip the horse's mane.

Her grey and white spotted Appaloosa nickered and looked back at them with unseeing milky eyes.

"I remember when you were just a colt in Padua Hills," Kat said. "Do you remember me?" His ears stood up. "He looks great, Allie."

"He's a wonderful horse, always has been." Big and imposing, galloping through the orange groves on moonlit nights, carrying her safely home.

"Good horse," Carlos patted him affectionately on the neck.

"Hey, Happy heart." Allison held out a handful of carrots. The Appaloosa took them with soft deft lips. Her best friend and companion since she was fourteen; his eyes were soft brown then. "You have a nice ride with Carlos, honey. Aunty Kat and I will be back in a while."

"But I want to go for a ride with Daddy!"

"Not today," she stammered. Too young to understand. "You go with Carlos and Happy." She leaned against her horse, holding onto his neck for support. "Take good care of my boy," she whispered.

"You go now, Mrs." Carlos gently pulled her away, handing the reins to Tristan. "Okay, hombre, now we ride like the cowboys, eh!"

DREAMS OF APPALOOSAS
Chapter Three: The View from Horse Heaven Hill

"Hey, girl, how you doing?" Exhilarated by the fresh morning air, determined to leave the night behind, Allison swung up on Moon Woman. The high stepping white Appaloosa with a heavy spray of rusty red and black spots was a foundation mare for the Howard line with all the traits they were looking for---confirmation, intelligence, endurance and the indomitable spirit of the original breed.

Kat was up on Tony. "Ready when you are."

"Well then, let's go." Allison waved goodbye to Tristan, backlit by hazy golden sunlight, an idyllic scene, one of hundreds of images that would remain forever fixed in her mind. "I love you, honey, have a good ride."

She started down the drive with a gentle touch of her boot, hardly necessary as Moon Woman, trained by Carlos, anticipated her every wish. "That man doesn't whisper to horses," Tom said, "he actually carries on long conversations with them."

Allison surrendered to the easy rolling flow of the mare. Tom was right; everything looked better from the back of a horse. The horses hooves crunched on the curving gravel drive covered with yellow poplar leaves. Mackay dashed ahead, chasing fat ground squirrels that popped up in front of him and, just as quickly, ducked back into their holes. The descending winter would soon drive them underground; she'd miss them.

A worm fence zigzagged along either side. The Howards had used this traditional style for generations, five split rails joined by alternately stacking one on the other, a structure of simple, practical beauty. Even the ranch gates were built without hardware.

Allison reached down and gave the mare a reassuring pat. She was there at Moon Woman's birth, a thrilling, anxious moment watching tiny black hooves emerge from the birth canal after hours of false starts, followed quickly by her white head, neck and spotted withers. A miracle.

A tiny, perfectly formed, long legged colt, delicate as porcelain, leaning against the sculpted bulk of her proud mother, fiery red patterns on her hindquarters. Looking on, the legendary stallion Shadowcatcher covered with a hail of black stars as if painted for war.

They reached the outer pasture and the yearlings, a flowing mass of earthy colors, manes flying, galloped down the fence line to greet them, led by Keith, Tom's powerful, brown, white and red spotted Appaloosa. He skidded to a stop directly in front of them, head and tail held high.

"That's still the most spectacular animal you have on the place," Kat said in admiration. "He's in your painting. Keith, right?"

"That's right. Tom's first love. Tristan and I come in a close second."

"I doubt that."

"I don't, but it's okay. We both feel the same way about horses."

Keith whirled in a tight circle, kicked up his heels and tracked them, light-footed, alert. Mackay ran with him, barking, careful to stay out from under his hooves.

"That's an odd name for a horse."

"Tom named him after Keith Richards, his favorite guitarist."

"You mean as in the Rolling Stones? Richards isn't an Indian, is he?" Kat laughed easily. They stopped, watching Keith charge up and down the fence, putting on a showy display, rolling his wild eyes.

"I doubt it. Tom bought him from a Nez Perce up in northern Idaho before we met. Keith was his first Appaloosa. He was trained as a roping horse, but Tom just likes to turn him loose on a flat piece of ground and let him fly. God, he loves that horse."

Keith executed another skidding stop and turned to face her, blowing hard. Allison leaned over the saddle horn. "Hey, take it easy, big boy, settle down, I miss him too." He was calm with Tom, almost serene.

The yearlings milled around. Keith turned on them,

ears flat, cutting out the fillies and driving the colts off until they were a comfortable distance away.

"So he's not the daddy of all these boys and girls?" Kat said, eyeing him closely.

"No, unfortunately he was a gelding when Tom bought him. We're still looking for the right stallion."

"He's very possessive of the girls, isn't he?"

Allison smiled. "He's "pride cut", gelded late; a lot of stallion blood still runs in his veins."

"Well, he's a fine looking horse, that's for sure. Do you ever ride him?"

"No, he's way too much for me," Allison nudged Moon Woman into a trot.

Keith ran with them to the far corner of the pasture worn down to bare dirt with his incessant, restless pacing. He whinnied loudly, throwing his head, as they rode off.

Tom wouldn't want her to leave him cooped up like this for long. One day soon, she'd work up the courage to ride him and let him run for the sheer joy of it.

It would be a glorious painting. *Keith bursting out of a blinding sun, flying with eagles, thundering across lemonade rivers in a rainbow spray, galloping down steep slopes in an avalanche of multicolored gum drops.*

"Is that Horse Heaven Hill over there?" Kat asked.

"That's it." A sacred place above it all where someday she would stay with Tom forever.

"The name fits."

"Yeah, it's sort of like being in heaven." Where all things are possible.

They rode under the Windhorse Ranch header Tom had carved and hung the week they got back from their honeymoon. The colorful prayer flags, decorated with stylized windhorses, fluttered and snapped in the breeze. Everything but a prayer wheel. If they'd had one, their life might have turned out differently.

A flash of wings above Horse Heaven Hill. Spirits riding the wind.

"What are you looking at?"

"A golden eagle."

"Where?"

"About eleven o'clock, circling the hill. See him?"

"Yeah! Wow, he's impressive."

"Tom always said he wanted to come back as an eagle."

Kat nodded, shading her eyes. "Wouldn't that be great."

Just beyond her reach. She nudged the mare into a trot, then a canter.

"Is this a race?" Kat pulled alongside.

"I don't want to lose him." Moon Woman coiled under her. "I need to get up there."

"Go ahead; we'll be along."

"See you at the top." She turned her loose. They galloped across a shallow creek in a sheet of silver spray. "Let's go, girl, let's go." A pair of mallards erupted into the air with a squawking protest. Mackay veered off to give chase.

Charging up the steep narrow trail, she hung on, feet locked under Moon Woman's belly, stealing a look skyward now and then until they reached that magical point where earth fell away and the whitish-blue sky faded into the endless vault of eternity. Only an eagle could take you there.

Allison reined in. With a shrill keening cry, he swooped past, wings so close they brushed her face; hope shot through her. Moon Woman jumped, but didn't bolt. "Easy, girl."

He soared out over the valley, wings spread wide, rising steadily on an updraft that effortlessly carried him higher. "Don't go, stay with me."

By the time Kat and Mackay arrived, she'd dismounted and was still watching the eagle as he grew smaller and smaller. Tony, blowing and snorting, was streaked with sweat. Mackay flopped on the ground beside him, panting hard.

"Well, I haven't had that much fun in years," Kat announced. Getting no response, she dismounted and walked over to Allison. "That was quite the ride, kiddo."

"I'm sorry I left you like that."

"No problem. I see you found your eagle."

"I did. Isn't he beautiful?" Hanging motionless on a current of air.

"Yes, he is. It's good to see you smile again, Allie."

"You too."

They carried the saddlebags to the crest of the hill. The Big Hole Valley spread out below, the river twisting and turning in and out of red and yellow aspens. Black Angus grazed on yellowing hay stubble. A pair of ravens circled in the cobalt sky; the eagle floated high above them. She longed to be with him.

Allison spread Tom's coat on the ground, canvas side down, and motioned Kat to sit beside her. The worn red, white and green stripped Hudson Bay lining was warm, stirring powerful memories.

An exhausted Mackay curled up next to her, put his head on her leg and promptly fell asleep. The lush high mountain meadow was dying. Faded flowers rustled like tissue paper in the breeze. Soon, brutally cold winds would sweep over the summit; everything would be buried under drifting snow. The prospect of a winter alone frightened her.

Allison poured coffee. To her surprise, Kat took out a cigarette and lit it with a gold lighter. "I thought you were going to quit."

"I did. So that's the Memorial by the river?"

"That's it. The next time you come, we'll go down there; it's a magical place." She pulled Tom's binoculars out of her saddle bag. "Here, take a look."

Kat braced her elbows on crossed legs, squinting into the binoculars, cigarette dangling from her lips.

"That's where the Nez Perce were camped, sleeping

peacefully when the General attacked just before dawn. He took them completely by surprise. The soldiers waded across the river and started shooting. It was a massacre."

The eagle swooped low over the river, tracking along the abandoned village.

"It's really eerie, all those bare tepee poles but nobody there." Kat lowered the binoculars and took her cigarette out of her mouth. "It's a reproduction of the place, right? Those couldn't be the originals."

"No, but the placement is supposed to be authentic. The tribe comes every year and holds a ceremony. I hear it's quite a show."

"You've never gone?" Kat ground out her cigarette in the dirt.

"No, what would I say? 'Hi, I'm related to the guy who slaughtered your relatives'."

"I can see how that might be awkward."

"Actually I like to go when it's just Tom, me and the river." She handed her sister a sandwich and took one for herself. The eagle was an indistinct blur in the arc of blue sky.

"This is beautiful." Kat threw her head back to catch the sun.

"Beautiful and haunted. There were probably a thousand Appaloosas down there that day. Their ghosts still roam these hills, and the first time we walked the river, I heard the murdered women and children calling out to me. I really did."

Kat sampled her sandwich, looking out over the valley. "I don't doubt it, Allie. I guess I missed out on the imagination gene, or I lost it somewhere back in law school."

"Or I got more than my share." Allison put her hand on Kat's arm.

"I'm not putting you down, Allie."

"I know you're not." Kat had flown over most weekends since the accident; she'd be lost without her.

"It's just that I can't manage to conjure up spirits of Indians and Conquistadors on an LA freeway while I'm doing seventy in four lanes of traffic; do you know what I mean?"

"Sure, that would be hard."

"It's probably a lot easier out here where things haven't changed all that much."

"Probably."

Kat finished her sandwich. "That was good. All this exercise and fresh air gives me one hell of an appetite."

Side by side, they watched Moon Woman and Tony graze. Allison looked across the river towards the ridge above the tree line where Tom saw Eagle from the Light in her dream. Veins of yellow rock slashed with grey-black granite glowed in the afternoon sun.

Kat finally broke the silence. "So you and Tom came here often?"

"Yes, it's our favorite spot." Where it all began and

would someday end.

"I can see why."

Mackay barked and they both stood up. "Who's that?" Kat asked, shading her eyes.

A man on horseback was coming up the hill at a gallop, clods of dirt arching out behind him. "Looks like Ben, Tom's brother." Mackay backed up against her and growled. She grabbed his collar. Ben Howard did not like dogs.

He reined in directly in front of them, turning the head of his big sorrel sharply. "Seen any strays, ladies?" He stared down at them with cold eyes.

"No, we haven't," Allison replied evenly. She didn't like the way he treated horses. His mount was in a lather and breathing in short gasps.

A big man with grey, tangled, shoulder length hair and a square, beefy, unshaven wind-burned face. Hatless, he wore a dirty Levi jacket, shotgun chaps that came to his knees, and high boots with spurs.

"Some calves gone missin'. Found their mommas, but no babies. Think a pack of coyotes got um." He patted the butt of the rifle in his saddle scabbard. "Or a wolf."

"Maybe they're mixed in with that herd across the river," Allison suggested hopefully. Did he know about Red Coyote?

He stood in the stirrups and stretched. "Just come from there," he replied dismissively, turning his head to spit a steam of brown tobacco juice over his shoulder.

Kat stepped forward. "Katherine Garnett." She extended a hand. "We met at the funeral."

He nodded. "Yeah, the sister." He took her hand and held it.

"Yes," she replied coolly.

Ben stared hard at Kat for a moment as if trying to remember something and then released her, turning to Allison. "Better tell that old Mexican to get them Indian ponies in close tonight, it's gonna snow hard."

"Thanks for the warning."

"All part of the service." He touched his forehead in a mock salute. "You gotta pay attention to the weather this time of year."

"I'm aware of that." Ben had always made her profoundly uneasy.

"Be over to see you soon and talk ranch business."

"Alright."

"Gotta go." He jerked his protesting horse around and spurred off down the hill as suddenly as he came.

"Mr. Personality," Kat commented dryly. "What's his problem, anyway?"

"Oh, lots of things I guess. Tom said he's been upset ever since their folks divided the ranch and left half to Tom. Apparently, it took Ben completely by surprise."

"Why should that have surprised him? They're brothers. What did he expect?"

"Well, by then Tom was long gone, living in California and doing well. Ben had always managed the place and was the older brother, so I think he assumed the ranch would all go to him---that it was his birthright."

A cold breeze swept across the hilltop. The horses stamped their feet impatiently, sensitive to the incoming weather.

"Jesus, Allie, this isn't the Bible; that's ridiculous."

"That may be, but you shouldn't underestimate the importance people put on keeping a legacy ranch intact out here. Anyway, Tom didn't want to upset Ben, so he let him manage the 7/7 and the Windhorse as one ranch and stayed out of the way."

"So nothing really changed."

"No, not until Tom and I got married and decided to come back here and breed Appaloosas. Needless to say, Ben wasn't very happy about that."

She looked to the sky. The eagle was gone. White lenticular clouds were piling up over the Bitterroots, layers on a wedding cake, a sure sign of turbulent weather on the way. "He was trying to buy us out when the accident happened. He's still running his cattle on both places, and now he's pushing me harder than ever to sell."

"Don't let him bully you, Allie. Tell him you're not selling and the management arrangement is terminated. There's nothing in writing, is there?"

"No, but it's not that simple. Our accountant told me I should wait until the estate is settled and I get Tom's life insurance money before I change things. The hay and cattle generate a lot of income."

Kat looked at her sharply. "The life insurance people haven't paid you yet? Are they contesting the claim?"

"I don't think so." She began to gather up her things and sent Mackay off to bring in the restless horses. "They said it's in process. Come on, let's go; I'm getting cold."

"It's been two months, Allie. This is a very straight forward situation. I'll call them when I get home and find out what's going on."

"You don't have to do that." A shiver ran through her. The light had gone flat. Acknowledging the slow moving machinery of death would destroy any fragile hope she had left.

"I know, but it's something I can do for you." Kat paused. "And while we're on the subject, let me ask you something else and don't take this the wrong way. Have you seriously considered you might be better off selling this place and moving back to California with Tristan?"

"I'm not going to do that, Kat." She faced her sister; the cold wind sent dust devils whirling around them. "This is our dream---to honor the Nez Perce by bringing back the Appaloosas in all their glory and creating a sanctuary where they can run wild and free."

"That's a huge undertaking, Allie. You've lost some

of your best horses and you've got Tristan to think about."

"I am thinking about Tristan. And Tom and the twins. And everything we've worked for and planned together." She felt herself faltering. "I can do it. I have the resources, and I'm going to see it through."

Kat took her in her arms. "You're a brave woman, kiddo, I'm very proud of you."

"Oh, not so brave, Kat." She rested her head on her sister's shoulder and let the tears come. "Last night I dreamed Tom and I were right here on this hill, making love, and then he was gone. I ran after him but I couldn't find him."

Kat pulled her close. "I'm so sorry, Allie, I know it's painful."

"I can't get the nightmares out of my head, Kat, no matter how hard I try. I keep seeing his truck go over that cliff and explode in a ball of fire. I hear Tom, the twins and our horses screaming and screaming. It's terrifying. I think about it every day, and I dream about it every night. I feel so alone."

"You're not alone, Allie. I'm right here with you." Kat took Tom's coat from Allison and held it out. "Here, put this on; you're shaking." Kat helped her button it up to her chin.

"Thanks."

"Come on, lean on me; I'll warm you up. That's what woke you up this morning, isn't it?"

"Yes, and there's more. I was back in college and Lyn was there, trying----trying to----it all seemed so real."

"Lyn Barnett?"

"Yes."

Kat stepped back, holding her by both shoulders. "Now you listen to me, that son of a bitch is history, over and done with a long time ago." There was a hard edge to her voice.

"But why would I dream about him now?" Allison wiped her tears away with the back of her hand.

"Because you've been through hell and that's bound to trigger all kinds of bad stuff." Kat released her.

"You think that's it? I feel so guilty just dreaming about him."

"That's bullshit, Allie; you've got nothing to be guilty about. You're just feeling overwhelmed with Tom and the twins gone. You're a strong woman, you'll make it through this."

"I don't feel very strong."

"But you are, and corny as it sounds, you know what they say about how time heals all wounds."

"I hope to God that's true." Kat handed her Moon Woman's reins and they mounted their horses. Mackay barked and ran ahead.

"Do you think Ben was right about the snow?" Kat asked, glancing at the darkening sky. "It's a little early, isn't it?"

"Not necessarily."

Kat reached over and took her hand. "Lyn Barnett is gone for good, kiddo. He won't be back. Don't give him another thought, okay?"

"I'll try." Tom's heavy coat warmed her, a strong protective shield. Allison held his gold horse pendant. He was close.

DREAMS OF APPALOOSAS
Chapter Four: Over the Rainbow

A cowgirl in purple buckskin splashed with pink stars, long blond hair flying, riding her Appaloosa, a smear of spots and splashes---brick red, chocolate brown, creamy white, school bus yellow---galloping across an aqua marine sky on a road of white clouds the size and shape of manhole covers toward a tiny rainbow in the top left corner of the painting.

"What do you call that, a Georgia O'Keeffe sky?" They were in her studio off the kitchen, drinking Tom's Black Label straight. Kat was smoking her third cigarette of the day.

"No, I call it my sky," Allison sipped her drink, wishing she had a cigarette too. One more shot and she might, but Tristan was there at his little table by the windows, happily smearing finger paint across a piece of butcher paper with Dotty Girl at his feet.

Kat stepped closer, examining the rainbow in Allison's painting. "Looks like one of those popsicles we used to buy at Ralph's. You remember those?"

"I do, they were great."

"What a cool painting, really fun, Allie."

"Thanks." She felt warm and tipsy.

"A woman flying free---almost anyway." Kat put out her cigarette in a jelly jar lid. "The question is what does she expect to find over that rainbow?"

"That's the big question, isn't it?"

"Well, it's your painting, kiddo."

Kat's green eyes were on her. "Something good, something wonderful or maybe just peace."

"You don't say," Kat smiled, finishing her whiskey.

"You want another?"

"Why not? We don't get to do this very often."

"No, we don't."

"Mommy, look at my pretty picture."

They both went over to admire his effort. "A major talent," Kat commented, looking at the whirling red and blue display. "Wonderful colors."

"That's a horse, isn't it?"

"Happy!"

"A great horse. Mommy and Daddy are very proud of you." Allison bent down and kissed him on the cheek, tears welling in her eyes.

Kat refilled their glasses at the drafting table. "I can't believe how big Tristan is. It seems like only yesterday when I flew to Missoula for the big event. He was so tiny; I was afraid to pick him up. He's an armload now."

"Yes, he is." Tom held her hand throughout the

delivery. "Do you remember the twins passing him back and forth, arguing about whether he was going to be a bull rider like Justin or a football player like JB?" She took a long drink. "Tom finally settled it when he said Tristan was pure quarterback material---it ran in the family."

"I think they were all wrong. Tristan's going to be an artist like his mom---that also runs in the family."

"I hope so." His birth was the greatest day of her life. She had everything in that one brief moment.

"And speaking of art, Allie, these paintings are terrific. I mean all of them---the ones in the kitchen and that great painting in the old living room. You're on a roll, girl."

"Well, I'm on something, that's for sure." Distraught, she looked out the window. Ben had been right about the weather. Yellow leaves swirled in the wind; snow was starting to fall.

"Don't be modest; it doesn't become you. You're doing good work. I think it's the best you've ever done."

The Bitterroot Range was imbued with the dark green-purple light of the approaching storm. She knew what it was like to be on one of those lonely, exposed ridges with no place to hide, feeling the tingle of electricity building in the air, waiting for the crack of lighting. They'd unsaddled their horses, turned them loose and huddled behind a rock. "Might as well enjoy the show," Tom had said, holding her close, "because there's not a damn thing we can do about it." Lightening flashed back and forth so close it sizzled; claps of deafening thunder shook the ground. The sharp smell of ozone filled the air.

"Allie? Are you with us?"

"Yes, sorry. I was thinking about something else."

"I know these people."

Kat was staring intently at the first painting she'd done after the accident, a happy blond cowgirl leaning into a smiling cowboy, arms around each other, boots, chaps, shirts and scarves covered with red hearts that peeled away in a funnel cloud. The lovers they once were and would be again.

Kat stayed in front of the painting. "I can't believe he's gone."

Allison was surprised to see tears running down her cheeks. "He's not gone---he's right there."

"These are very powerful, kiddo." Kat's voice was thick with emotion.

Allison put an arm around her sister's shoulder and felt tension. "I'm glad you like them." She'd only seen Kat really cry once before---when she walked out on her husband. That had been one hell of a cry.

"Sorry." Kat downed the rest of her whiskey and set the empty glass down with a thump.

"You're the one who said crying is a good thing, remember?"

"I did?" Kat wiped her eyes. "Anyway, I want to tell

you---how proud I am---of how you're handling this. I'm supposed to be the tough one."

"You still are, Kat, I'm barely hanging on here." Saved from crying right along with her by the honk of a horn announcing their dinner guests. "Come on, Tristan, we'd better get you cleaned up. Uncle Dave and Jim and Betty are here."

Kat helped her pick up the crayons and finger paint. "It will be great to see Dave. He wrote me from wherever he was in South America and said he felt guilty about leaving you so soon after the funeral."

"Listen, I told him to go ahead with his trip and I'm glad he did. Why don't you say hello to everyone for me. Tristan and I will be down in a minute; we need to wash up."

By the time they arrived, Kat was helping Betty set the table in the dining room. "Hi, Betty, it's good to see you." Her dear friend and only confidant in Wisdom where they both taught high school.

Betty Christian, in a green polyester pants suit, bleached blond hair piled high, stopped what she was doing and folded her into an enthusiastic embrace. "How's my favorite person in the whole world?"

"I'm okay. Thanks so much for coming." A warm hug from Betty, a big, forceful, mother of five, invited inclusion and inspired confidence.

"I love your paintings in the kitchen. It's like having the boys back home, isn't it?"

Allison nodded, unable to speak.

"But you're looking a little peaked, girl. You need some more sleep."

"I probably do."

Mackay, Dotty Girl and Tiger Cat slept in front of the blazing fireplace. Tristan went over to pet them. The large formal room had views of the creek, pond and lower pastures.

They'd spent so many happy evenings in this room with family and friends. Joyous times. Tom's leather bound books lined one wall in leaded glass cases, and on the other, a selection of her watercolors of hills and seascapes around Cambria on California's central coast where they first met. A life time ago. Tom loved these paintings. He said he could smell salt water and feel gentle ocean breezes when he walked into the room.

"And you could also use a little meat on your bones." Betty grabbed a handful of her loose fitting jeans and pulled. "What do you think, Katherine?"

Kat, still busy setting the table, laughed. "I couldn't agree more, Betty. She definitely needs to put on some weight."

It was impossible to be depressed with Betty around. When she could barely get out of bed, eat, or speak coherently, Betty had come out every day with lunch, wouldn't leave until she ate something and then insisted they walk to the ranch gate and back.

"Once school starts, we'll have my Home Ec girls whip up some heavy duty desserts. That'll fatten her up," she assured Kat. "Our Allison has a weakness for pecan pie, don't you, honey?"

"I like all your desserts, Betty." School started in a week. Allison refused to take a leave but was beginning to have doubts about leaving Tristan, the security of the ranch, and confronting a room full of students without the twins just down the hall.

The smell of Mexican food wafted in from the kitchen---chicken enchiladas, vegetarian burritos, chilies rellenos---the dinner Afracela usually made when Betty and her husband Jim, the county Sheriff, Tom's oldest friend, came over for an evening of conversation and cards. They played Hearts.

Betty carried a box of plastic dinosaurs over to Tristan. "So did you gals have a good ride today?" she asked over her shoulder, helping him arrange the prehistoric animals in a semi-circle around the dogs and cat.

"We had a great ride." Kat appraised her finished table setting. "It's such a relief from being in LA and we saw a fantastic eagle, didn't we, Allie?"

"Yes, we did." On Wings of Eagles. The poem was in her shirt pocket; she would finish it tonight, for Tom's sake.

"I also lost a horse race. It was quite a day. Allison

tends to forget I'm not one of her cowboys."

"Oh, don't feel bad about that," Betty chuckled. "Nobody can keep up with our girl on horseback when she gets up a head of steam."

"And speaking of the boys, Jim and Dave came with you, didn't they?"

"Sure did. They'd never miss one of Afracela's dinners. They're out with Carlos, talking horses. Men and their horses," she added with a booming laugh. "I'll go whistle them up."

"Now there's a woman who can really fill up a room," Kat said when Betty had gone.

"She's a force alright. Tom calls her the original pioneer woman."

"I can see why."

The men arrived in a rush of cold air. "Good evening, ladies." Jim Christian's broad shoulders filled the doorway. He shook the snow off his white Stetson and stepped inside. "I'll bet the temperature's dropped twenty degrees in the last half hour."

Dave followed in a snow covered black ski jacket and went straight to Allison. "How are you, sis? It's great to be back. I really missed you." He kissed her lightly on both cheeks and hugged her.

"Me too." Solid feeling yet somehow frail. "I'm so glad you're safe. How were things in the mountains?" Melting snow off his jacket made a cold trail down the front of her shirt.

"Good. Great, as a matter of fact. The higher I went, the better I felt. It was really something."

"That's wonderful." Aged beyond his years, but looking much better than he had at the funeral. Progress to be celebrated.

"We want to hear all about it at dinner, Dave," Kat chimed in.

"Oh, I've got stories to tell you guys."

"You're my favorite storyteller," she replied, putting an arm around his shoulder. "You always have been."

Kat towered over him; they both did. They'd been his protectors since he was fourteen.

"So how are you, Allison?" Jim stepped in to give her a hug.

She was always surprised by how muscular he felt for a man who looked so lean. "Getting through one day at a time. How are you?"

"I'm doing okay. The horses look good. Carlos says you've become quite the trainer."

"He's a great teacher, but we're short of help without Tom and the boys, and when school starts, I won't be able to do as much. Do you think Henry would be interested?"

"I think he'd jump at the chance to work with Carlos, but he couldn't start until after football season. My rule: study and football; that's it."

"That would work out fine."

"It will probably be a short season without JB and

Justin. I don't think they'll make the playoffs."

"What about the Snook boys? They're big, aren't they?"

"Yeah, but they're all talk and no show when the going gets tough. Look, I'll have Henry give you a call. I know he'd love to do it. He's our best hope for taking over the ranch someday and he's great with horses."

"We'll pay him, of course."

"Even better, thanks."

Jim turned to Tristan. "Hey, that's a good lookin' herd of dinosaurs you got there, young fella," he said, bending over to examine them.

At that Dotty Girl struggled to her feet and growled.

"It's okay," Jim assured the old dog with good humored authority, "this is official dinosaur business." Dotty stood her ground.

The Sheriff pointed to the biggest one. "So what do you call this guy?"

"T Rex," Tristan announced proudly, handing it to him.

"Well, thanks."

Tristan reached up and touched Jim's crew cut. "Daddy."

Taken aback, he patted him on the head, a smile radiating across his weathered face. "I'm not your dad, but I knew him well."

Allison turned away. Tristan's godfather, an honor Tom formally offered him at dinner in this very room.

She was six months pregnant and they knew it was a boy. "You're my best friend, Jim. In the unlikely event something should happen to both of us, I know you'll take care of him." In the unlikely event. The furthest thing from their mind.

Seeing her distress, Dave came over and took her hand. "It really is good to see you. How are you holding up anyway?"

"Not great, but I'm doing my best for Tristan's sake."

"That's all you can do."

"You're right. So how are you feeling?"

"Actually pretty good."

"You picked up some color down there." His curly light brown hair showed more white around the temples than she remembered.

"At altitude, you're a lot closer to the sun."

"So did you make it to the top of whatever it was you were trying to climb?" He was a handsome young man with a solid jaw and aquiline nose, but his light brown eyes, always steady and determined, looked tired.

"Aconcagua. And yes, I did."

Mackay and Tiger left their spot by the fireplace to sniff his heavy wool socks. Dave got down on one knee to pet them. "So how are you guys anyway? This dog is getting fat."

"Big. He grew into those feet this summer but he still acts like a puppy."

She remembered how Dave sat on their patio in Padua Hills during his high school years and fed the birds, patiently waiting for them to land on his outstretched hands. Their parents had been horrified when she and Kat showed up with him, an emaciated, battered street kid from the homeless shelter where they were volunteers.

Dave---a long suffering St. Francis figure in flowing white robes, standing defiantly against the elements, oblivious to threatening dark grey clouds, rolling thunder and lightning…….

"Come on," Betty called. "I'm getting hungry; what do you say we eat?"

On the summit of Aconcagua---arms outstretched, welcoming the circling hawks, eagles and falcons. A heroic figure.

"Allison?"

"I'm coming."

"So how big is that mountain anyway?" Jim asked as they collected their plates.

"Twenty two thousand eight hundred forty feet, the tallest mountain in the Americas."

"Was it tough?"

"Not technically, but weather and altitude make it dangerous. I passed a dead guy in a sleeping bag near the top; that was a little unnerving. He looked like a mummy, probably been there awhile."

"Jesus," Betty exclaimed, "that doesn't sound like

much fun."

"I didn't do it for fun, Betty," he replied as they moved down the buffet line, "I did it to see if I could make it."

Allison seated Tristan but remained standing while the others took their places, determined to finish what she had started. "It's wonderful to have our friends and family around our table again. I want to thank you from the bottom of my heart for everything you've done for Tristan and me these last months. I couldn't have done it without you."

Her hands shook as she took the folded paper out of her breast pocket, damp from the melting snow off Dave's jacket. "Today when Kat and I were out riding, we saw a magnificent golden eagle."

A powerful gust of wind hit the house with a hollow thump. Sparks flew; smoke puffed out into the room and retreated, leaving behind the sweet smell of pine. The dogs stirred; the cat ran under the dining table.

"We followed him all the way to the top of Horse Heaven Hill, and he stayed with us for the longest time." Holding the paper in trembling hands, she looked at Kat. "He came very close to me at one point. I felt the brush of his wings on my face and I remembered the wonderful poem I tried to read at Tom's funeral."

The lights flickered twice and surged back on. "So with your help, I thought I'd try to get through it tonight." Wind whistled in the eves; snow flew by the windows.

She felt his presence urging her on. "I am the sunlight on ripened grain. I am the gentle autumn rain. When you awaken in the morning's hush, I am the swift uplifting rush of eagles in circled flight. I am the soft stars that shine at night...."

Mackay let out a crashing bark and ran to the window; Dotty Girl followed. A shadowy figure was moving by in the driving snow. Everyone turned.

Allison dropped the poem and went to the window; the dogs ran back and forth. "Quiet!" Sit!" To her surprise, they obeyed, staring out into the storm.

Tom was on Keith, bundled up in his canvas drover's coat, wearing the black cowboy hat with raven feathers in the silver band and the red and black scarf she'd given him for his 50th birthday.

"You alright, honey?" Betty was beside her.

He'd come home! "Yes, I am."

"I wonder what set those dogs off? They sure saw something."

Jim joined them. "Maybe an elk," he suggested, squatting to pet the dogs. "Who knows? Whatever it was, guys, it's gone now."

She'd seen fully rendered compositions in her head ever since she was a girl, but nothing like this.

"Come on, honey." Betty took her hand. "Like Jim said, something set them off. Come back and finish the poem for us."

Dave and Kat nodded encouragement.

"I'll try." Tom was home. How could she tell them? Tears coursed down her cheeks; she let them fall. Allison picked up the poem and continued, "So do not stand at my grave and cry. I am not there, I did not die."

Only the crackling fire disturbed the deep silence that engulfed the room. Wings brushed her face again.

"That was wonderful, Allison," Betty said quietly. "We love you so very much."

Jim sat silently beside his wife, rigid, stone-faced. What had he seen?

Dotty girl was still at the window, staring out into the flying, dizzying snow. Overcome by the sight of Tom's dog waiting patiently for him, Allison looked away. "Just give me a minute."

She slowly folded the poem and put it back in her pocket. "It means so much to me---to us---to have you here tonight." She heard herself whispering in a husky voice.

"Let's sit down, sis." Dave pulled back her chair. "That was a wonderful tribute. I think we ought to drink a toast to Tom, don't you?"

"Yes, that would be nice."

Jim raised his wine glass. "To my good friend Tom Howard, the finest man I've ever known---and the twins, terrific young men who made their dad proud every day of their lives."

His voice choked; he stopped, then recovered. "I miss them."

Dave joined him, looking directly at Allison. "I loved Tom because he was so good to you, sis. And because he was the big brother I never had but always wanted. To Tom, my hero."

"Hear, hear," Kat joined in.

"I think out of respect to Tom we ought to finish this on a happier note, don't you, Allison?" Jim asked. "After all, he was a pretty happy guy."

Tears streamed down his craggy, lined face. Very unlike the Jim Christian she knew. He caught her eye and forced a smile.

"So here's to our great teachers, Betty, Dave and Allison who are about to start a new school year. Good luck, guys." He drained his glass. "I don't know about you, but I'm ready to eat."

Allison looked out the window, a blank white canvas. Dotty Girl still waited just as she'd stoically waited for days at the ranch gate for Tom to come home until Carlos finally brought her inside.

Were the twins out there with him in the numbing cold? She'd been brooding about facing school without them for weeks. No more driving back and forth together singing along with Tom's Rolling Stones CDs. The halls would seem empty.

"I understand Reverend Snook is going on the warpath again about getting me to teach Intelligent

Design in my science class," Dave commented as they began to eat.

She missed JB and Justin terribly. On her first day teaching, they'd introduced her to their fellow students as their mother. Not new mother or stepmother, but our mother.

"Ah, yes, Reverend Randy Snook," Betty snorted. "He should concentrate on disciplining those sons of his instead of trying to dictate the curriculum. They're totally out of control."

"I think the twins like you, honey," Tom remarked as they celebrated her first school day with wine in front of the fire. "Pretty good for a couple of surly teenagers."

It was better than good. Like her marriage, it was a dream come true. "I don't think they're surly," she'd protested; "they're wonderful boys. I'll always love them like my own."

"Intelligent Design is nothing but Creationism in sheep's clothing," Dave insisted. "Same old witchcraft."

"I'd be a careful about taking on Reverend Snook," Jim said mildly. "He's got a lot of community support."

"Spoken like a true politician, Sheriff," Betty retorted.

The conversation whirled around her, but Allison's attention stayed on the window, hoping for another miracle.

"I thought Intelligent Design was pretty thoroughly discredited," Kat interjected. "Nobody takes that stuff seriously, do they?"

Betty laughed. "You're not in California, Katherine. This is Montana."

Tristan pulled on Allison's arm. "Why's Dotty Girl over there?"

"She's being a good guard dog, honey. I'll get her for you." The dog had never left Tom's side from the day she met him at the horse show in Cambria.

She excused herself and went to get Dotty while Dave poured himself another glass of wine. "Come on, Girl." If it weren't for Tristan, she'd go to Tom right now and cling to him with all her might. I will never let you go.

"Hell, I never said I wouldn't teach it; I said it wasn't science. Darwin is science; Intelligent Design is religion, pure and simple, right, Allison?"

"Allison?"

She got Dotty Girl settled in beside Tristan's chair. "I don't know, Dave."

"I understand the argument," Jim replied thoughtfully, hands steepled in front of him. "But my point is Randy Snook, no matter what you think of him, is not a man to take lightly. His kin folk paid their way West by pushing hand carts for the Mormons and a lot of them died on the way. Did you know that?"

"No, I didn't."

"Well, it's true. All I'm saying is when you combine that kind of background with a guy who takes his Bible literally, you need to give him some respect."

Tristan was asleep. Afracela was serving coffee and dessert. Tom had come and gone too quickly. She needed to paint him as she'd seen him tonight, capture the great uplift she felt as he passed by.

"Point well taken," Dave replied cheerfully. "I'll do that."

Jim turned to her. "I assume you ladies intend to go to the school board meeting and defend your friend here."

"Probably, we really haven't talked about it."

"Of course, we will!" Betty insisted. "Dave is a wonderful teacher, one of the best we've got, and we're not gonna let Reverend Snook or anybody else intimidate him."

"I never suggested, Betty…."

"You may be afraid of Snook, Sheriff, but we're not."

Jim shook his head in amusement. "I'm not afraid of him, honey; I'm just saying it might be a good idea to think it through."

Tristan revived long enough to kiss everyone goodnight before Afracela took him up to bed with Dotty Girl. Dave excused himself too, complaining of jet lag. He would stay in a guest room and the Christians in another as they frequently did on late nights like this. It was a hard twenty mile drive into town on unimproved roads, and she liked having a house full of people.

It was snowing harder than ever; the conversation

lagged. Allison volunteered to help with the dishes, but Betty turned her down. "Sit and relax, honey, I like being in kitchens, particularly yours. You've had a long day."

A day of uplifting miracles that wiped out the drag of nightmares, a soaring eagle, a startling vision of the man she loved. Images to capture in paintings and discuss with him in her journal while they were fresh and vital.

"Good thing Dave decided to stay." Jim leaned back in his chair. "He looks pretty beat. That's one hell of a mountain. Anybody want some of this in their coffee? Allison?" He held up the bottle of Black Label he always brought for Tom.

"Thanks, but I think I'd better stick to coffee." Her faith vindicated, but so tired. Already Tom was slipping away.

"Dave's always been a fanatic climber," Kat was saying. "Dad encouraged it. He said it would help him forget the past and make him feel better physically. Something about the production of more red blood cells at altitude."

"That's interesting." Jim shifted in his chair and leaned forward. "You know I don't think he understood what I was trying to tell him about Snook."

"Frankly, I didn't quite get it either," Kat said.

Allison stood up. If she excused herself now while the day's events were still fresh, there might be time to turn them into the reality she longed to create.

"I'm worried about what might happen if he finds out Dave has AIDS. That could get ugly."

The word jolted her back into the conversation she was vaguely following. "For Christ sake, Jim, he was a victim, an innocent child."

"I understand that Allison, even so....."

The phone began to ring; she ignored it. "And he's not gay, never has been."

"There are federal laws about making unfounded accusations like that," Kat interrupted forcefully. "And I can assure you they apply, even in Montana."

The phone continued to ring. "Could you get that please," Allison called to Betty in the kitchen.

Jim leaned forward. "Look, Katherine, I'm on your side. I wasn't talking about the law; I was referring to the reaction of certain people in this community."

"Reaction to what, exactly?"

Betty came into the dining room and handed Allison a portable phone. "Sorry, but he insists on talking to you."

"Who is it?"

Betty shook her head.

"Hello."

"Allison, I finally found you."

"Lyn?"

"I was so sorry to hear about Tom. I want to offer my sincere condolences."

This couldn't be happening. Not now. She felt dizzy.

"I still love you, and I want to help any way I can."

"Stay away from me, you bastard!"

Kat grabbed the phone. "This is Katherine Garnett, Assistant District Attorney for Los Angeles County. If you ever call my sister again, Mr. Barnett, I'll have you arrested and put in jail where you belong, you miserable son of a bitch."

DREAMS OF APPALOOSAS
Chapter Five: My Journal

Midnight, September 4, 2007

My dearest Tom,

What an incredible joy to see you ride by tonight! Thank you for coming home! I felt certain you were close by today, watching over us, feeling the touch of your wings on my face. And tonight, Dotty Girl certainly knew you were here, and I think Jim might have too. Unfortunately, Tristan was half asleep, and I don't know about Betty, Dave or Kat. I love them all dearly, but I don't think they're ready to make that leap yet, so I didn't say anything. Maybe later.

But you've come back just as you promised and not a moment too soon. Our wonderful gathering was interrupted when, of all people, Lyn called me out of the blue. I couldn't believe it! I had a horrible nightmare about him last night and there he was on the phone after all these years. Will I ever be rid of him?

Fortunately, Kat was right beside me and read him the riot act. And thank God I'd just seen you which gave me enough of your famous "Faith and Courage" to get me through the rest of the evening.

Oh, Tom, I can't tell you how much it means to me to have you home. I hope it's not my overactive imagination. Are you really here? I long to be in your arms, feel your touch, see you smile, hear you laugh, turn over in bed to find you reading, those silly granny glasses on the end of your nose. I know that is probably too much to ask, but seeing you put me on such a high.

I still wait for you in the dark, look for the lights of your truck coming up the drive, listen for the sound of your horse. I have been heartbroken since you and the twins left us. It's been so desperately lonely without you. Tristan wants to see you and the boys and he doesn't understand why you're not here. I'm afraid he's starting to forget you. Sometimes, in my darkest moments, I wish Tristan and I had gone with you on that trip.

Will it ever stop hurting? Each day seems like forever. I feel as if I'm on the edge of a dark abyss, clinging to life, hanging on for Tristan's sake---only because you expect me to---and so does everyone else.

Tomorrow I take Kat to the airport and I miss her already. Thank God for Kat. We are planning to stop at the memorial. I think I can do it if she's with me, especially after seeing you tonight and knowing you are not up there on that lonely pass or in the cemetery, but here with us. But I am afraid of the nightmares it might trigger---you and the twins and our beautiful horses, burning, screaming.

Then I have to turn right around and go to school next week; my first time alone. I know I'm not being as brave as I should be, Tom, but I'm trying with all my might to keep moving forward for Tristan's sake and I won't give up.

I'm wound tight after seeing you and feel so full of wonder and hope that I won't be able to sleep, so I'm going down to paint.   I'll paint you as I saw you tonight and that will bring you alive in my hands once again and comfort me. I will hold onto my vision of you and make our dreams come true.

All my love,
Allie

P.S. This is the wonderful "Red Coyote" who appeared in my dream.

Red Coyote

DREAMS OF APPALOOSAS
Chapter Six: Lost Trail Pass

Allison woke to the rich smell of Afracela's coffee and a crackling fire, head cradled in her arms on the drafting table, the sketch of Tom riding Keith into the storm beside her. He was home. Refreshed and alert after a dreamless night, she stood and stretched. Morning sun warmed her. The call from Lyn seemed far away.

Snow framed the studio windows, clung to trees and bushes, stood on the picket fence like cotton puffballs, and hung off the eves of the barn roof in fantastic scallops, frosting on one of the gingerbread houses her grandmother used to make at Christmas. The first snowfall of the year, a new beginning.

She poured herself a cup of coffee and studied the drawing. There was something familiar about the line that flowed from horse to rider, heads down, leaning forward into the storm. It wasn't original; she'd seen it before. An Earle Fraser sculpture, "the End of the Trail", one of Tom's favorites. "Sorry, honey, my heart was in it but my head was fuzzy. I'll give it another go tonight. I'll get it right, I promise."

Her studio was where she created the reality that

sustained her. Here she and Tom could smile at each other for all eternity, arms intertwined in a passionate embrace, ride across the endless sky together on a highway of clouds. And the twins would always be with them, forever young.

Tom was everywhere in this room. He'd wired the halogen lights, laid the hardwood floor, painted the walls with a warm neutral color to showcase her paintings. They installed the Franklin stove together and made love in front of its inaugural fire as a full yellow moon rose over jagged outlines of indigo mountains.

After she took Kat to the airport, she would come back and redo the sketch. Tom would sit straight, defying the storm; the twins would be with him. He'd like that.

By the time she'd showered and dressed, Dave and the Christian's were gone. Kat and Tristan were playing with his wooden blocks on the kitchen floor. The dogs snoozed in the corner. "What is that, guys, a fort?" She leaned down to kiss them. Tristan smelled of lemon bath soap.

"Yeah, we call it Fort Howard, don't we, Tristan?"

Nodding in agreement, he continued stacking blocks, higher and higher, red letters on one side, green numbers on the other.

Kat got slowly to her feet. "I'm really stiff. I thought I was finally getting used to being on a horse again."

"It was a hard ride; we went a long way."

"Well, I enjoyed it. Afracela left us some breakfast." Kat turned her head from side to side to relieve the soreness. "So how are you holding up this morning after the call from Lyn?"

"I don't know. I actually got a pretty good night's sleep, believe it or not, and now I'm doing my best to put it behind me. But it was a shock."

"Of course it was, especially after dreaming about him the other night."

"That's something, isn't it, a nightmare on top of a nightmare." The same soothing, seductive voice. She'd been such a fool.

"He's got one hell of a nerve calling you at a time like this, and believe me, it's not going to happen again if I have anything to do with it."

"God, I hope not."

Kat went to the window. "It's so gorgeous out there with the new snow. Look at all the elk in your lower pasture. How do they get in?"

"We open the gates for them in the fall. They're safe from hunters and Carlos puts hay out when the snow gets too deep." As if he knew they were talking about him, a magnificent bull turned his head towards the house. "He is beautiful, isn't he?"

"Yes. Don't the dogs chase them?"

Allison laughed, joining her sister at the window. "No, these are Tom's dogs; they do as they're told---

most of the time. I don't think there's anything prettier than a wild animal in his element, undisturbed. I love to watch them."

"The Peaceable Kingdom," Kat nodded. "You always were a pushover for animals."

"I don't know if I'm a pushover, but you're right, I do love them." She saw Kat's carry-on bag next to the door, packed and ready to go. She didn't want her to leave.

"You relate to them on a personal level, don't you?"

"Yes, I guess I do. Ever since moving here, I feel more connected to all living things. Maybe it's because we live such a relatively isolated life---about as close to the natural world as you can get---and it's forced me to see that we're all part of something much bigger and more complex than I ever imagined."

"I can see how that might happen, Allie."

They ate a leisurely breakfast and watched the elk while Tristan expanded his fort. She didn't want to face the day or the scene of the accident. Better to stay in their sunlit kitchen and hold on to this precious moment of peace and contentment, surrounded by paintings of Tom, the twins and their horses.

They were clearing the dishes when Afracela came in, carrying a wicker basket of flowers---daisies, yellow roses, and blue and purple stock---tied into three bundles, each wrapped in royal blue paper and tied with wide white ribbons. "For Mr. Tom and the boys," she said, holding them out to her.

Allison blinked back tears. "Thank you so much." Blue, his favorite color.

"God be with you, Mrs."

Tom had built the greenhouse for Afracela at the south end of the new horse barn. She could see its red roof and sage grey board and batten siding from where she stood. His pride and joy. He used to kid her that the ten stalls were nicer than their house.

She'd never stopped at the roadside memorial and only agreed today because Kat thought it was important. Allison wasn't sure if she could do it.

"Give Mommy a big hug, Tristan. I'll be home tonight to tuck you in."

He put his arms around her neck and clung to her. "I want to come too."

"I'm sorry, honey, you and the dogs have to stay here with Afracela." She held him for a long, lingering moment, just as she held Tom on that last morning, not wanting to let him go. "I'll be back before you know it," she said, kissing him again, "I promise." Tom's exact words.

Slinging the overnight bag over her shoulder, Kat picked up the flowers while Allison struggled into Tom's drover coat, buttoning the stiff corduroy collar high against her neck. My fortress, my shield, my sword. Inspirational words from Sunday school days. She stepped into the cold, clear morning.

Snow covered hills, massive sleeping white bulls. Mountain castles all around. Colorful Windhorse prayer flags streaming from jagged turrets and towers under an intense royal blue cloudless sky. Tristan's Fort Howard.

"God, what a beautiful day." Tom's diesel pickup started with a satisfying roar.

"It is that and then some," Kat settled back in the wide bench seat.

They drove past corrals with horses bunched around feeding troughs; steam rising from their warm bodies. She lowered the window. "Hey, you beauties, have a great day, see you later." The horses looked up and went back to their grain. Tom's horses, their horses. Was he still here?

They clattered over the plank bridge that crossed the Big Hole River, banks rimmed with crumbling ice, mirrored surfaces reflecting blues, greens and golds in the intense, dancing sunlight. Stones shimmered beneath the surface---Indian red, cobalt turquoise, ultra marine violet---a carpet of changing shapes and colors. On the far horizon, towering zinc white thunderheads boiled over the Bitterroot Range. The background for her painting to celebrate Tom's return.

"Snow doesn't seem to bother the horses," Kat remarked.

Allison regretted not bringing her sketch book. Clouds on such a grand scale were hard to duplicate from memory.

"Earth to Allison, where are you?"

"Sorry, I was thinking about those clouds."

"And I was saying the horses seem to be doing fine in the snow."

"They're tough; they're used to it." There was such an inspiring, ever-changing world in the sky where man had no impact whatsoever.

"So what was Ben so worried about?"

"Oh, he was just being Ben. He doesn't like our Appaloosas, never has."

"Why not?"

"Because he thinks they're an Indian horse and basically good for nothing---like Indians. To Ben a horse is a horse. He uses them like farm machinery. He raises prize winning Angus bulls; that's his thing."

"How could two brothers be so different?" Kat took out a pack of cigarettes.

"I honestly don't know, but Betty said they were very close once. They worked together on the ranch, went hunting, and all that stuff boys do out here."

"Really. You'd never know it now. Mind if I smoke?"

"Go ahead but crack the window, will you?"

"Something must have happened because I never met two more dissimilar people in my life."

"Well, for one thing, they got into a big fight over Priscilla."

"Tom's first wife?"

"Yes. I guess they both had their eye on her. Betty

said she was not only the prettiest girl in town and the Homecoming Queen, but the brightest as well."

"You mean a real fight?"

"According to Betty, Ben beat up Tom pretty bad. He was older and a lot bigger, but neither of them quit. Apparently they finally just walked away from each other."

Kat exhaled a long stream of smoke that hung high in the cab for a moment before being sucked out the window. "That must have put a strain on the relationship, to say the least."

"I'm sure it did, but Tom never said a word to me about it. In fact, I never heard him say anything bad about Ben. But that's Tom. He doesn't waste time and energy on stuff like that."

"Well, Tom got the girl."

Allison slowed as they turned onto the freshly plowed country road, snow piled on either side. "He did. Betty said Ben went down and joined the Marine Corp the next day and ended up in Viet Nam. By the time he got back to Wisdom, Tom had married Priscilla and was going to Stanford."

"That didn't work out too well for Tom or the boys when she walked out on them."

"That's true, but she was sick, Kat. Priscilla's still sick; she's bipolar. It's a terrible disease. People can go from being straight A students to drop outs and from loving wives to runaways."

95

The road was straight and narrow, rolling gently over low hills. Black Angus grazed in endless fields of azo yellow stubble poking through the snow. Tom and the twins had driven down this same road, towing a load of their best mares. She ran down the window to get some fresh air.

"That's must be why Tom set up the trust fund for her."

"Yes, it is. He never blamed her. In fact, he felt he might have triggered it by moving her into a world that was totally foreign to her. They never intended to stay in Palo Alto, but the business took off on him and he worked all the time. She found herself isolated with a couple of kids. It was a long way from Wisdom, Montana."

"So where is she now?"

"In a rest home in Long Beach. She tried to commit suicide after---after the accident." Allison gripped the wheel until her knuckles turned white. She understood.

"That's awful."

"Betty's been over to see her. They're old friends, of course. Fortunately, Tom feels very strongly about taking care of her and so do I. They all grew up together, you know---Tom, Jim, Betty and Priscilla---the whole crowd."

"And Ben. He's sort of the odd man out, isn't he?"

"Betty said he was never the same when he got back from the war. He ignored old friends and retreated to his half of the ranch and has lived there alone ever since." She wasn't looking forward to meeting with Ben. She'd be glad when the estate was settled and they could get his cows off their land.

A blur of sleek tawny bodies and white rumps zigzagged in unison across the highway at high speed. "My God, what are those?"

"Pronghorn antelope---aren't they great! The fastest thing on four legs in North America---nothing faster in the world except a cheetah. They're also a native species, like our horses."

Kat watched as they disappeared. "I thought the Spanish brought the horses over here."

"They did, but fossils of Eocene horses were found in Chalk Hills, Wyoming. They were only three hands high and something like forty million years old."

"You and Mom never cease to surprise me with your encyclopedic knowledge of history. That's really amazing."

They drove on in silence through the pristine day. Allison fought to hold onto the powerful image of Tom and the twins with ever shifting clouds in the background, so clear and compelling only moments ago.

Kat opened the ashtray and put out her cigarette. "I feel like I'm in a time warp out here."

"In what way?" With the cigarette gone, the smell of flowers was strong; her stomach tightened in anticipation. Everyone expected her to pay her respects at the memorial.

"It's light years away from where I live---and how I live, kiddo. I think I told you I'm prosecuting a big time drug dealer, Manuel Rodriquez. It's made me a prisoner in my own home."

"What do you mean?"

"Manuel's in jail, but his brother Pedro isn't, and he's threatened to kill me, so I have twenty-four hour security."

"My God, that's terrible. Why didn't you tell me?" Losing Kat would be unbearable.

"Don't worry; I've got lots of good people watching out for me, Allie. It's not as bad as it sounds."

"It sounds bad to me. Do Mom and Dad know?"

"No, and I don't intend to tell them, so don't you." Kat shrugged. "Comes with the territory, I guess, but sometimes I wonder if it's worth it. There seems to be an endless supply of these guys in LA and we're not making much headway."

Allison slowed as she passed the weatherworn wood sign marking the city limits: "Welcome to Wisdom, Montana, Population 652, Home of the Wolves, State Football Champions 1973, 2007".

Tom and Jim were on one team, the twins on the other. Cold fall evenings, the smell of fires on the sidelines, huddled together under a blanket drinking coffee. Rosy cheeked, bare-legged cheerleaders in heavy wool sweaters, the twins giving them a thumbs up when they scored. Tom called it "pigskin weather".

"God, this place is deserted. What's up?"

"It's Sunday." A battered Western movie set except for the modern Sinclair station with the huge green trademark dinosaur on the roof that Tristan loved. The only sign of life was a parking lot full of cars and pickups around the former bowling alley, now home to the Church of the Divine Light Reformed, Reverend Randolph Snook.

"Your old friend," Kat commented dryly as they drove by. "When is that school board meeting anyway? I'd sure like to be here for that."

"I don't think they've set a date yet." Going back to school would be hard enough without contemplating what was certain to be an unpleasant confrontation.

There was snow on the lawn around the city park, the stone County Court House and adjoining two-story red brick high school. An electronic reader board flashed "Welcome Back Students" to an empty street.

"Pretty fancy sign."

"Yes, we have a four day school week, thirty-five kids in each classroom, no art and no music, but somehow the District managed to get federal funds for that sign."

"I thought you taught history and art appreciation."

"I do, but art is strictly on a volunteer basis."

"They're sure lucky to have you."

"Thanks. It will probably be good for me to go back

99

to work."

As they left Wisdom behind, she realized Kat was right. The Big Hole Valley was like being in a time warp. Only an occasional gate or mail box marked the sprawling third and fourth generation ranches. Still the vast empty space the Nez Perce passed through every year on their way to hunt buffalo on the Great Plains.

A huge canvas painted in shades of white with something very small in one corner. A bird, powerful and symbolic. An eagle. A pair of eagles. A time warp with a sense of hope. A reaffirmation of life in a void.

She visualized the painting as she drove, reassured by the solid vibration of the diesel engine through the steering wheel.

It would have to be big. The eagles very small to force viewers close enough to see them and be overwhelmed by the vastness of white. I don't know where we're going to find that kind of space. We might have to build something---a whole new wall. That's your department, Tom.

"I worry about you out here, Allie," Kat said, breaking the silence.

"Why?"

"Because I honestly think you and Tristan might be better off back home in California."

"So we can live in fear and have security guards like you? I'm sorry; I didn't mean it that way."

"That's okay."

"It's true I'm not exactly a great fit with some of the local folks, but I have good friends here, I do, Kat--- Dave, the Christians, the Garcias, teachers at school and parents at Tristan's day school. They're very nice people, really quite progressive, all things considered."

"I'm sure they are. I was just suggesting that you and Tristan might be more comfortable in another setting, and you've got so much work to do on the ranch, in addition to your teaching and painting."

"That may be, Kat, but this in our home now. Tom and I came here with a dream and I intend to see it through for Tristan's sake."

Kat didn't reply. Forested evergreen hills replaced hay fields as they climbed toward the pass. The truck began to labor. The smell of flowers made her anxious. Allison downshifted and missed, grinding the gear. "Damn, sorry." The curves and switchbacks were getting tighter.

"Sorry about what?"

"I blew the shift."

"Don't worry about it, I can't even drive a stick like this. I think you're doing fine."

"I'm not doing fine at all." How far past the summit was the memorial? She couldn't remember. She didn't want to remember. Was it on the first sweeping curve or the next? "I don't think I can stop the memories."

"Of course, you can, Allie."

A wave of sadness engulfed her as they crossed

over Lost Trail Pass at 7,000 feet. Lewis and Clark, the Nez Perce and the Seventh Infantry had come this way. The last great Indian uprising, a brilliant but futile fighting retreat with thousands of Appaloosas, followed doggedly by Tom's great grandfather and his bloody Bannock scouts, murdering and scalping stragglers. The exhausted Nez Perce thought they had outdistanced their pursuers and could rest overnight along the peaceful Big Hole River. A fatal miscalculation.

Allison vowed to get the General out of their living room when she got home. She eased off the gas, engaged the four wheel drive, and glanced at the odometer as they started down toward Missoula. "Warning, 6% grade. Trucks use low gear. First escape route, four miles."

"Carlos says it's 26.7 miles from the ranch gate." Her chest constricted; it was hard to breath. The odometer read 26.1. She downshifted and slowed. "I don't see it."

"Over there," Kat pointed. "On the left."

Allison pulled onto the right shoulder and stopped, letting the truck idle. She hesitated, forcing herself to look up.

"I'll come with you."

"Let me try this alone." She closed her eyes for a moment, prayed for faith and courage, unfastened her seat belt and picked up the flowers. "I'll just be a minute."

She couldn't let Tom and the boys down. The wind was biting cold. Silence. A painful, throbbing pressure pounded in her ears. She was across the northbound lane when a violent gust of wind tore the flowers out of her hand. Desperately, she grabbed for them and slipped, falling hard. "Damn!" The flower basket rolled away toward the guard rail. Stunned, she burst into tears. "God, I can't do this."

"I've got you." Kat was instantly at her side, pulling her to her feet.

"The flowers," Allison sobbed, eyes blurring with tears.

"Don't worry, we'll get them."

A semi-truck and trailer bore down on them, stopping in a hiss of airbrakes and a cloud of exhaust. "You gals, okay? You broke down or something?" The driver shouted over the idling diesel.

"No, we're fine," Kat yelled back. "Thanks." She pointed to three white crosses set in the narrow turnout.

The errant flower basket was wedged under a long section of new steel guard rail dripping with melting ice. Allison backed away. "I can't stand this." It was here at the end of a long, sickening skid.

"Steady." Kat held her arm.

"Sure you don't need some help, ladies?" She tried to concentrate on the silver cattle trailer's elaborate black cursive sign, "Blackjack Ranch, Bruneau, Idaho". Anywhere but the abyss.

"No thanks, we're alright," Kat called back.

"You be careful, hear?" He gave them a tip of his green baseball cap and was gone, two black streams of smoke pouring out of tall chrome exhaust stacks.

The smell of diesel made her stomach turn. They were in front of the crosses at the edge of a drop-off so steep the thundering river at the bottom was hidden from view. She leaned heavily against Kat. "I feel sick. Stay with me, please."

"Of course, just let me get the flowers." Kat knelt down and dislodged the basket. "Alright, let's do what we came to do."

Allison kept her eyes on the ground while Kat helped her remove the dead flowers. They crumbled in her hand. Carlos had left them two days before when he picked up Kat at the airport. Nothing lasts here. Too cold. Windy. Hot. Dry. Harsh. Everything dies. Allison bowed her head. "Look what's happened," she murmured to Kat, throwing the dead flowers aside.

"That's why we brought fresh ones, kiddo." Kat handed her the bouquets and helped her fit them into the cans.

"These are from Afracela," Allison said quietly. A gum wrapper and a yellow shotgun shell were frozen in the gravel in front of the crosses.

She struggled to her feet, finding it hard to keep her balance. "I want to go." But the empty, yawning space beyond the guard rail held her in its grip, pulling, inviting her to step over.

Kat reached out. "Well then, come on."

With Kat's arm around her waist, Allison turned away. She'd often seen crosses along highways and wondered what stories they told. Now she knew. Tragedy and heartbreak. Leaning heavily on Kat for support, they carefully crossed the road as the afternoon sun dropped behind the mountains. Freezing slush crackled under their feet.

"I'll drive," Kat announced, holding out her hand for the keys.

"I thought you said you couldn't handle a stick shift."

"I lied. I wanted to make you feel better. I can drive anything."

Retrieving the keys from the deep pockets of Tom's coat, she felt a cork screw, a broken carpenter's pencil and handful of horseshoe nails mixed with hay. Tom was ready for anything---almost. She burst into tears.

"Oh, Allie." Kat held her in her arms.

"Thanks for being here."

"You're welcome. Come on, let's go; it's freezing out here."

Kat started the truck and lit another cigarette. "Did I ever tell you about the Lamborghini John Henry bought me right after we were married?"

"I don't even know what a Lamborghini is, Kat."

"It's a very expensive Italian sports car, and I swear it had more gears than this truck. God I loved to drive that car."

"So what happened to it?" Allison asked, grateful for the change of subject.

Kat, cigarette dangling from her lips, released the emergency brake, put the pickup in gear and pulled onto the highway. "When I left him, I decided to leave the car too."

"You should have taken it with you; he owed you."

"Maybe, but all things considered I figured I was better off without either one of them."

"You could have sold it."

"Yeah, I know, but the truth was I didn't care. I was so glad to be rid of the bastard and anything that reminded me of him."

Allison looked out the window at the passing thick wall of evergreens flocked with last night's snow, her attention wandering.

A winding dark highway littered with dried, crumbling bouquets of gun powder gray dead flowers scattered by the wind. Giant white memorial crosses lining either side, becoming smaller and smaller as they marched to the horizon, disappearing into a lamp black sky.

Gone forever. Allison closed her eyes. Men and horses falling. Endless rows of crosses.

The smell of cigarette smoke was tempting and she opened her eyes. "Give me one of those, will you?" If she allowed that horror to invade her creative world, all would be lost.

"You sure?" Kat looked at her skeptically. "They're not good for you."

"The hell with it; it might help."

"I know the feeling, kiddo, but Mom and Dad would be disappointed," Kat noted, handing her the pack. "They never knew you smoked." A faint smile flickered on her lips and was gone.

"Mom and Dad didn't know about a lot of things." The first drag transported her back into another life of reckless excitement.

"So what's it like?"

"What's what like?"

"Smoking again."

"Just the same---like I never stopped." She and Lyn had a ritual cigarette after making love. It was better than the sex. Her parents didn't know a thing about that either until he hit her hard enough to put her in the hospital for three days while her jaw was reconstructed. Six miserable, humiliating weeks of pain, drinking through a straw.

On the second drag, nicotine rushed to her head like an express train. "I haven't had a cigarette since the Lyn days," she admitted, crushing it out with disgust. "You know that call really did upset me. It came at the worst possible time."

"He can't hurt you again, Allie, it was over years ago. You have to do your best to forget it and move on."

"I know, but all the shame and guilt came pouring back when I heard his voice."

"You and your guilt. Why, for Christ's sake?"

"Because he helped me get established in the art world."

"It was your talent not his."

"That's not really true. Talent isn't always enough. Lyn had connections. He pushed and promoted me, and I let him."

"He took advantage of you, kiddo. He's an abusive, self-centered coward who beats up women."

"I had no idea he actually loved me. I thought it was one grand adventure. I was so young and naïve. I ruined his life."

"Bullshit. He didn't love you. He was a married man who fooled around with students. He held a prestigious job in a position of trust. He ruined his own goddamn life."

"I just want him to leave me alone."

"I know you do. I told Dad we should have pressed charges and put the bastard in jail instead of quietly ruining his academic career. That was a major mistake. We sure picked a couple of losers, didn't we?"

"I guess we did."

"The only good thing about John Henry was that he didn't smoke---and he didn't hit me."

"That's two good things, Kat."

"One, two, who cares? He's a great lawyer but a lousy womanizing husband."

"And then along came Tom. My lucky day." The most romantic man she'd ever known.

"What in the world are you smiling about?" Kat asked.

"Tom."

"You know, it's a damn good thing I wasn't with you at that horse show, I'd have grabbed him so fast you wouldn't have seen me drag him away." Kat laughed quietly.

"Ah, but I saw him first."

"That you did, kiddo."

Tom had walked over to Happy's stall at the Cambria Horse Show. "That's a good lookin' Appaloosa you got there, lady." They'd just won honorable mention in the Novice Halter Showmanship Class, a remarkable feat considering Happy's encroaching blindness.

She couldn't remember what she'd said, only the electric sexual jolt when he took her arm and they walked the grounds looking at horses. A moment she would never forget. They had Chinese take-out and talked most of the night in camp chairs by her trailer with the smell and sounds of horses all round. Tom said that a love of Appaloosas and an interest in western US history brought them together---and passion, making love wherever they happened to be. That night it was on a picnic blanket in tall grass behind the Pavilion.

Kat drove the rest of the way in silence as she dozed. The cattle truck came at her over and over as she lay paralyzed in the road. "You gals okay?" He had no trouble stopping. Tom would never have been speeding down that hill in bad weather. Never. What happened? Drifting, half awake, half asleep, Kat nudged her.

"We're here. Are you awake enough to drive home?"

Rubbing her eyes, she tried to organize scattered thoughts. They were parked at the airport's main entrance under lights in a loading zone.

"Maybe you should stay here overnight," Kat suggested, pulling her bag out of the back seat.

"I'm fine; I just need to wake up. It's only a couple of hours home."

"Whatever you say. I don't want you to wait for me, Allie," Kat said firmly, consulting her watch. "My plane doesn't leave for an hour."

"I don't mind." She was anticipating the loneliness she would feel when Kat's plane took off heading for another world where the breeze was warm and soft and the smell of the ocean filled the air and maybe the pain wouldn't be so great.

"But I do. I want you to go home, now." Kat smiled. "Hell, you'll be there with Tristan before I get to my condo."

"Good point." Kat's beach front condo, so beautiful, so empty. "I'll miss you."

Two little boys walked by with their parents. One of them waved and Allison waved back. It would have been wonderful to have known Justin and JB when they were that age.

"Me too. Listen, I don't know if I can make it next week; I've got the Rodriguez trial coming up."

"I understand." She dreaded a lonely weekend without her. They'd spent more time together in the last six weeks than they had in years.

"I'll do my best."

"I know you will, Kat. I know you're busy....."

"Never too busy for you." Kat reached across the seat and hugged her.

Allison clung to her, crying. "I'm so grateful to have you. I couldn't do this without you; I just couldn't."

They were both crying. "You were very brave today, Allie. I'm proud of you."

"I wasn't brave at all, but I tried. I'm going to miss you."

"I'll miss you too. I know you might not believe this, but I need you just as much as you need me." Kat wiped away her tears. "I guess we'll have to hold each other up, won't we?"

"We always have; we always will. Call me when you get home."

"It will be late."

"I don't care. I love you, Kat."

"Me too. And give my love to Tristan. Tell him---

never mind---just tell him I love him."

Allison watched her beautiful sister walk into the terminal, a tall lonely figure in the gathering dusk, going home to an empty condo by the sea, and knew that Tristan was all either of them had in the corner of their blank white canvas.

DREAMS OF APPALOOSAS
Chapter Seven: The Stalker

Tired and lonely, Allison fought to stay awake in the dark overheated truck, trying to compose a life affirming painting while her headlights swung hypnotically back and forth on each sweeping curve as she climbed toward the desolate summit of Lost Trail Pass.

Kat and Tristan on a fence rail, dogs at their feet, yearlings behind them; a Tom Howard bluebird day. Her big sister, tall and beautiful, a commanding figure in blue jeans, boots, white shirt, red scarf, flowing red hair, emerald green eyes and that radiant smile that could light up the darkest night.

The memorial crosses were somewhere ahead. She longed to have Kat beside her. Kat held her on course, steadied her when she faltered and tethered her to earth when she wanted to let go. The smell of cigarette smoke lingered in the cab. Black walls closed in on either side. She leaned over the steering wheel, staring ahead, determined to concentrate on the good.

Kat's protective arm around a grinning, blond-haired Tristan with Tom's sky blue eyes, wearing his red cowboy hat, clutching a green T Rex. A subtle wash on the Appaloosas and dogs to emphasize the importance of the figures in the foreground. If anything happened to her, Kat would take care of Tristan.

The warning whine of tires jolted her out of her reverie as she crossed the fog line, careening toward the edge in the unrelenting grip of centrifugal force. She jammed on the brakes, fishtailing on the ice, skidding to a stop inches from the guard rail.

"My God." The three white crosses were directly in front to her, shrouded in a gossamer ground fog that curled over the rail from the river below. The diesel engine thumped steadily under her feet with clock like precision. Wind rocked the truck. Scattered flowers blew over the edge. Falling! Screaming! Fire! Death! The pull of the abyss beckoned her.

Do not stand at my grave and cry, I am not here, I did not die. Only fog, wind, and crosses frozen in time. "Oh, Tom, what am I doing here? Tristan is waiting. I promised him."

Weeping, Allison put the truck in reverse and backed onto the highway. Pausing, she wiped her eyes, then reluctantly pushed on toward the summit, driving slowly, carefully, trying to force the row of crosses from her mind.

Tuscan gold, Navajo white, barn red. She would give the painting to Kat, a reminder that when she felt surrounded by enemies, she was loved by a little boy in Montana. A good way to thank her for all she'd done.

Separate the dogs. Dottie Girl lying down and Mackay with his paws up on the rail. Perhaps red-winged blackbirds with the horses. As she went over the composition, the line of dark crosses drifted onto her canvas, growing larger, forcing Kat and Tristan into the background. The red-haired twins wandered in the distance. "Oh, Christ, Allie, concentrate!"

Headlights blazed in the rear view mirrors. "Sorry." Embarrassed, Allison moved over to let him pass, but the car stayed directly behind her. "Okay, have it your way." Not many people went to Wisdom this time of night. When she turned, he would go on down the highway.

At the summit, she put on her turn signal and slowed. He signaled and slowed too. A wave of fear engulfed her as poignant as a decade ago. It couldn't be Lyn. Her hand automatically went to her jaw.

She pressed the automatic door locks. A dull click, the doors were already locked. There was no help here. No cell phone service. She put her foot down hard on the accelerator, a welcome surge of power. "Go!"

Lyn made random appearances in Cambria, following her home at night, passing her on the freeway, until Tom confronted him in a supermarket parking lot, and he'd disappeared for good. Then the call last night. "Tom, I need you."

The blacktop road rippled with frost heaves. The truck bounced and swayed; tires howled. He kept pace,

115

headlights right behind her. It was Lyn!

Fighting panic, Allison threw open the glove compartment searching for Tom's pistol, frantically pulling out maps, gloves, ice scrapers. No pistol! "Damn!" She'd left it in his desk drawer.

Look in the side pocket!

"Tom?" Allison reached down with her left hand, searching for a weapon. Hoof picks, screw drivers, a flashlight. Her hand closed over the cold canister of bear mace. Jamming it between her legs, she glanced in the rear view mirror. Still there.

"Get a grip." The sound of her voice echoed in the cab. Someone unfamiliar with the road? Someone who had a hard time seeing at night, or a drunk.

Dark trees flashed by. How long had he been there? Where did he come from? Lyn called; that wasn't her imagination. Finally the familiar "North 1060" sign marking the road to the ranch. Home. Safety, minutes away. She downshifted, braked, and made the turn, fighting to stay on the road.

He had gone on to Wisdom. Massive relief.

But then the headlights reappeared. "Goddamn it." She stepped on the gas. Close to home; one more hill. Pull the orange tab---up, down or out? Don't point the mace into the wind. The ranch gate came up fast; she locked the brakes. The truck stalled in a cloud of diesel exhaust. "Shit!" He was right behind her.

You forgot to put in the clutch, Allie; get it started.

"Tom!" She turned the key; the engine cranked over and over, finally surging back to life.

Thank God. Adrenaline pumping, she threw it in gear and turned down their gravel drive. "Not this time, you bastard!" The lights of the ranch came up fast. She leaned on the horn.

The front door opened; Mackay charged out to meet her, Afracela close behind in her Coat of Many Colors, glowing in the headlights. Allison jumped out of the truck, almost falling. Carlos caught her by the arm, his white hair a silver aura.

"Somebody's following me."

"Where is he?" Carlos asked calmly.

The headlights were gone. "He was right behind me all the way from the summit." Breathless. Heart hammering.

Carlos stared intently down the deserted road. "Go inside, Mrs. Call the Sheriff. I will take Mr. Tom's shotgun and go look."

He'd found her again. For a year, she'd been safe in Cambria until she glanced up from her desk at school and saw him casually sitting across the street, one arm draped over the back of a park bench as if waiting for her to come out and sit beside him. By the time the police arrived, Lyn was gone, but never for long.

Afracela took her arm. "Come inside, Mrs."

She felt her hold on life slipping away. Was the idyllic time with Tom and the twins a romantic dream and Lyn her only reality?

"Where's Tristan?"

"Sleeping."

"I promised I'd be here to tuck him in." Afracela put a restraining hand on her arm.

"He is fine, Mrs."

Allison hesitated. Lyn had broken into her life. "You don't know him. We need to call Jim; this man is dangerous."

"I'll call. Go and sit by the fire. I made you dinner."

Her face was serene, the warm touch of her hand a transfusion of confidence. Afracela's healing hands.

Allison bent down to pet Mackay, ears soft as velvet. "You're a good boy." His eyes narrowed to slits of pleasure. "Next time, I'll take you with me." Next time she would take Mackay and Tom's pistol. Get Lyn out of her life forever.

"The Sheriff is coming, Mrs. He will hurry." Afracela placed a tray with dinner before her.

The smell of soup made her sick; she pushed it away. "Has Kat called yet?"

"No, Mrs."

"I need to talk to her." She dialed Kat's number and waited and waited. Why didn't she answer? Was her flight delayed? She answered on the 7th ring just as the recording came on. Her voice strange and far away. "Kat?" A rush of traffic noise.

"Allison? Where are you?"

"Home. Where are you?"

"Turning into my garage. What's the matter? You sound upset."

"Lyn followed me home." Allison reached into her shirt, found Tom's horse pendant and began turning it over and over.

There was a crash on Kat's end. "Say again?"

"I said Lyn followed me home. He was right behind me. It was awful, just like Cambria." She gripped the pendant tightly, trying to keep her voice under control.

"Sorry, that was my garage door. That's what I thought you said. What do you mean followed you, from where?"

"I don't know, I just looked up and he was right behind me on the pass." Talking too fast, she slowed down. "He followed me all the way to the ranch gate."

"Are Carlos and Afracela there?"

"Yes, Carlos went out to find him." Afracela, arms folded, stood by the window, staring intently into the night. Headlights were coming up the drive.

"Did you call Jim?"

"I did---Afracela did."

"Are you sure it was Lyn, Allie? Did you actually see him?"

"Of course, I'm sure, Kat, I'm telling you it was him. Hell, he called me last night; you talked to him."

"Okay, okay. I was just wondering how he got over there so fast."

"He was probably here when he called. God, this is unbelievable."

Carlos came in carrying a shotgun; a cold wind followed. She shivered.

"Allie, are you still there?"

"Yes, just a minute, Carlos is back." Afracela and Carlos were conferring in low voices. "Did you find him?"

"No, he turned around at the gate," the old Mexican replied. "I go wait for the Sheriff."

Allison relayed the information to Kat.

"That's good, kiddo, sounds like they've got it under control."

"I'm scared, Kat."

Lyn had watched her working in her garden from a vantage point across the street, exactly the prescribed 100 yards required by the restraining order. It was happening all over again.

"Listen to me, Allie; you're safe. He won't mess around with Jim or Carlos. Hold on a minute."

Kat was breathing hard. "Are you all right?"

"Yeah, I'm climbing the stairs. The damn elevator's been giving me claustrophobia lately."

"I know that feeling."

"Hang on, I screwed up the code, and if I don't get it right, the county security guys will be out here to see what's going on."

"Did it work?" Afracela came over and took her

hand.

"Yeah, sorry, I'm inside now. The code's "Shadowcat"; do you remember him?"

"Sure, a great cat." Innocent days.

"He was, wasn't he? Listen, Allie, let Jim handle this. Lyn might kick women around but Jim will set him straight just like Tom did."

"You're right, he was afraid of Tom. God how I wish he was here."

Afracela smiled, dropped her hand, went to the table and poured tea.

"My guess is that Jim will scare him right back to California."

Afracela motioned to her, pulling out a chair.

"You know, I bet Lyn still lives over here. I'm going to have John Henry pay him a personal visit. We're going to stop this son of a bitch once and for all."

"John Henry? I can't imagine you asking him for anything."

"Well, he's the guy who can find Lyn, and when he does, you won't ever have to worry about him again."

Allison stared out the window. Where was Tom? Had she really heard his voice in the truck? The minestrone soup was getting cold, congealing. Her stomach rebelled.

"And while I'm at it, I'm going to have him contact the insurance company and see about your money. I hate to admit it, but he's the best man for that job too."

Allison touched her jaw, remembering the pain. "If you think we should."

"I do. Leave all this to me. You take care of yourself and Tristan."

"I'll do my best." She forced her hand away from her jaw and stretched her fingers wide. Her wide gold wedding band caught the light. "Thanks so much, Kat."

"You're welcome. Call me if Jim finds him and try not to worry too much. We'll get through this together, kiddo. I'm with you all the way."

"I love you, Kat."

"Love you too. Love to Tristan. Good night, Allie. Call me anytime."

The fire burned low. She stared at the soup and bread and mumbled an apology.

"Hot tea, then?" Afracela urged, sliding the cup in front of her.

"Yes, that would be nice, just give me a minute." She put her head down on her arms and closed her eyes. "Goddamn it," she mumbled. Grief over what she had lost sank its cold talons into her heart once again.

"Drink your tea, Mrs."

Afracela's hand touched her shoulder, an amazing infusion of energy. The dog looked up at her, concern in his yellow eyes. "It's okay, Mackay."

Afracela sat down at the table. "You, me and the Mackay dog," she smiled. "All good friends here." She pushed the gold gilt sugar bowl over to her.

Allison spooned in more sugar than usual and stirred. How could she lose her faith and courage so quickly? Tom would expect better than this.

The two women sipped their tea in silence. The log house creaked and settled around them. A living thing, built out of trees, mud, and rock. Mackay laid his warm body across her feet and went to sleep like Red Coyote in her dreams. Profoundly comforting.

Allison looked at her seascapes of Cambria. Her painting of Murden's Cove was Tom's favorite, an isolated spot where he walked Happy, totally blind by then, when he came on weekends. She was thrilled when he took such an interest, insisting Happy was still a great horse who just needed his confidence restored.

She had wonderful memories of those days leading up to their marriage. Tom had moved back to the ranch with the twins but was still wrapping up his business in Palo Alto and visited her often. They rode bikes in the hills, walked on the beach, ate dinner at intimate restaurants, went to bed early, got up late, and had scones and coffee while reading the Sunday Los Angeles Times in her pocket garden.

But when Tom took Happy to Murden's Cove, he always went alone. Until one summer morning, he asked her to meet them there. She waited, barefoot in the sand, shading her eyes until she saw them coming around the point along the surf line---Tom riding Happy at a full gallop in a cloud of spray, seagulls scattering in front of them.

"Tea gives you color," Afracela commented with her all knowing look.

Horse and rider thundering down a dazzling white sand beach on the edge of tumbling blue-green surf, a strip of burning orange-red sky above. Spray flying, gulls in wild, erratic flight in the intense clarity of morning light. Tom, shirtless, riding bareback in his distinctive, comfortable slouch, knees up and forward; Happy running free, mane flying, head turned to show his noble profile, chartreuse hand print on his flank. Man and horse on the verge of flight.

"There's nothing like a good cup of tea," Allison replied. "It always helps." She slipped her feet out from under Mackay. "Can I pour you some more?"

Afracela smiled and nodded.

She refilled their cups from the beautiful teapot Tom bought her at the Cambria Arts and Crafts Fair before moving to Montana, decorated with lilies, poppies, and pansies---like her garden there. "Now you'll always have your flowers with you, Allie." She glanced up again at the painting.

If her blind horse had enough faith in Tom to gallop down a beach through the waves, then she could carry on at the Windhorse. She prayed his presence and love would be there to guide her.

She felt calmer, more confident. Kat and Afracela were right; good people surrounded her and she had

Tristan. And Tom. He had spoken to her tonight; she was sure of it.

"Call me when Jim gets here. I'm going up and kiss Tristan goodnight." She had a promise to keep.

DREAMS OF APPALOOSAS
Chapter Eight: My Journal

September 28, 1 a.m.

My dear Tom,

I'm not too steady at the moment so bear with me and I'll get a better grip on my emotions. One day I'm up, the next day I'm in the black pit of despair. There are times when I honestly don't know if I can go on. But then I think of Tristan, our dreams for the Windhorse, the dogs and horses who all count on me, and I know I must find your Faith and Courage to get through each day. Kat assures me it will get better.

It's been one hell of a two weeks. I can't believe that after all these years Lyn is back. I don't know how he found me on that empty road, but fortunately, you were there when I needed you. Jim has been scouring the countryside ever since, but hasn't found a trace of him. I think he and Kat wonder if it really was Lyn stalking me again or just my conditioned response to his phone call. As for me, I know it was him.

Anyway, to make sure he gets the message to stay away, Kat asked John Henry to see if he can track Lyn down in California. She also asked him to see why the life insurance company hasn't paid us. That's the farthest thing from my mind at the moment, but she thinks it's important to get it settled.

Tom, you are the only one I can pour my heart out to completely. I long to see you again. The nights are the worst. Unless I paint myself to sleep, the nightmares return, and I despair that you are gone forever. But each morning gives me renewed hope. When I am in that blissful state of half wakefulness, I feel you next to me, your hands on my body, and we make love.

Tonight, I imagine we are together, catching up on our day---or in this case weeks---the way we used to, sitting on the porch, having a drink, watching the horses graze and Tristan play. God, how I miss you. So, in honor of the occasion, I have poured a shot of Black Label for both of us and we'll adhere to your rule of focusing on good news first.

So here it is. When I get home from school, if the weather's good, Carlos has Five Wounds, Moon Woman, and Happy saddled and ready to go and insists Tristan and I go riding with him where he's plowed a trail. "Good for you and the boy, Mrs." And he's right, of course. I feel so much better about everything on a horse.

Tristan rides Happy without a lead now. At first, I was anxious about his safety, but Carlos assured me there was nothing to be afraid of and gave me an incredible demonstration. He makes a series of clicking *sounds and Happy turns, stops, backs, trots and canters under perfect control while our Tristan hangs on to the saddle horn and reins, laughing and giggling.*

Carlos has also been busy halter breaking the weanlings. I love to watch him work and help when I have time. I talked to Henry and he'll start work after football. He's very excited about it and he'll be a big help. Maybe in the spring Carlos and I can get serious about finding your perfect stallion and replacing our lost mares. But it's too much now.

Carlos has also started basic ground training for the yearlings---following on a lead, circling in the arena on a long line and getting them used to the noisy plastic bag he waves around. Sunrise Princess is my favorite. What a beauty with her light golden body and beige and white spots. She is so very spirited but allows Carlos to lift her feet now and she's way ahead of the others, learning to back and step to the side. What a smart girl!

What else is in our good news column? There's so much more about Tristan to catch up on. When he's not riding, he's running. Afracela and I have to watch him like a hawk. He's a little wind up toy, put him down and he takes off at high speed--- he can be out of the house before you know it. Even Dotty Girl has a hard time keeping up with him. She tries to herd him around but is beginning to realize that, like you, he has a mind of his own. Mackay, of course, thinks it's all fun and games. I can't believe you are missing this. Perhaps you're not.

Tristan is constantly asking me about you, JB and Justin. He wants to know where his big brothers are who throw him up in the air and make him fly. And most of all, he wants to know why his father doesn't come home. He's really become quite persistent, even demanding. Last week we went to "Dad's Night" at his day school and one of the little girls asked him why his dad wasn't there. He looked over at me and said that was because his daddy was in the cemetery. I had to turn away so I wouldn't cry.

It's a hard thing to explain to a three-year-old. I tried using the example of the magnificent Merlin Falcon, with his golden breast and spotted white and dark elegant wings that died after hitting our window. How the two of you buried him in the garden with seeds for his journey into the next world while his mate circled overhead, waiting for his spirit to join her, as it surely would.

I told him the little cross you put over his body was only a marker and the grave was not the final resting place for birds, animals or people. Their spirits live on forever in our hearts just as you and Justin and JB always will.

I wish you could have seen his face, Tom. Talk about concentration. God knows, he's trying, but I don't know if he can yet understand what I'm trying to tell him. I guess that shouldn't surprise me. I can't even start to explain how I feel about your presence---or my vision of you riding by--- to those closest to me, including Kat, much less anyone else.

Making the transition from my private reality has been particularly difficult at school. In spite of myself, I still expect to see Justin and JB in the halls with their friends, and when they don't materialize, I feel an incredible sadness. However, thanks to Betty, the kindness of the kids and my fellow teachers, I was getting along pretty well until I had an unfortunate run in with the Snook boys. God knows why they're in my art appreciation class except it keeps them eligible for football.

They were snickering and making crude remarks about a classic Rubens nude I was using as an example of how the ideal woman used to look before the age of anorexia. I understood they were playing to their adoring female audience but I firmly told them to knock it off about the lady's big ass. It could have remained a humorous incident, but Dan decided to get belligerent. He told me that he didn't have to listen to a word I said because I was going to get fired along with my "fag" friend, Mr. Anderson.

With that, I escorted them out of class, and in the process, Dan brushed against my breast. I suppose it could have been accidental, but I don't think so because he only grinned and certainly didn't apologize. Anyway, I totally lost it and told him if he ever touched me again,

I'd file charges.

By the time I stormed down to the principal's office, I'd cooled off a bit and Hal assured me the boys wouldn't get back in school until they had personally apologized. He didn't seem overly concerned, however, that they called Dave a fag or that they implied I was going to be fired right along with him. Hal's attitude was boys will be boys; don't worry about it.

I reminded him Reverend Snook would be leading the opposition to Dave and Darwin at the school board meeting. I also put him on notice that I would be there to defend Dave's personal and professional integrity. He seemed a little taken aback but didn't take the opportunity to offer his support for either one of us.

Anyway, Betty is standing with us one hundred percent---as you would expect---including phoning parents to solicit support. But I'm afraid the damage has been done. It makes me want to weep or throw bricks, depending on the time of day. They don't appreciate what a battle Dave is fighting or what an extraordinary teacher he is and how lucky we are to have him. Now I regret persuading him to move here. I sure didn't do him any favors, did I?

So Betty (God bless her!) and I are going into this meeting loaded for bear. We plan to fight Reverend Snook every step of the way on Dave's behalf. I know you will approve because you love Dave as much as I do. I wish you were coming with us.

Finally---my God it's getting late, isn't it? I've decided to have a come-to-Jesus meeting with Ben over his constant pressure to buy the Windhorse. As you know, I don't like confrontations and I honestly don't want to upset your brother, but enough is enough. It's time he understands we're here to stay. To be quite frank, I find Ben intimidating. If you've got any good ideas on how to handle him, I sure wish you'd let me know.

I am hopeful that Ben will see the benefit of our plan, although I'm not counting on it given his hostility to everything Indian and our Appaloosas. I plan to offer him the Howard family photos, especially the big one of the General. And I'm going to take down the dead animals; perhaps Ben would like them too. The room is full of death and destruction and I have enough of that in the present and don't need to be reminded daily of the past; it's too depressing. I'll brighten it up with Eagle from the Light and my current Howard ranch series.

In the meantime, Kat---what would we do without her?---has been helping us finalize our conservation agreement with the estate lawyers so we can realize our dream of Appaloosas running free and letting the ranch go back to nature. Then, hopefully, the restless spirits of the Nez Perce can finally return home and have the peace they never found in this life. Appaloosas once again roaming next to the Memorial--- eagles riding the wind in an eternally blue sky—grazing elk, deer and antelope and, of course, Red Coyote and all his friends. A SPIRITUAL, MAGICAL, HISTORICAL PLACE that will never change. Our LIVING MEMORIAL. Something for Tristan so he will always remember us.

Once again I'm thinking about my big painting to match our big dreams. Hundreds of Appaloosas with all their streaks, spots, and stripped hooves, painted with fantastic yellow, black, and crimson lightening designs, galloping out of monumental boiling white clouds over the Big Hole River. Maybe one of your Cumulonimbus Mammas? I have no idea what they look like, but I always love to hear you say it. I'm going to call it "Dreams of Appaloosas." What do you think?

Well, I'm out of Black Label. I hope you don't mind if I borrow a little from you, perhaps it will help me get to sleep. It's a cold clear night, and if I hold my breath and listen, I can hear you and Keith coming up the drive. God, wouldn't that be great! I'm here. Waiting.

As always, all my love forever,

Allie

DREAMS OF APPALOOSAS
Chapter Nine: Eyes of the Elk

A dark wintery evening, no stars. Snow glittered in the headlights, a narrow path of diamonds leading her home from school. Old fears and habits reasserted themselves, constantly checking the rear view mirrors for any sign of Lyn. Nothing but empty road and the lonely whine of tires.

Allison took Tom's loaded pistol out of the glove compartment and put it on the seat beside her. "Remember, Allie, the only reason to load a pistol is because you intend to use it." A cold, menacing, weapon.

Her meeting that afternoon with the Snook boys had not gone well. Their required, perfunctory apology could never repair the damage done by their sneering reference to Dave as a fag, and she told them so. They shrugged. The principal seemed unconcerned. So unfair, so ugly.

Feeling cold, she turned up the heat and thought about putting in a CD. Something, anything to relieve her frustration and loneliness. The Rolling Stones "Wild

Horses"? No, she wasn't in the mood. All wrong without Tom or the twins, it would only make things worse.

But once home, there would be Tristan. They'd have a quiet, peaceful time together in front of the fire, playing with his dinosaurs or reading Green Eggs and Ham for the thousandth time. Her mother had given it to him for his third birthday. She thought it might be too sophisticated, but it wasn't. He loved that book and she loved reading it to him.

Except Ben was coming over. She'd promised Tom to put it on the line with him once and for all. They were not going to sell the ranch or run his cows; they were going to raise Appaloosas.

Anxiously, she touched the feathered necklace Carlos had given her that morning, a surprise. Soft and smooth against her skin. Raven and flicker feathers, Indian trade beads collected by Tom's mother, tiny sea shells from Cambria. "This will protect you, Mrs." And he'd made a bracelet out of Happy's tail hairs for Tristan.

But would it? And from what? Lyn? Grief? Sadness?

The necklace was certainly beautiful. *A field of Mars Black with a single narrow band of light cutting diagonally across it, leading to this magic talisman high in one corner.* A companion piece to her white void painting with its tiny eagles. Big pieces, side by side, light and dark, hope and despair.

The glowing red eyes came out of nowhere. She locked the brakes. The truck came to a shuddering, skidding stop as the elk bounded across the road and leaped the fence.

A second slower would have been too late. A jarring impact, flesh on metal. "Oh God, I'm so sorry." A magnificent cow elk, an unforgivable lapse. "Pay attention, Allison!" A horrible thing to live with, saved only by an instinctive reaction. And luck.

Heart pounding, she put the truck in gear and drove on slowly, deliberately, images of what might have been, scenes of carnage turning over and over, the glowing eyes, foot on the brake too late, a crushed body, or worse, wounded, legs broken. Could she use Tom's pistol to put the poor animal out of its misery?

Ben's muddy pickup was parked in front of the house. He was early, that wasn't good. She sat for a moment, trying to gather herself for the ordeal ahead. There was something in the back of his truck, something big, out of place. She stepped out to take a closer look.

The head and wide rack of a bull elk hung over the tailgate. Blood dripped steadily from his mouth, forming a red pool in the slushy snow. "You murdering bastard!" Soft brown eyes glassed over with a hazy film of death. The elk she and Kat had seen grazing peacefully in their pasture only weeks ago.

"I've had it with your goddamn brother, Tom!" Allison stormed up the front walk, hot fury building with each long stride. "Absolutely had it!"

A grim faced Afracela met her at the door.

"Where's Ben? Where's Tristan?"

The old lady pointed silently to the living room. "Little boy is upstairs with the dogs. Mr. Ben don't like dogs."

"I know, but this is my house, Afracela, our house, not his. Please go up and sit with Tristan until we're finished. This won't take long."

He was standing in front of the smoldering fireplace, staring at her Eagle from the Light painting. A thin layer of smoke drifted along the high ceiling. He turned, half filled shot glass in hand. "Evenin'."

He wore a quilted, camouflage hunting suit turned down at the waist and a dirty sweatshirt. "I want to talk to you, Ben." She landed on his name like a hammer.

"What's the problem? You look like you seen a ghost."

There was a half empty bottle of Black Label on the coffee table. Tom always told him to help himself, and he always did. "How dare you park in front of our house with that dead elk where my little boy can see it?"

He shrugged his heavy shoulders. "Where the hell do you want me to park?"

She ignored his question. "And you better not have shot him on our property."

He finished his whiskey with a dismissive toss and gave her a lopsided smile.

"Jesus, take it easy, will ya? I got him up on the Big Black Dome, fair and square, that's way, way off your place."

He stared at her feathered necklace as if he might tear it off. Unnerved, she stepped back. "You know how I feel about hunting, Ben, about killing animals, any animal, and I expect you to respect that." A weak pleading statement. That wouldn't do.

"No problem. Want a shot?" He bent down to refill his glass, holding up the bottle when he was done.

"I won't tolerate it, Ben, and I don't want a drink."

"Okay, okay, you made your point. Anyway, what I shoot is my business." He drained the whiskey in one gulp and set the glass down on the coffee table, appraising her with cold grey eyes.

In vain, she looked for some resemblance to Tom but found none.

"Did you know Tom used to be a hunter?" he asked casually.

"So he said."

"Him and me hunted together all the time when we was kids. Shot that big old moose there. Tom was maybe, I don't know, thirteen. Dad was mighty proud."

Old enough to know better, she thought grimly.

"That was before he went off to California," Ben went on conversationally. "California. That sure changed old Tom all around."

"Really." Thank God.

Ben turned back to her painting as the grandfather clock struck the hour with strident, hollow clangs. "So what's this supposed to be anyway?"

"What does it look like?"

"Some kind of Indian. Why have you got him here?"

"You mean in this room?"

"Yeah, he don't belong with them." Ben waved a big hand at the row of family photographs.

"Why not?"

"Because this is their place, that's why." Ben went over to the photograph of the General. "This old man was murdered by an Indian right here in this room. Did you know that?"

He moved gracefully for such a big man, cat like. It was the first time she'd seen him animated and it alarmed her. "I did."

"It took our people four generations to build this ranch into what it is today. They worked like slaves. Took a goddamn piece of worthless wilderness and made somethin' out of it with their bare hands."

"But it didn't belong to them, Ben," Allison countered heatedly. "They just took it; did you ever consider that?"

Meaty lips curled in contempt, eyes narrowed. "You got it all wrong about these goddamn Indians, you know that?" He pointed at the painting. "He never lived here; he was just a murderin', uncivilized savage passin' through."

"He's not the only murderer in this room, Ben Howard," she countered angrily.

"Them Nez Perce bastards killed white settlers, whole families, tortured them, cut off their hands and legs and stuff you don't even want to know about and watched um die," he rumbled on. "You can look it up."

"That may be, but those were isolated incidents involving young men drunk on white man's whiskey who had been abused and humiliated by settlers and missionaries who stole their land," she snapped back angrily. "And you can look that up."

"Uncivilized bastards," he growled.

"If General Howard was so civilized, why didn't he let them go?" she countered stridently. "I mean seriously, they'd already been driven out of their homeland, they knew they couldn't win, they were on the run. They just wanted to be left alone."

"Because somebody had to get rid of them that's why."

"Get rid of them? These were human beings, Ben, like you and me."

"Not to me, they aren't." He fixed her with grey unblinking eyes.

Allison met his stare, wanting to unleash her anger. There were so many things she wanted to say. "This isn't getting us anywhere, Ben." Kat said some people were killers, and her brother-in-law was one of them.

"I guess not."

Then she saw the family resemblance. The arrogant lift of the jaw, the granite profile. *Ben and General*

Howard posed together---Ben with his foot on the head of the dead elk---Zachery Howard with his foot on the head of a dead Indian. Vain, proud, foolish men, oblivious to the raging prairie fire about to engulf them.

"Why don't you take that photo of the General home with you?"

"This one?"

She felt the tension ease. "Yes, I'd like you to have it."

He looked as if he didn't believe her. "In fact, you can have most of the photographs in this room along with the animal heads. Do you want them?"

"Sure, I guess so."

"Good. Look, it's getting late. There's something I want to tell you." The grandfather clock ticked off each second as it had been doing for more than a hundred years.

"Oh, yeah? Well I got something over here for you too."

They went back to the coffee table, sitting on opposite sides, but before she could say anything, Ben picked up a manila envelope with her name scrawled on the front in black marker.

"Like I told you, you can't make a go of this place on your own. You need me to run the Windhorse and the 7/7 together, like I did for Tom."

"We've been over and over this," she replied impatiently. "Tom and I don't intend to run it as a hay

142

and cattle ranch any more. It's going to be a preserve for our Appaloosas."

"In the first place them Indian ponies can't winter here and wander around on their own. This is the coldest place in the lower forty-eight. You gotta bring um in and feed um hay," he snorted.

"I'm aware of that."

"Well, where you gonna get the hay and who's gonna haul it and who's gonna go out there in the dead of winter to feed? And who's gonna repair all the machinery, the trucks, the tractors and stuff, like I've been doin' since I was a kid---that broken down old Mexican?"

"We can do it."

"Hell, it's a waste of prime land, Allison. The 7/7 was the best goddamn ranch in Montana before my folks broke it up, and it can still be if you'd give it a chance….."

He stopped and poured another shot. "Look, the thing is, you can't break it up and make money. I know. I spent thirty years figurin' it out. We got 10,000 acres here and it all works together, but not in two pieces, you understand? You got your bottom land and your water and I got the high grazing land. We need it all."

The conversation was getting away from her. She tried to interrupt and explain they weren't doing it to make money, but he cut her off, face flushed.

"The 7/7 ain't gonna end up being one of those

hobby outfits owned by some stockbroker back East or busted up into pieces for big houses so fat ass fly-fishermen can get their rocks off on the weekend." He swallowed the last of his whiskey. "While I was in Nam gettin' shot at by gooks, they were buyin' up every good ranch in Montana. That ain't goin' happen here."

"That's enough, Ben. This isn't getting us anywhere."

"You don't know what you're doing, lady," he went on, waving the manila envelope at her. "You just got a lot of fancy ideas, but take it from me….."

Angrily, Allison stood up. "Tom and I know what we're doing."

"What's Tom got to do with it?"

"He and I planned this together. It will work; we'll make it work. We…." She stopped, feeling tears coming. I need your help, Tom.

"Jesus Christ," he muttered, glancing again at her feather necklace. He opened the envelope. "Look, I got somethin' for you."

Reluctantly, Allison sat, reaching into her shirt collar for Tom's gold horse, fighting back tears.

"Here."

He handed her a cashier's check made out to Mrs. Allison Howard. Caught by surprise, she counted the zeroes. Nine million dollars. "That's a lot of money."

"Had the Windhorse appraised; that's what it's worth. I mortgaged the 7/7 to raise the cash. It's a fair

144

price."

"I'm sure it is." She felt his eyes on her as she pushed the check aside.

"Well?"

"I don't know what to say."

"Say yes. Hell, you don't really care about the ranch or the people who built it. You just give me all their pictures."

Aroused, she looked up at him intently. Ben was smiling. He thought she would cave in. "I care about our place, just not the way you do."

The smile vanished. "I guess not. Look, I'll stop back and pick up the ancestors and the trophies another time. I'll leave the check here. You think about it."

"I won't change my mind."

"We'll see about that."

DREAMS OF APPALOOSAS
Chapter Ten: One of the Blood

Kat arrived early Saturday morning and they had coffee sitting on the top rail of the round pen while Carlos warmed up Poker Joe, Justin's three-year-old Appaloosa gelding, on a long line. A clear crisp morning, the rugged Beaverhead Mountains stood guard to the west, a row of granite warriors dressed for winter. Brilliant, sharply defined colors, red vine maple, shimmering yellow aspen, clumps of silver white iridescent grasses poking through sparkling snow.

"Are you really going to ride that horse?" Kat asked skeptically.

It was hard to work in the round pen and not think about the twins. Justin, their long-haired, independent, rough tough outspoken bull rider. "Pardon?" So different from JB, team leader, quiet, crew-cut quarterback, everybody's friend.

"I said are you going to ride that horse? He looks a little squirrelly to me."

"Poker Joe? You bet I am, and he's spirited, not squirrely." Still haunted by the horrible sight of the dead elk and the unsettling meeting with Ben, it was the last thing she wanted to do. But Justin had great hopes for this horse and she always felt better riding.

"Another great name. Who was Poker Joe?"

"A Nez Perce hero who led the escape after the disaster here. The Army thought they had them surrounded in Yellowstone Park, but Poker Joe got them out of the trap. He knew that country like the back of his hand."

"It wasn't a park then, was it?"

"Ironically it was a brand new park, and believe it or not, there were already tourists there. Some of them ran into the Nez Perce and got killed. The Indians were in a bad mood after the Big Hole and felt like everyone had turned on them."

"How so?"

"Well, they'd gone through Montana many times in the past on their way to hunt buffalo and always got along with whites along the way. They traded with them; there were few conflicts. But after the ambush at the Big Hole and the wanton killing of women and children, the Nez Perce decided it was a fight to the finish."

They silently watched as Poker Joe, with his impressive display of brown and white spots, trotted steadily around in wide circles, trailing a fine mist of powder snow and dust while Carlos, Dodger blue baseball cap on backwards, remained stationary, deftly shifting the long line from one gloved hand to the other.

She felt Kat studying her. She had to clear her mind and concentrate. It would not be good to get on Poker Joe angry and upset. As Tom constantly reminded her, horses know when you aren't on top of your game and that can be dangerous.

"Maybe you ought to wait for another day to ride him, Allie," Kat suggested, clearly sensing her mood.

"I'll be fine. This is what I do, Kat, it's important to me." For Justin, JB and most of all, Tom. If she quit on them now, she'd lose them forever.

With a snap of the long line, Carlos moved the horse from a trot to a canter. Tail and head high, gait smooth and seemingly effortless, although streaks of sweat were beginning to mark his dusty flanks.

Kat leaned forward. "You know, that man is remarkable."

"He is, isn't he?" The rhythm of the light-footed horse was hypnotic. *Two shadows in a haze of brick red layered dust back-lit by the morning sun in bands of Naples Yellow, Potter's Pink, Violet and yellow ochre. Carlos, stationery in the center of the ring, a bull fighter in a glittering Suit of Lights, the illusive spirit of Poker Joe flying around him.*

She closed her eyes, trying to hold this inspiring image, but the colors faded into a twisting swirl. Dizzy with fatigue, she gripped the fence rail for support.

Kat reached over to steady her. "You all right, kiddo?"

"Not really, I had an awful day yesterday, and I didn't sleep much last night."

Carlos slowed Poker Joe to a trot, then a walk and led him over to the far rail where there was a saddle waiting.

Kat took out a cigarette. "You want one?"

"No thanks. I've got to go to work here in a minute." Despite losing their best brood mares in the accident, there were a lot of horses to finish; Carlos couldn't do it alone.

"So what happened yesterday, Allie?" Kat exhaled a long stream of smoke into the pristine air and stepped down off the railing.

Allison got down with her. "Oh, everything. The Snook boys apologized to me because they had to, but if you call somebody a fag in a place like this, there's no way to take it back."

"Well, Jim was pretty emphatic about nipping that sort of thing in the bud."

"I know, but he's the exception to the rule around here."

"A rather important exception, Allie. And speaking of Jim, did he ever come up with anything on Lyn?"

"No, but that doesn't mean he wasn't here."

"I didn't say that."

"But you were thinking it."

"No, I was thinking John Henry didn't have any better luck in California. Apparently Lyn was teaching at the La Jolla Art Institute but got fired six months ago for improper conduct with a female student. No surprise there, and no forwarding address either."

"God, I was so naïve, it's embarrassing just thinking about it."

Kat put an arm around her shoulder. "You were young, kiddo, that's not a crime."

"Maybe not, but did you ever see any of his paintings?"

"I don't believe I did. They were very modern, right?"

"And violent and chaotic in a disturbing sort of way. I guess I should have paid more attention to them."

"Well, it's over and done with now."

"I sure hope so." Carlos was leading a saddled Poker Joe across the arena, Mackay ran out to meet them. She couldn't have all these distractions weighing her down; she had to tell Kat about the elk and Ben before she got on him. "And then I came home last night and Ben's truck was parked right in front of the house with a bleeding dead elk in the back, it was just awful."

"I'm so sorry, Allie."

"He denied it, but I'm sure it was the same one we saw in the pasture before you left last time. I just can't get that picture out of my mind."

"For good reason. Why the hell was he here in the first place? What did he want?

"He wants to buy the Windhorse. He gave me a

check for nine million dollars."

Kat's emerald green eyes fastened on her. "Where would he get money like that?"

"He said he mortgaged the 7/7."

Carlos brought Poker Joe up to the rail. They were both covered with a fine layer of red dust, giving them a wild, primitive look. "Ready, Mrs.?"

"Yes." Time to put on what Justin called her "game face". It was so lonely without the boys; they had such great faith she could rise to any challenge.

"Drawn on a local bank?"

"I don't know. It doesn't matter. I told him I'm not selling." She looked away to the snow covered hills, glowing pink in the morning light, then climbed over the rail into the arena. "Let all your energy go into your feet, Mom. Concentrate, feel it." Lessons from her stepson, the bull rider.

Carlos handed her the reins and stepped back. Allison ran her hand down the big gelding's sweating flank, rubbed his head and withers. "Don't get in a hurry, wait until you both relax. Let your tension go."

Now it was just the two of them. And when the unmistakable waves of calm finally came, she gathered the reins loosely in one hand, grasped the saddle horn with the other, and put a boot in the stirrup.

Poker Joe didn't move. Solid. Stoic. Ready. Slowly, she stepped up, flexing her knee, putting more weight in the stirrup. "How we doing, big boy?"

He turned his head slightly toward her. She didn't look at him. "All set?" Allison took a deep breath, swung her free leg over and sat, leaving her right foot out of the dangling stirrup on the opposite side, just in case.

Poker Joe let out an audible sigh. "Looks like we're good." She slipped the right foot into the stirrup and adjusted her seat until she felt centered, remembering Justin's creed, "It doesn't matter what you say, Mom, it's how you say it."

"Let's go, Joe." A light touch of the heel, forward in the saddle, and they walked past Kat just as a red pickup truck towing a silver horse trailer came up the driveway. "Will you go see who that is please?" She moved her hips with the horse; they were on the way. Go with the flow.

"Will do. You're looking good, kiddo."

"Thanks."

Kat watched a man get out of the truck, say a few words to Afracela, then go in the house. The shiny red pickup had a gold framed license plate that read "Horsedoc". She heard a horse kicking and snorting inside the trailer as she walked by.

Kat paused in the living room doorway to adjust her eyes to the dark interior. The man stood with his back to her, looking at the Eagle from the Light painting. Tall, wide shoulders, raven black hair wrapped in a tight pony tail with colored yarn.

He turned. "Mrs. Howard?"

"No." Kat stared as he held out his hand, focusing on his well manicured nails, a heavy silver and turquoise bracelet and ring. "I'm her sister, Katherine."

"My mistake."

His handshake was gentle. Kat withdrew her hand. "She's out riding, Mr.?"

"Billy. Billy Blackmere. I was an old friend of Tom's, but I've never met his wife."

"She'll be in soon," Kat replied briskly. He had a classic, chiseled, copper face. High, sharply defined cheek bones, a slightly hooked nose with flared nostrils. They were about the same height.

"This is a great painting," he commented.

"Mrs. Howard---Allison---is the artist."

"Who is this anyway?"

"Eagle from the Light, a Nez Perce war chief."

"I saw a photograph of him once, but he was in his ceremonial gear. I like this better," Billy replied, touching her lightly on the waist, inviting her to share his impression.

Kat looked at him closely.

He smiled. "What?"

"Nothing. I was just thinking that you look quite a bit like him, if you don't mind my saying so."

"Well, we're both Nez Perce if that's what you mean---one of the blood." He gave her a forgiving smile. "And how about you? Are you from California like your sister?"

They looked directly at each other. "What makes you think that?"

"The suntan. It goes nicely with your red hair---if you don't mind my saying so."

Kat laughed. "You're an admirer of red hair, Mr. Blackmere?"

"Please call me Billy. My great grandfather had red hair, or so I'm told. He was a Scottish trapper."

"Really?" Kat looked uncomfortably around the cold living room. "I'll tell you what, Billy, let's go find my sister."

"Okay."

"What are you here to see her about?"

"Actually, I brought her a present; it's supposed to be a surprise."

"A present?" They walked out and stopped by his truck and trailer. "Is it inside?"

"If I told you, Katherine, it wouldn't be a surprise, would it?"

"No, I guess not. I'll go get her."

Allison was circling the round pen on Poker Joe, relaxed and in control. "Hey there, cowgirl," Kat called out as she loped past, "there's a tall, dark, handsome guy here who says he's got a present for you."

She reined in the horse. They were doing well together, a flawless ride so far. Good things were definitely beginning to happen. A present sounded

154

intriguing. She stepped down, gave the reins to Carlos and followed her sister. Halfway across the driveway, she realized Carlos and Mackay were coming too.

There was an unmistakable sparkle in Kat's eyes, and when she introduced her to Billy, Allison knew why. A gorgeous man by any standard. So this was the accomplished vet she'd heard so much about from Tom. "It's very nice to meet you, Mr. Blackmere," she said formally, giving Kat what she hoped was a private knowing glance as she introduced Carlos.

"Mucho gusto." Carlos inclined his head politely.

The First Americans. *Horses, beads, feathers, blood and gold. Carlos in his priestly regalia, robes and snakes, curved silver dagger poised; Billy in war paint, a long trailing feathered headdress, lance at the ready. Buffalo running, volcanoes smoldering, eagles back lit by a smoky sun.*

"Tom told me a lot about you, Mr. Garcia. I'd like to watch you work sometime."

"Como no, senor."

Billy turned to Allison. "Your sister said you painted that portrait in the living room. I really like it."

"Thank you." This was Eagle from the Light in blue jeans and cowboy boots.

"I apologize for dropping in unannounced."

"That's alright. I remember Tom mentioning you many times. You're the vet. He bought Keith from your uncle, up near Moscow, or was it Pullman?"

155

Billy nodded. "That's right, from my namesake Uncle Billy. He actually lives in Lapwai on the reservation. Keith was quite a horse. How is he anyway?"

"As lively as ever."

Billy Blackmere took off his flat Navajo hat. "I'm really sorry I wasn't here for the funeral, Mrs. Howard. I was on the East Coast at the time. I am sincerely sorry for your loss. Tom and the boys were wonderful people."

Allison turned away. "There's no need to apologize; I know he'll understand." Mare's tails on the horizon. God's most beautiful clouds. Tom's barometer of changing weather.

"Actually, I don't know if Tom told you, but he and I worked together on an Appaloosa project whenever we had time. I specialize in equine genetics at Washington State University." He replaced the flat hat, carefully adjusting it until it sat level on his head, and glanced at Kat.

"Tom and I were both interested in bringing the Appaloosa back. Our goal was to find the best original bloodline available which wasn't easy because the breed has been scattered and not well recorded."

The trailer rocked back and forth as the horse stomped his feet. "Which is why it took me so long to get here. I actually talked to Tom earlier this year and told him I thought we were finally getting somewhere."

Allison looked at him questioningly.

Kat stepped forward. "Well, Mr. Blackmere, I don't know about everyone else, but the suspense is killing me." Mackay barked at Billy, wagging his tail in anticipation.

"Sure, of course."

He seemed embarrassed by Kat's attention. Allison stole a look at her sister and Kat winked at her. Despite his alarming good looks, he was a shy man.

"I only wish Tom and his boys were here to see this, Mrs. Howard, but I promised him I'd be here on your 5th anniversary and I'm pretty close, aren't I?"

Next Tuesday. She clutched Tom's horse pendant and nodded, unable to speak.

Billy went to the trailer, opened the back gate, and pulled down the loading ramp. The Appaloosa horse colt came prancing out, tail and head high, ears alert. He was dark, almost black, with a spray of white spots spreading across his hindquarters like scattered stars.

"My God, look at that beautiful horse," Kat exclaimed.

Billy gave the colt his head. He circled once and went straight to Carlos. The old man swept off his hat and bowed. "Ah, que caballo," he exclaimed reverently.

Billy took Allison's arm. "This is your anniversary present from Tom. His name is Eagle's Light. There isn't another one like him in the world, and considering your painting, Tom named him well."

Eagle looked at her curiously.   Allison burst into tears.

"*Don't cry, Allie. This is the one we've been waiting for.*"

DREAMS OF APPALOOSAS
Chapter Eleven: My Journal

October 15

My dear Tom,

What a great day! I still can't believe I heard your voice again, but I did; you were right next to me. Your presence was so strong it sent a chill up my spine. And Eagle's Light---your fantastic anniversary present! What could be better than that beautiful little horse colt? He's given us all such a boost---me, Tristan who loves him, and Carlos who is absolutely thrilled. You're right; this is the stallion we've been waiting for. Thank you, thank you for lifting us up.

As you can tell, I'm still on quite a high, wandering pleasantly on this occasion of our anniversary, marveling that it's been five years since we said our vows in the little Episcopal Church in Claremont---you and me, Mom, Dad, Kat, Dave and the twins---and your friend Vicar Bill who read that inspiring passage from Corinthians: "Faith, hope and love abide….and the greatest of these is love."

And then we had that wonderful wedding reception at the ranch. I think everyone in the valley was there, the country and western band, dancing, hay rides, fishing, games for the kids, and that giant barbeque, steak, salmon and endless vegetables from Afracela's garden.

And, of course, Betty. It was the first time I met her and I'll never forget how she took me aside and said in her imitable Betty way: "Hey, girl, you've got to be a dandy if Tom married you. I know we're going to be the best of friends."

And we have been ever since, what a blessing.

I remember how she and her boys brought in that giant wedding cake she made for the occasion. It must have been three stories high, bright yellow frosting with little plastic horses prancing around the edge, Congratulations Tom and Allison! Tristan plays with those horses now and I always smile when I see them.

And did you see how Carlos, looking for all the world like a Mayan pied piper, led Eagle into the barn with Tristan and Dotty and Mackay marching along behind? God, what a fantastic picture. I've never seen Carlos so enthralled with a horse. He is such a gorgeous little creature, so proud, so self possessed, already prancing around giving the mares the eye. Thank you! I love him! I love you! You have always been the most incredibly thoughtful person.

And speaking of love, Kat seems quite taken with

Billy Blackmere and was chatting away like a school girl at dinner tonight. It does my heart good to see her happy and I'm sure it's a relief to have someone to talk to besides her grief stricken sister.

Anyway, I have no idea if anything will come of it, but I persuaded Billy to stay the night and suggested he and Kat might like to go riding in the morning. You know what kind of good things can happen between a man and woman on horseback!

I hope you had a chance to see me up on Poker Joe this afternoon. I'll admit I was apprehensive, but I think Justin would be proud of us both. Joe was a perfect gentleman, filling me with confidence and hope, thanks no doubt to those hours and hours your son spent with him.

So all in all, Tom, this was the best day I've had in a long, long time. I was thinking about going down to the studio to start a portrait of our new arrival, Eagle's Light, along with Tristan and the dogs, but all this happy excitement makes me very sleepy and that is rare so I best take advantage of it.

Goodnight my love. Thanks for staying close. I'll see you in my dreams.

Love,

A

DREAMS OF APPALOOSAS
Chapter Twelve: Midnight Riders

———————

Snow crunched under his boots. "Good morning, Mama, I have tea."

"Come in, Lalman." She unzipped her red mummy bag. Bitter cold. He pulled the tent flap back. A flood of brilliant, blinding light; air filled with dancing feathery ice crystals.

Crouching, he set a tray down. She longed to huddle in her bag but felt obligated to this polite young Nepalese guide who got up in the dark so they could have morning tea like British lords and ladies of old. "Thank you."

He smiled and nodded, pouring from a battered copper kettle into two tin cups.

Stiff from their long climb up from deep valleys. Herds of wild Mongol ponies grazing along rushing dirty-white glacier fed rivers. Villages of crude stone houses, green fields cultivated on steep slopes, high snow covered passes, prayer flags flying straight out in the wind.

Their honeymoon trek.

Today they were going to the base camp of Dhaulagiri, higher than either of them had ever been. "Come on, Tom, get up, time to rise and shine."

His sleeping bag was empty. "Tom, where are you?" The tent was bigger than she remembered, full of oriental rugs and people sleeping under piles of animal skins.

"Gone," Lalman announced solemnly.

"Gone? Gone where?"

"To climb the mountain."

"No!" He would die! She struggled out of the bag; freezing air fastened on her like a claw. "I have to stop him." Desperately, she collected her climbing gear. "Where are my boots? I can't find my boots."

"Don't worry, Allison, I'll help you find them." An old haggard Lyn got up from under a pile of skins, shedding them one by one, coming toward her, dark and threatening.

"I don't want your help! I have to save Tom!"

"I need you, Allison."

"I have a gun!" Where was it in the chaos of the tent?

As he raised his hand to strike; she heard a chilling animal growl. Red Coyote was at her side, fangs bared.

———————

"Get up, Mrs." The lights were blinding. She sat up with a jolt. Startled, Mackay jumped off the bed, barking.

"What's wrong?" Why had Tom gone without her?

"Mr. Billy needs you downstairs."

"Who?"

"Mr. Billy."

"Now?" It was 2 a.m. Acid fear rose in her throat. Another call from the State Police? Mrs. Howard?---Mrs. Allison Howard?----Your husband.......

"He needs help with the horses. Get dressed, please."

"Why?" She got unsteadily to her feet. Where were her boots?

"Somebody painted them."

Lalman's eyes, dark, mysterious, foreign. "Painted the horses?" Her jaw ached where it had been broken so many years ago. Tom's pistol was on top of his desk in the burnished leather holster.

"Yes, the young horses, very bad. Here." Afracela laid jeans and a wool shirt on the bed beside her. "Mr. Billy is in the kitchen. I take care of Tristan; you don't worry about him."

"Thank you." She pulled on her pants and shirt. Her boots were beside the bed where she'd left them. Her heart was racing. Why would somebody paint their horses? She grabbed her pendant and necklace off the bureau.

A frightening, confusing dream. Why had Tom gone to climb Dhaulagiri? Lyn, sick and old, reaching out to her.

Afracela helped her fasten the gold horse and feathered necklace around her neck. "I'll be back as soon as I can."

"God be with you, Mrs."

There had been a tragic death on the mountain. Kind, gentle Lalman, their guide and friend, lost in a massive avalanche with three Swiss climbers shortly after they got back to Montana.

Should she take Tom's pistol? No. She touched the horse pendant and talisman. What else? Mackay. Keep him close. He was waiting at the bedroom door, tail wagging.

One more ritual. She quickly traced the silver cross and letters on Tom's black granite paper weight, one letter at a time. "Faith and Courage."

"Come on, Mackay, let's go."

———————

He had his back to her, filling buckets in the kitchen sink, wearing his classic blue down Powderhorn ski jacket. "Tom!"

"Mrs. Howard." He turned toward her, wiping his hands on a red and white checkered towel.

"Oh, I'm sorry, for a moment I thought you were my husband." One thrilling moment.

"Well, it's probably his jacket. I got cold and found it in the mud room. I hope you don't mind."

"Of course not." It fit him well.

"Did Afracela tell you what happened to the horses?"

"Yes, but I don't understand why would someone do this." Innocent flight animals.

"I don't either, Mrs. Howard, but right now I need you to help Carlos calm them down so Katherine and I can do the clean up." He stepped closer. "I know it's a shock, but I think we can take care of it with soap, water and a little paint thinner. I found some of that in the barn."

"They painted all the horses? What about the new colt? What about our little ones?" The last descendants of the mares who had perished on Lost Trail Pass. Eagle's Light, their hope for the future.

"Fortunately, the weanlings were in the barn with the colt. They went after the yearlings in the outer pasture down by the road. They tried to rope Keith but he broke loose and showed up here raising hell. That's what woke us all up."

"He's a strong horse." Tom's horse. The Spirit of Windhorse. Who hated them enough to do such a despicable thing? Lyn, Ben, the Snooks? Not possible, or was it?

"Can you help Carlos get them calmed down and into

the barn for us?" He took the foaming buckets out of the sink and set them down.

"Of course. Mackay will help." He looked up at her eagerly. He wasn't afraid.

Billy picked up the buckets, one in each hand. "I'll see you out there then, Mrs. Howard."

"Alright, and it's Allison, please call me Allison."

She lingered in the kitchen for a moment while she put on Tom's drover coat and found warm gloves. The paintings of Tom and the boys boosted her confidence. They were with her.

But the images of loved ones and the security of Tom's rugged old coat didn't protect her against what she saw in the arena under the ghosting midnight moon and harsh glare of ranch lights. Eight yearlings bunched together, charging back and forth in the dust, whinnying, snorting, rolling their eyes, covered with florescent pink spray paint.

"My God, Tom, look what they've done to our horses!" She felt Billy's grip on her arm.

"Mrs. Howard, Allison, are you up to this?"

Faith and courage, Allie, faith and courage.

Allison swallowed hard. "Yes."

Carlos moved slowly and deliberately behind the darting herd, swinging an open loop in slow motion. Jim's pickup was parked next to the barn. "Is the Sheriff here?"

"Yes. He's out in the pasture where this happened.

168

I'll be in the barn with Katherine."

She forced herself to step into the corral, Mackay at her side. "Stay back," she ordered him sharply. Carlos dropped a rope over a bucking, whirling yearling and braced his feet. Rainbow, a dark roan, fine limbed, rising withers and well slopped back, a beautiful splattering of cream colored spots over his body, covered with vile pink swastikas, "DEVIL" sprayed across one flank.

"Oh, Tom, this is horrible. What am I going to do?"

Carlos snubbed Rainbow tight and held his head down, sides heaving. His eyes rolled white as the old man calmed him, stroking his neck, whispering to him.

Get a halter on him. Walk him. Let him feel your touch. Talk to him.

Thank God, you're here.

She slipped the halter over Rainbow's head as Carlos held him. "I'm so sorry. It's going to be alright; we'll take care of you." He quivered. She stroked his neck and felt tense knotted muscles, but he didn't bolt.

Carlos nodded encouragingly and slipped the lasso off. "You take him, Mrs."

The yearlings parted around them wildly, a sea of beautiful colors defiled by harsh pink. Strong Eagle. Bird Alighting. Brave Wolf. "WHORE, BITCH, FAG, FUCK."

Visions of Carlos in the foaling shed for three nights after the dam's two false labors before Rainbow finally arrived. Forelegs folded, Carlos gently pushing him back into the birth canal, grasping and extending each leg, bringing him into the world with tenderness. "He saved you once; he'll save you again."

Now these horrible violations. Allison cried silently. Their beautiful, precious Appaloosas, proud descendents of ancient spotted horses from Asia and Spanish Mustangs. Survivors of long stormy ocean crossings, left behind by Conquistadors to fend for themselves. Premier mounts of Native American buffalo hunters and warriors, last remnants of Nez Perce herds that stretched as far as the eye could see. "Who would do something like this?"

Hateful people, Allie. Cowards.

"I won't let this happen again." Determined, she led the young horse out of the arena into the barn with Mackay on her heel, tears streaming down her face.

You can do this, Allie.

Rainbow's head, warm and solid, rested on her shoulder. Animal energy that sustained his ancestors flooded into her. "Come on, baby, let's get this paint off." These horses embodied everything good in this world---beauty, trust, loyalty--- to have them terrorized and defiled stirred a primitive rage.

For the next several hours they worked silently with the spooked yearlings. Carlos and Mackay cut out a horse; she calmed and haltered him then led the frightened animal into the barn, stroking him, humming wordless tunes.

Kat took the horse from her and held it while Billy swabbed and cleaned off the paint. He worked fast, his handsome copper face bathed in sweat, scrubbing with a stiff brush and repeating the process until the coat came clean. "A lot of these horses have rope burns on their neck and legs," he said, applying salve. "Looks like they were tied down."

"Goddamn them!" She'd find the people who did this.

"The burns look ugly right now, but they probably won't leave much of a scar," Billy assured her.

"They look pretty bad to me."

"They'll heal, Allison, we'll keep an eye on them." Billy kept his head down, concentrating on his work. When he finished cleaning a horse, he turned it back to her with encouraging words. "This one's a hundred percent; he cleaned up real nice," or "this girl's ready to go."

She understood he was trying to keep her focused on the job so she kept her anger in check. The freshly cleaned horses gathered in the corral, still skittish but no longer panicked. Their indomitable spirit persevering against all odds.

Horses carrying men into battle when their instinct was to flee, a wandering herd animal isolated, reduced to plowing fields, towing wagons, working underground in mines, never seeing the light of day. Horses used and

171

abused for every conceivable purpose. Slaughtered and stolen, dispersed to break the fighting spirit of the Nez Perce. But not their Windhorse Appaloosas. "Nobody will ever hurt you again," Allison promised each one as she turned them loose. "Never."

With the barn clear, she and Kat went out to the corral and watched the herd settle as the moon faded behind high clouds and purple shadows fell over the arena.

Kat lit a cigarette, squinting at her through the smoke. "How are you doing, kiddo?"

"I'm angry. I don't think I've ever been this angry."

"You should be, Allie. This is despicable."

"I could shoot whoever did this; I really could."

Kat took a long drag and exhaled. "The question is who would you shoot? This doesn't seem like a Lyn thing."

"No, it doesn't. I thought about that but it's ridiculous. He couldn't catch them and wouldn't know what to do if he could. He was even afraid of Happy, wouldn't come near him."

"Seems like something kids might do. Maybe those boys at school."

"Maybe, or Ben. He hates our horses." Allison shivered in the night air. Jim was coming across the field toward them with a flashlight through a low hanging sea of ground fog; he would know what to do.

"Yeah, but I can't see Ben spray painting horses. I

can see a lethal weapon in his hand, but not a can of spray paint. I think it's those boys trying to get back at you for getting them kicked out of school."

"I don't know, Kat, they're just a bunch of ignorant kids. This is cruel."

"Never underestimate the cruelty of an ignorant kid, Allie."

Jim greeted them, taking off his white Stetson. "How you holding up, Allison? How are the horses?"

She forced a smile. "We're both okay, thanks to Billy." He was unshaven and looked tired. There were deep squinting furrows around his eyes.

"Met him on the way in; lucky he was here. I found a hell of a mess out there, tire tracks, footprints and spray cans all over the place. Looks like we've got us some vandals on a rampage who've got it in for you guys and Dave."

"What's Dave got to do with this?" Kat asked sharply.

"That's where I was when Carlos called me. Somebody sprayed graffiti all over his trailer, nasty ugly stuff, same color of paint. Broke a few windows while they were at it."

Allison felt her heart jump. "Was he hurt?" Kat was right. It was the Snooks; it had to be. Vicious bastards, like those football players in California who had taunted Dave years ago.

"No, fortunately, he was at a parent teacher

conference at school, but he was pretty shook up as you might imagine...."

Kat interrupted. "I told Allie it was those Snook boys and what happened to Dave confirms it. This has gone well beyond a cruel prank, Jim. There's the Wyoming case; that boy was tortured and killed by local kids in a rural community just like this one because he was different, because they thought he was gay."

"Well, that's not going to happen here, Katherine." He put on his Stetson and zipped up his jacket. "Believe me, one way or the other, I'll put a stop to this."

Knee level ground fog swirled around them. Allison's face burned in the cold, fired by visions of the Snook's rampaging through Dave's trailer and tying down her horses. "He's family to us, Jim, our brother, and we're not going to stand by and let this happen ever again. You tell those bastards I have a gun and I know how to use it."

"Let us handle it, Allison. I left my deputy back at Dave's trailer and he'll stay there until we get this cleared up. I don't want to hear anymore talk like that."

"He's right, Allie, let him do his job."

The horses stomped their feet in the corral, waiting for the sun. She looked in vain to the hills for an eagle in the false dawn. "It's just so horrible, how could this happen?"

"I can't answer that yet, but remember you're not

alone. You have good friends here, all around you. And if I know Dave, he won't let this intimidate him either, he's tough."

"We know he's tough," Kat agreed, lighting another cigarette. "Hell, he's a survivor. But all the same, I think I'll give him a call and see if he'd like to come out and stay awhile until you get things sorted out."

"That's an excellent idea." He turned to Allison and put his arm around her. "And you should get some rest, young lady. I'll call as soon as I know something, okay?"

"Okay." It felt good to be held and reassured. "But first I've got to go out and see our new colt. He's quite a horse, Jim. He's the one Tom and I have been looking for all these years."

"So I hear." He gave her a squeeze and kissed her lightly on the cheek.

There was sadness in his voice. She watched him walk slowly back to his truck as a faint strip of dull light appeared on the highest summits of the Beaverheads and then fell back. He was more stooped than she remembered. They both loved Tom. She wondered if Jim talked to him like she did. It was such a comfort at a time like this.

DREAMS OF APPALOOSAS
Chapter Thirteen: Carlos

Peaceful silence. The steady, pulsing light of a Coleman lantern at the far end of the barn, showing the way past stalls of curious weanlings. Allison and Mackay moved toward it, embraced by soft shadows.

Carlos sat cross-legged on a bale of hay with the orange barn cat beside him, still as an Egyptian statue. Behind them, Eagle's Light munched grain out of a red tub. The colt looked up as they approached, wary, alert. "Buenos noches, Mrs. Come, sit." He moved to one side, offering her a place on the hay bale.

"Thanks." She gratefully sat down amidst the rich smell of hay and horse manure, surrounded by animal warmth. Mackay jumped up beside her. Annoyed, the barn cat sprang down and stiffly marched away.

The double doors of the stable faced into the main corral where the traumatized yearlings huddled. A murky dawn crept toward them. The air was heavy. More snow on the way. Mackay leaned protectively against her.

"I have coffee, Mrs."

"Just what I need, that sounds wonderful." A steaming cup to warm cold hands; the exotic smell of Afracela's strong Mexican coffee. "I'm so glad our colt is safe with you, Carlos." Eagle touched the back of her neck. She turned and stroked his nose, soft and delicate. Their anniversary horse. The gift of new life. Dark, intelligent watchful eyes.

"I will keep him safe always, Mrs." He stood and moved to the stable door, looking out into the corral.

Tom's rifle and shotgun were leaning against the wall. "Are you expecting more trouble?"

He acknowledged her with a nod but remained in the doorway, waiting, watching as the subdued light spread across fences and outbuildings. "I will be here."

Carlos, Master of Horses. Guardian of Eagle's Light. "Tristan and I couldn't stay here alone without you and Afracela," she said softly. "I want you to know how very grateful we are for helping us keep our dream alive." A debt that could never be repaid.

"You are not alone, Mrs." His back was still to her. "Come. Look. He's here."

"Who?" She went to the stable door followed by Mackay.

"Your spirit guide, the Red Coyote."

Breath caught in her throat. Not just in her dreams. On a low hill overlooking the corral, sitting on his haunches in a veil of mist rising off the river. "How long has he been there?"

"All night while we were in the corral with the horses."

"Look, Mackay, it's Red Coyote." Too short to see over the door, his ears went up and he wagged his tail. She'd never told Carlos about Red Coyote. She'd never told anyone but Tom.

"He sees more trouble coming, Mrs. Danger." He looked directly at her.

"Danger?" Eyes so dark she felt as if he was looking through her rather than at her. A snow flake landed on her face, then another and another. "What kind of danger?"

"I don't know, but he will tell you. It will come to you in your dreams and you must listen." He pulled a tobacco pouch and papers out of his jacket pocket and began to roll a cigarette.

Strong, workman's hands, steady and sure. Eagle came up behind them and nudged her. Mackay barked but the little colt ignored him. "We have to protect this horse, Carlos, all our horses but especially this one."

He nodded, wetting the papers with his tongue, shaking out a line of tobacco and rolling an uneven cigarette.

"And Tristan, we must guard him with our lives. Nothing bad must happen to him."

"Afracela will keep him safe." He lit the cigarette with a wooden kitchen match by scraping it across his jagged thumb nail.

"Why Afracela?" She'd never heard him use her Christian name.

"Because she is strong, Mrs.; she saved me from the fire."

A cold breeze drove a flurry of snow into the stall. "I don't understand, what fire?"

"In Vera Cruz, when I was a boy."

The yearlings trotted along the corral fence, seeking shelter from the approaching storm in the lee of the stable. Red Coyote had disappeared behind the fast moving wall of snow bearing down on them.

His cigarette smoldered. "The soldiers burned the church. They hung the priest from the bell rope. I was there."

The smell of sharp, crude tobacco filled the air. "That must have been horrible. Why did they do it?" The poor boy in Wyoming, hung on a barbed wire fence in the snow, left to freeze to death.

"I don't know." He took a long drag. "He was my father."

"Your real father?"

He nodded, crushing the burning tobacco out between calloused thumb and forefinger. "Afracela saved me from the fire; we ran away together."

Carlos looked at Eagle's Light. "The priest gave me a burro. He put a red ribbon around his neck." He stroked the colt. "Now he has come back to me."

Eagle nickered and moved his head under the old

Mexican's hand. "The little boat took us across the river to safety. There were parrots, green parrots and banana trees."

"Oh Carlos." He had fallen into a dreamlike trance. Flight from Vera Cruz. *Erupting volcanoes, a verdant plain of Malachite, Terre Verte and Amanozite green. Two brown children leading a burro with a red ribbon around his neck away from a burning church, angry orange flames, clouds of green parrots fleeing into a smoke filled sky.*

Moved, she was going to put her arms around him but he stepped back, producing a quiver of eagle feathers from inside his jacket and presented them to her.

"For Mr. Tom, for his hat."

"Thank you so much. He'll love them."

"Mr. Tom flies with the eagles."

She clutched the feathers, tears running down her cheeks. "Yes, he does."

"He rides with spirits in the hills, Mrs."

"Do you really think so?"

"Oh yes, I hear the sound of their horses every night, the ground shakes there are so many.

DREAMS OF APPALOOSAS
Chapter Fourteen: My Journal

November 3, 6 a.m.

Dear Tom,

Sorry I haven't kept you up to date lately, but so many things have happened since our long agonizing night with the painted yearlings. They've all settled down although it took awhile, especially with the change in weather. You know how jumpy our horses get with the first storms. We've continued to put ointment on their burns and they are healing nicely, only Bird Alighting has needed antibiotic cream for a minor infection. Thanks again for being here with your encouraging words that I so desperately need. I've come to rely on you.

I had a revealing conversation with Carlos late that night, or more accurately, early morning. I knew from the day I met her that Afracela was a gifted woman, but Carlos made me realize that it had to be destiny, not blind luck, that led these two amazing people to the Windhorse. I mean, what are the chances that these children (and that's what they were when they fled Mexico), after traveling thousands of miles on their own, would end up on a deserted Montana highway in the middle of winter to be picked up by your father, with Afracela pregnant and about to give birth?

I think the odds of that happening without some higher purpose are just about zero, don't you? So it is with a grateful heart that I thank your mother and father for taking them in because, as I told Carlos, without the two of them, Tristan and I simply couldn't stay on here.

I remember you once casually described Carlos to me as a shaman. I realize now you were serious, for he certainly has those qualities associated with being an inspired medium, including a profound sensitivity to the spiritual world that surrounds us.

Not only does he hear the same thunder of Appaloosa hoof beats passing by in the night you once described to me (that I could never hear), but assures me you fly with eagles, which is my profound belief as well. And I was totally surprised when he introduced me to the Red Coyote in my dreams, sitting on that hill in back of our corral, watching over me.

According to Carlos, Red Coyote is my spirit guide sent here to warn me of more danger to come, and he advised me to keep Tristan close to Afracela because she has the power to protect him. I instinctively knew she *was destined to play a big role in our lives. Carlos, in the meantime, has taken it upon himself to become the protector of Eagle's Light and my guardian as well, for which I am so grateful.*

The unexpected call from Lyn and attack on our horses and Dave's trailer weighs heavily on my mind, day and night. Thank God Lyn hasn't called again, but I feel the constant pressure of unresolved threats everywhere. Jim has been doing everything he can to tie the Snooks to both incidents, but they absolutely deny any involvement and so far he can't prove anything.

The consensus around school is that they're guilty as sin on both counts, but none of the kids are willing to speak up. The Snooks are bullies, grown men physically, and without Justin and JB to restrain them, they've become very intimidating to the other boys who are no match. All except Henry who did speak up and got in a horrible fight with them and broke his hand.

While I can understand kids being intimidated, I can't excuse the teachers, many of whom just want to stay clear of this controversy. Unfortunately, one of those is the football coach who claimed Henry started the fight. He didn't even suspend the Snooks from the team as they have a big game coming up this weekend!

Betty said Jim was so furious he told the boys if they ever met him on the street, they'd better cross over to the other side. As a result, Reverend Snook is talking about starting a petition to recall Jim---can you believe that?

I know none of this is my fault, Tom, but if I hadn't gone back to school, I never would have had that run-in with the Snooks over what, in retrospect, was a trivial incident (although I didn't think so at the time), and this wouldn't have escalated into the mess it is today.

Anyway, I'm beginning to wonder if I shouldn't quit teaching and be done with it. But then I'm the one who persuaded Dave to move here in the first place and I simply can't abandon him. Incidentally, he's been very supportive. You'd be so proud of him. He comes over on weekends to help out, often stays for dinner and the night, and plays with Tristan for hours. Dave calls him the dinosaur boy.

So as you can see, I really have no choice but to go into the school board meeting and defend him to the best of my ability, despite my apprehension. Betty will be there, of course. She's gone to a lot of trouble to collect testimonials on his behalf from parents, and she's counting on me to do my part. Kat has a trial so I won't have the usual moral support of my big sister, but it's probably time I finally step out of her long shadow.

I'm happy to report she did go riding with your friend Billy and he took her to the airport on his way home, so stay tuned for further developments there! I also finished her painting last night of Tristan and Kat sitting on the corral rail with the dogs and horses. He's very special to her. I think it turned out well. I'll give it to her for Christmas.

So anyway, tomorrow night is the big night. It's often occurred to me that if you'd been here, none of this would have happened. Nobody, least of all the Snooks, would have dared come anywhere near our place or made a personal attack on Dave. But while that may be true, and I wish with all my heart you were here to defend us, I have decided not to hide behind that excuse any longer.

So I'm going into that meeting armed with a big dose of your faith and courage--- and whatever else I can lay my hands on----not only to defend Dave, but let Reverend Snook know I hold him personally responsible for his boy's behavior. I'm counting on you to be there with me.

Wish me luck.

Your loving wife, for better or worse,

Allie

P.S. You'll be glad to know Carlos has taken it upon himself to drive me back and forth to school. When we were coming home yesterday, he stopped and pointed out what he said were two riders on the far high ridge. Although he seemed very sure, I couldn't see them. You and Eagle from the Light? I hope so. Guess I better put your spotting scope in the truck for our next sighting!

DREAMS OF APPALOOSAS
Chapter Fifteen: The Garden of Eden

The overheated school cafeteria, heavy with the smell of institutional food and wet clothes, was filled to capacity. Allison stepped to the podium, flanked by the principal and the school board, sitting on folding chairs. "Good evening, ladies and gentlemen." The microphone screeched and echoed, she stepped back. "Is that better?"

No response from Reverend Snook and his Church of the Divine Light Reformed congregation who packed the first three rows, a sea of staring faces. Florescent lights reflected off their gold rimmed glasses like sparklers. "My name is Allison Howard, and, as many of you know, I teach History and Art Appreciation at Wisdom High School."

The Divine Light congregation stirred restlessly. Disapproving stares. Beefy fundamentalists and their wives who, according to Reverend Snook, emerged as fully developed human beings sent by God to dominate the earth. Snook, in the center of the first row, a mountain in black, arms folded, staring at her in a pose of moral superiority. The man who condoned the cruel painting of their Appaloosas and the attacks on Dave and Henry. Her adrenalin surged.

Stick to the script, Allie. You're here for Dave, not to get in a fight with Reverend Snook.

Right! Thank you, Tom. Nervous, she adjusted the black and white wool running horses blanket coat around her, the concealed pistol heavy on her hip. "I've come here this evening to tell you how important I think it is that we continue teaching evolution and resist efforts to introduce Intelligent Design into our science classes."

The words fell heavily, drawing a few coughs. Toward the back of the room Betty, sitting with Jim, gave her a thumbs up. Directly in front of them, Dave and parents of students waited, ready to give testimony on his behalf. Friend and allies. Allison pushed on. "Unfortunately, the on-going controversy over this issue not only involves the integrity of our curriculum, but has also come to threaten the career of our excellent science teacher, my good friend and colleague, Dave Anderson."

Calm, rational arguments she had gone over and over while driving slowly in from the ranch. "I know Dave Anderson to be an excellent teacher and a man of high moral standards." She forced herself to return the hostile stare of Reverend Snook. "And given the condition of our school system, we simply cannot afford to lose a teacher of his caliber and integrity over an issue like this.

"For those of you who don't know him, Dave has been our science teacher at Wisdom High for the past four years." She motioned him to come up and join her. "He has a Master's Degree and a teaching certificate in physical science from the University of California at Santa Barbara and almost ten years of experience in K through 12, as well as the community college level."

Dave came slowly up the aisle past the Divine Light Congregation and stood beside her, starring at the floor the way he had when she and Kat brought him home from the shelter. They had written a letter to introduce him to their parents. Dear Mom and Dad: Dave's been living on the street since he was twelve when he ran away from his alcoholic, physically abusive parents. He's very bright. He deserves a second chance, and we hope you'll let him live with us. He needs love and stability, and most of all, somebody who believes in him. You won't be sorry; you'll be as proud of him as you are of us.

"Dave is not only a highly qualified, gifted teacher but a dedicated one who has given your sons and daughters freely of his time, tutoring them before and after school with truly impressive results. In the last four years, half our seniors have been admitted to four year colleges---an unprecedented record of success in Wisdom. For these reasons, I hope you will give him the continuing support he deserves." Surely, the good people here, and there were many, would not turn against him.

Good job, Allie! A great introduction.

Thanks. "Dave?"

Tentatively, he stepped forward as he had on that day in their Padua Hills garden when he explained to her parents that he wanted to be a teacher and help young people. Stepping aside, she stole a glance at Betty who smiled and nodded encouragement.

"Thank you, Mrs. Howard." He cleared his throat, raised his head, acknowledged the principal and school board and turned to the audience. "Teaching is not only my chosen profession but my life, and I regret very much having to respectfully disagree with Reverend Snook---and others---over this contentious issue of Intelligent Design." He put his hands in his pockets. "So I will state my point of view as briefly as possible so that others will have equal time to air theirs."

He spoke slowly and distinctly, calmly and reasonably, as if he were in a classroom setting, as he had when he was valedictorian at Claremont High School and dedicated his speech---on tolerance in modern society---to their proud parents.

"In short, Darwin's thesis, explaining the evolution of life---both animal and human---over the millions of years since our earth was created by the so-called Big Bang, is not in dispute anywhere in this country, or the world for that matter."

Several people in the front row turned to Reverend

Snook and started to whisper. *Worried ranchers in cowboy boots and jeans, knee deep in bright green cultivated crops, surrounded by cows and sheep, meeting their ancestors, an incoming orange tide of dull blue primitive organisms slowly emerging from the evolutionary muck of time.*

"The knowledge of this well established evolutionary theory is what I teach my students so they will be properly equipped to go forward with their education and into their chosen professions as truly educated people."

"Well, that's just the problem, Mr. Anderson," Reverend Snook interrupted loudly. "It's a theory, not a fact. It can't be proven. It's a sham and we….."

"Excuse me, sir," Dave replied forcefully, speaking directly to him, "I'm not sure you understand how the scientific process works. Evolution is an accepted theory which has met, over and over again, the repeated application of hypothesis and proof, whereas Intelligent Design…."

"Is the hand of God at work, Mr. Anderson, the sole creator of the universe and mankind, and that's the truth!"

Allison was about to protest, but the principal stood and signaled for quiet with a wave of his hand. "Let's let Mr. Anderson finish, shall we, Reverend Snook? There will more than enough time for rebuttal."

"Of course," Snook responded. "I simply didn't feel I could let his statement go unchallenged in view of our faith. I'm sure you understand."

A faint smile crept across Dave's face. "And I respect your faith, sir, and may I add that personally I don't think religious faith is necessarily incompatible with evolution. I just don't think Intelligent Design has any place in a science classroom. It's theology, not science."

The first rows remained silent but there was an encouraging smattering of applause around the rest of the room. She felt a rush of pride for her foster brother, for his courage and ability to remain reasonable in the face of such hostility, especially considering the ugly threats and vandalism directed at him.

"Thank you for hearing me out and allowing me to express my views." He gave a bow and stepped back to join her.

"You did good, Dave, just great." She gave him a hug. He looked exhausted. The skin on his face paper thin, his black beard painted on.

"Thanks, so did you."

Dave with Charles Darwin on the deck of the Beagle, crowded with animals and birds, a Noah's ark sailing into billowing white clouds, the turbulent dawn of life, and blended into those clouds, the hint of a Supreme Being, white hair streaming in the wind.

The Reverend Snook took the floor, turning his back on them, addressing his congregation and the audience beyond. "It's always interesting to hear the distorted views of an atheist, ladies and gentlemen, but we certainly don't want one teaching that sort of nonsense in our school, do we?" His deep penetrating voice filled the room.

"The problem with Mr. Anderson is that besides being an atheist, he doesn't have his facts straight about the creation. We all know it didn't start with his big bang millions of years ago, and he can't prove it did. But we know for certain when and where it started. Exactly 5,000 years ago in the Garden of Eden."

Loud applause from his congregation.

"Because the Bible tells us so."

Halleluiahs.

Allison shifted her feet, hot, trapped in the wool coat that hid the pistol. She should have left it in the car.

Reverend Snook rolled on. "I would also like to ask Mr. Anderson if there is no God and there is only his so-called theory of evolution, where do his morals come from? How can he tell right from wrong? Or can he?"

Allison felt Dave stiffen next to her.

"The answer is, of course, that in a Godless world ruled only by evolution, there are no moral values. None-what-so-ever, ladies and gentlemen!" He paused. "None. Zero." He opened his arms wide. "Which is reason enough to make sure this man is not permitted to teach and influence our innocent children any longer. He is not fit---morally or spiritually---for that task. He is, in point of fact, a degenerate, an immoral unchristian person!"

Burning with rage, Allison found herself standing at the edge of the stage, shouting down at his broad back. "How dare you say things like that about people you don't even know!"

"Judgment is mine, sayeth the Lord!" Snook thundered, turning on her.

Rein it in, Allie.

I will not! The room went silent, blood pounded in her ears. Rainbow, that gentle young horse, burned with ropes, covered with vile pink paint. Whore, Fuck, Fag. "I'm sick and tired of you trying to intimidate my good friend Dave Anderson by spreading vicious lies and encouraging wanton vandalism."

"Allison, Mrs. Howard, please." The principal took her arm, trying to move her back.

Allie!

She pushed his arm away. Warning flares went off in her head as Snook advanced toward her. "And I will not tolerate being assaulted and insulted by your sons any longer, sir. We all know what's going on here, and if those little cowards ever go after our horses again, they'll have to deal with me." She threw her coat open revealing Tom's pistol.

Jesus, Allie.

Snook stepped awkwardly back. "What do you think you're doing?"

"Real men don't hide behind a pulpit or send their sons out to do their dirty work in the middle of the night,

Reverend."

The school board jumped to their feet, the principal signaled wildly to Jim Christian who was talking on his cell phone in the back of the room. A camera flashed in her face.

"These are lies, all lies," Snook protested, but his voice no longer boomed.

The principal rushed to meet Jim as he came up the aisle. They conferred briefly.

Allison closed the coat over the pistol. What had she done?

The Sheriff shook his head emphatically, ended the conversation, and hurried toward her.

He bounded up on the low stage, took her firmly by the arm, and led her toward the back door. "You need to come with me, Allison."

"Am I under arrest?"

"No, we found Lyn Barnett over at the Three Bears Motel. He's threatening to kill himself unless you talk to him."

DREAMS OF APPALOOSAS
Chapter Sixteen: Judgment Day

Allison followed Jim down the deserted hallway, neither of them spoke, their booted feet echoed on the battered brown linoleum floor.   Past empty classrooms and the dimly lit trophy case with its dusty awards and photographs of Wisdom's sports heroes, past and present.   They were all there in uniform, heroic, indestructible. Justin, JB, Tom and Jim. Forever young and smiling. How had it come to this?

They stepped outside. Dark and snowing hard. Jim led her across the parking lot to his truck through ankle deep snow, walking so fast it was hard to keep up. Tristan would be waiting for his bedtime story, another one from their inexhaustible supply of Dr. Seuss.   If she'd stayed home, this might not have happened. Except Lyn was here. There was no way out.

He opened the passenger door and took her arm. "Watch your step there."

"How did you find him?"

"The guy from the motel called us." He closed the door for her, went around to the driver's side and got in.

"I'm sorry, Jim, really sorry."   Unlike her, he'd held

his temper in check, despite extreme provocation from Reverend Snook. She'd let him down at the worst possible time.

"Sorry for what?" He started the truck. The heater came to life; windshield wipers swept a heavy load of snow away and settled to a steady beat.

"The gun, I know I put you in a really bad spot."

"Hell, Allison, I'm already in a bad spot with a lot of those folks, don't worry about it." He made a tight, skidding U turn and headed down the snowy main street.

"I don't know what I was thinking; I guess I wasn't thinking; I really lost it. I probably cost Dave his job--- and mine too." The pistol felt heavy and awkward under her coat.

He looked across at her. "I don't know about that, Allison, but it wasn't the smartest thing you've ever done. I know Tom got you a concealed permit but you can't take a gun onto school grounds."

"I know that. I'll just have to take the consequences. Do you want me to give you the pistol?"

"No, we'll worry about that later." He slowed and turned onto an unpaved road marked "Dead End". "Right now I need you to tell me more about this Lyn Barnett guy. Do you think he really has a gun?"

"I don't know. He's a college professor---was." A long time ago. What was he now?

"A lot of times guys like this are just bluffing. It makes a big difference in how we handle it."

"What do you mean?" The Three Bears Motel emerged through the driving snow. Three red neon bears marched jerkily up and over a lurid blue mountain, transforming snowflakes into darting red sparklers. Tristan loved bears. They'd seen a cinnamon colored one in the high meadow last spring. He'd be waiting for her to come home, asking Afracela where she was.

"We want to talk him out of there if we can, but you never know what might set somebody off."

You disgust me, I never want to see you again, Lyn. "I don't want anybody to get hurt." I just want him to get out of my life forever. I don't care how you do it.

"Believe me, neither do I." He pulled in behind a green and white county patrol car parked across from the motel. "How do you feel about talking to him?"

"I can do it if I have to." It was an old stucco 50's building with individual cabins and attached wooden lattice carports. This might be nothing more than another bad dream.

This isn't a bad dream, Allie; you've got to deal with it.

"I think it will help."

"I need to call Tristan first, Jim, he'll be worried about me." It was all that mattered.

"Go ahead."

She felt the butt of Tom's pistol as she dug the cell phone out of her coat pocket. Afracela answered on the first ring and gave the phone to Tristan. He was playing with his Thomas the Train set. "That sounds like fun. I'm sorry I going to be a little late, honey, but I'll be there. Please give the dogs a big hug for me."

He asked her if she was with daddy. "No, I'm with Uncle Jim. Daddy's not here right now, but I love you and he loves you too." She clicked the phone shut and glanced at Jim who was staring straight ahead. "Let's get this over with, shall we?"

He nodded, took his automatic pistol out of the glove compartment, chambered a round and holstered it. "When we get out, stay right behind me, okay?"

Ducking low, she followed him through trampled snow to the patrol car where an overweight man in a maroon bathrobe and cowboy boots crouched with Jim's deputy, a laconic cowboy she knew only as Jake.

The man had a hunting rifle. "You get that crazy son of a bitch otta my place, Sheriff, or I damn sure will," he rasped in a hoarse voice.

"Shut up, Harvey," Jim snapped, turning to Jake. "What's the situation?"

"All quiet on the Western Front, boss." The deputy handed him a cell phone. "Still on the line last time I checked."

The motel was dark except for one dim cabin light glowing through the falling snow. It was hard to believe he was really in there. Lover and mentor who took her on field trips to paint the California coast, bought her romantic dinners, made love to her in soft sand while the sun sank in the West.

"Mr. Barnett, this is Sheriff Christian, I have Allison Howard here with me." He handed her the phone. "You ready?"

"What should I say?" The man who turned on her in a drunken fury. Please don't shoot yourself? The noisy neon sign clicked off and on as it sent the red bears over the blue mountain again and again.

"Try to calm him down. Ask him to walk out now before anybody gets hurt. Tell him you care about him."

But she didn't. Shoot yourself, don't shoot yourself. Just go away. She cleared her throat. "Lyn?" No answer. "Lyn, it's me, Allison." She wanted to be home with Tristan, reading Dr. Seuss, playing with Thomas the Train.

Muffled sobbing. Her anger flared. He'd shamed her again by coming back to Tom's home town; thank goodness Tristan wasn't old enough to understand. "Come on, Lyn, you said you wanted to talk to me. Here I am." Jim nodded encouragingly.

"I---I---can't go on without you, Allison. I---I tried, but I can't. I'm going to end it."

"Stop that kind of talk." She would get on Happy and ride out of this nightmare.

"I lost everything when I lost you. Everything. I didn't mean to hurt you." His voice quavered.

"For Christ's sake, Lyn."

"I'm freezing out here," the owner complained

200

loudly.

"Lyn?" Silence.   Allison shivered.

"You must hate me."

"Jake, put Harvey in the car and lock that damn rifle in the trunk," Jim ordered his deputy. "What's going on?" he asked her.

"I don't hate you." A lie. "Lyn?"

"I called and called but that Mexican lady wouldn't let me to talk to you."

"There's nothing to talk about."

"But I've always loved you. I can't go on......."

"It was over fifteen years ago, Lyn." She was not going to be held hostage to these threats.

"He's not going to shoot himself or anybody else. I'll put a stop to this." She handed Jim the phone and impulsively headed down the walk, seeing everything clearly---beautiful stalactites of ice hanging from dark viridian pines, raw umber cracks in the stucco. Snow crystals crunched under her boots.

Jim caught up with her at the door. A dirty white plastic number 9 hung at an angle on a single rusty nail. "I know this man; he won't hurt me."

Jim took her arm. "He broke your jaw, Allison."

She shook him off and knocked five times, their old signal at the Golden Palms Motel in Pasadena. No answer. She pushed the door open and stared into the gloom.

"Lyn?" Gray carpet, a low single bed, covers thrown

back in disarray, an overturned bureau and brown plastic chairs, the old-fashioned console TV lying on its side, screen shattered. Broken glass everywhere. A shabby room, not a good place to die.

He was crouched in the far corner; a yellow towel soaked with blood wrapped around one hand. She felt Jim beside her. "Wait here; I'll do this." She stepped inside. "My God, what have you done?" This was pitiful.

"I hurt myself," he whispered.

"Let me see that." Gray and unshaven, he looked as old as he had in her Dhaulagiri dream.

"No, don't." He pulled his injured hand back.

"Let me look." Two empty wine bottles on the floor. He'd never been a good drinker. Red wine turned the demons loose that marched across his violent canvasses.

Even as the old fear rose that he would strike out at her again, she finally understood. He'd taken such pride in grooming her for success, put so much of his personal reputation and influence on the line. When success came and she rejected him, he felt betrayed. He not only lost control, he destroyed his life.

Jim stood motionless in the doorway, watching, one hand on the butt of his pistol. Snow was sucked into the room in a tiny funnel cloud.

"It's Tom!" Lyn recoiled. "He's going to kill me!"

"It's not Tom; it's the Sheriff."

Jim stepped forward. "If you have a gun, sir, now is the time to tell me where it is so nobody gets hurt."

She saw the fear in Lyn's eyes, once his finest feature, those soft brown eyes that invited confidence and intimacy. No more.

"I don't have one," he admitted, hanging his head. "I made that up so I could see Allison again."

"You scared the hell out of me."

"I know, but I had to see you again. I love you. You were so talented." A ghost of that once radiant smile played across his face, the pockmarked face of a nobleman in some dark, cracked 18th century painting. "You never understood what great things we could have done together."

"That's over, Lyn."

"Such a waste." He held the bloody towel to his chest. "What do you think they'll do to me?"

The self confident professor who had swept her off her feet and into his bed was gone. Wine, urine and fear. Disgusting. "I don't know."

"Please stand up, sir," Jim ordered him.

Tired and weary of it all, she found herself extending a hand. "Here, let me help you."

Clinging to her, he got unsteadily to his feet. "Thank you, Allison."

He leaned on her, surprisingly light and frail, as Jim waited. She caught a glimpse of them in a mirror on the wall, a defeated, stooped old man supported by a tall, gaunt strawberry blond going gray, face pale with sadness and heartbreak.

Her last kind gesture to the man she now despised and pitied. "This is it for us, Lyn," she said softly as they stepped through the doorway into the glare of headlights. "I don't want to ever see or hear from you again. Do you understand?"

"Yes," he replied in a secretive whisper, "I understand. Please forgive me."

Allison walked away without responding.

DREAMS OF APPALOOSAS
Chapter Seventeen: My Journal

November 4, 2 a.m.

My dear Tom,

What a ghastly day! First, I walk into the school board meeting with your pistol, shocking you and everyone else, not the best decision I've ever made as Jim pointed out. Then Lyn shows up at the Three Bears of all places, threatening to kill himself.

I can't imagine a more disastrous combination of events piling up on top of everything else we've had to deal with lately, can you? It's way past midnight and I'm so wound up and distraught I can't sleep. Even worse, I can't paint, my only salvation at times like this.

So I'm doing my best to concentrate on the good in our lives, starting with Tristan who represents our bright shining future. He was sound asleep by the time I got home tonight, surrounded by his books and Thomas the Train. The very picture of innocent tranquility. Just as well. I carried him upstairs (he's getting heavy!) and put him in our bed under your mother's down comforter, you know, that old faded pink one that smells of lavender and is about a foot thick.

Our faithful dogs are here too, of course, a great comfort to have them close at a time like this. It calms me and reminds me where my responsibilities lie, come what may. Love fills our room; Faith and Courage will see us through.

I'm honestly don't know what possessed me to take your pistol into the meeting, Tom. I know I surprised you. Fear, protection, security? I must admit, I've kept it close at hand and loaded since Lyn followed me home that night even though in my wildest dreams I can't imagine actually using it. Or maybe I could. Certainly in defense of Tristan.

Or maybe I knew exactly what I was doing. When Reverend Snook saw your pistol, there was a brief moment of genuine fear on his face. He got the message: steer clear of this crazy lady. I'll never admit this to anyone else, but I'm actually glad I did it.

At any rate, I was saved from the immediate aftermath of that mess when things went from bad to worse and Lyn barricaded himself in that seedy motel. I suppose I should blame myself, but the truth is I don't and I found myself wishing someone, anyone, would shoot him and get him out of my life. Isn't that awful? Your sweet Allison!

Fortunately, our dear friend Jim was there to minimize my embarrassment and hustle Lyn out of town after he got his hand stitched up (minor injuries according to Jim,) with the admonition never to contact me again or come back to Montana. At Jim's suggestion, I'm going to write the motel a check for the breakage. The last thing I want to do is have him sitting around Wisdom in jail so I would have to testify at a trial. I hope and pray he's finally out of my life. It's amazing how one mistake keeps coming back to haunt me.

The damage has been done, of course. I'm sure the boys at the Circle K Diner are having a field day discussing my love life over coffee. The truth is, between Lyn, the meeting, the Snook boys, Dave and Henry, the town had become divided over who is guilty of what and whether man was created in the Garden of Eden or evolved after a big bang, and who knows what else!

Thank God, Tristan is too young to understand any of this, and there's not a thing I can do about it anyway, so I've decided to hunker down with Tristan and the dogs and enjoy the view. I'm in our rocking chair in front of the window. Can you see me? I miss you terribly. This is our kind of night! The snow has stopped; the moon is high, almost full, and way off in the distance, I can hear coyotes yipping away. I pray Red Coyote is with them.

I'm hoping you will ride by and pick me up for a romantic rendezvous. Do you remember the time you woke me up in the middle of the night and we rode up to Boulder Lake in a foot of snow to watch the sunrise? I thought you were crazy.   I remember every detail of that glorious night---the moonlight reflecting off the snow making the hills glow, the Milky Way, shooting stars, horses snorting, the only sound in the incredible silence as we climbed higher and higher.   But when we got there and you built a fire big enough to be seen from Mars and we huddled around it in our blankets and made love standing up---not an easy thing to do in a foot of snow---I thought you were the most romantic man I'd ever met and I was the luckiest girl in the world.   I still do.

With memories like this, I should be able to look at the upside of things no matter how awful they seem at the moment.   Sometimes I think I have a lot in common with those Nez Perce Dreamers like Eagle from the Light. Those poor souls, overwhelmed by Western civilization, who thought that if they withdrew to the hills, stayed apart and honored their old ways, someday they would be reunited with their ancestors and once again be able live in peace and happiness with dignity.

The Dreamers were a phenomenon born of utter desperation, of course, but it has occurred to me that life is pretty desperate for everyone when you get right down to it.   Don't we all want to believe there is *something better in store for us? Even Reverend Snook must be looking forward to the bliss of his heaven where he can join his fellows in paradise and no one will have to push carts across the desert--- or put up with Dave and me!*

I couldn't go on without my conversations with you. Most of the time, I feel your presence and love, and I fervently believe that someday all of us will be reunited in a life of peace, happiness and love, the same thing the Nez Perce longed for.

So I'm going ahead with our dreams for the Windhorse---a vast spiritual high mountain prairie where Appaloosas, Red Coyote and all his animal friends can wander safely for eternity with the Nez Perce, living and dead. A memorial to the history and people of this wonderful place where you brought me to live with you forever.

I know we can't do this alone, but major reinforcements have arrived in the person of your good friend Billy. He's going to pick up Kat when she flies into Missoula tonight. The key thing about that, and I've underlined it so you can't possibly miss it, is they aren't arriving here until tomorrow morning!

I have a very good feeling about this liaison! I'm happy for Kat! God knows she deserves a good man, and if that works out, I think we should involve Billy in our plans. I really like him and he has a lot to offer. This is a man with a foot in both worlds. A fascinating mixture of ancestors and intellect, don't you agree? A good combination all the way around!

Finally, my parents are very pleased we're coming for Thanksgiving; I know they constantly worry about us. I'm sure they think I'm a little unstable and not capable of making rational decisions, but I'll just have to explain things as best I can. Maybe a change of scene will be a good thing, who knows? Tristan is really excited about going; I know he'll have fun.

God, I am suddenly so exhausted. I'm going to go out and check the horses and Eagle's Light and then turn in. Do you think you and I and Tristan can all fit in that bed with the dogs on top? We'll give it a try. It's cold, and like they say, it's a two dog night for sure!

My love, always and forever,
Allie.

DREAMS OF APPALOOSAS
Chapter Eighteen: The Confidential Report

She tossed and turned most of the night, trapped between Tristan and the two dogs crowding in on her to stay warm. She and Tom always slept with the windows open, even in winter, and made blind sweaty love buried under down comforters. Not tonight. She considered painting but couldn't work up the willpower to get out of bed and instead fell into a restless sleep, concentrating on Tristan's soft, regular breathing.

———————

She and Red Coyote watched Appaloosas running wild and free from the top of Horse Heaven Hill. White, brown, black and burnt sienna spots blending in visual harmony, transforming into a river of horses flowing along the turning, twisting Big Hole River. Shape changers, pronghorn antelope, Indians in skins of animals they worshipped and hunted, all moving across shimmering Cascade green grass.

Where have you been?

Right here, waiting for you. Red Coyote stretched

and sat on his haunches, back to the rising wind that swept over the hill.

Shivering in the cold, she sat beside him, pulling her knees up against her chest. I'm glad I found you again. I feel so alone and afraid. So many bad things have happened. Dangerous, evil things.

Red Coyote tipped his head, looking at her with sympathetic eyes. Black thunderheads filled the sky, fading to grey as they rose in boiling towers topped with brilliant pink crowns backlit by a hidden sun. He moved in front of her to block the wind.

Grateful, Allison sank against him and closed her eyes, dreaming of Appaloosas, feeling the warmth of his rough coat and the steady thump of his heart joining hers.

———————

Pale dawn flooded in; Tristan and the dogs were gone. There were voices downstairs, coming and going, as distant as her fading dream. Shivering, she got up and hurried over to close the windows. Afracela had left coffee on the nightstand but she didn't want to lose the comforting presence of Red Coyote. She fell back in bed, pulled the covers over her head, closed her eyes and went back to find him.

———————

She rode across icy creeks into high, dry bare meadows gone dormant, through stands of aspen

stripped of their leaves by cold and wind. She called
out to him; there was no answer. She had lost the trail
to the top of Horse Heaven Hill. Lightening flashed,
thunder rumbled, Moon Woman was jumpy, ears flat,
prancing from side to side. "Easy, girl." The horse
coiled under her, ready to run. Red Coyote was gone.

Laughter, joyous, uninhibited, and the staccato bark
of dogs. Kat was here. Time to face the day. She
listened for the familiar sounds of Tom in the shower,
the clank of hangers in the closet as he dressed, the soft
tread of stocking feet on carpet as he came into the
bedroom, sat down across from her and pulled on high
boots with the two silver plated hooks inherited from his
grandfather. Or was it his father? If she was very still,
the memories might go on.

Allison pressed his gold horse pendant against her
breast and traced Faith and Courage as she left the
room, praying things would be better by the light of this
new day.

Kat and the dogs were sitting on the kitchen floor,
watching Tristan assemble a green plastic dinosaur that
was almost as big as he was.

"A little something I picked up for the cowboy," Kat
explained. She was wearing blue jeans and a grey Yale
Law sweatshirt; her lustrous red hair flowed free.

"Tyrannosaurus Rex," Tristan proudly announced.

Bright sunlight streamed through the kitchen widows on shafts of fine dust. Sunbeams from the Gods, warming the earth and all living creatures. The sun did not distinguish between the mysterious long-legged spiders that crawled over the snow or a horse, coyote, or woman dozing in her rocking chair. It warmed them all and gave them hope.

Allison knelt down and kissed their son.

"This little boy has a big vocabulary," Kat commented, getting to her feet. "He also has well developed problem solving skills. I don't think I ever would have been able to put this thing together on my own."

Kat looked radiant. "It's good to see you." She hugged her sister, confident that whatever happened, Kat would be there for her. "You look great. Rested." She was wearing perfume. Unusual.

"You don't look so bad yourself."

"Thanks. Where is everyone? Where's Billy?" She wanted to ask Kat about him in the worst way.

"Out with Carlos, checking on your favorite colt."

"Come see my dinosaur, Mommy," Tristan insisted. She sat down beside him, cross-legged, and examined the complex construction. "Kat's right, honey, you are a problem solving genius like your dad."

As a high tech engineer who invented software to program implantable cardiac defibrillators, Tom always knew which piece went where before he started. She, on the other hand, relied on inspiration, creativity, and occasional prayer. They were a great combination, a woman who liked to go places and a man who always knew how to get there.

She looked up at her sister, eager to hear about Billy and their night in Missoula, but Kat turned away and went to the kitchen table.

"We need to talk, Allison. Come over here and sit down a minute, please."

The sudden change of tone took her by surprise. "Talk about what?" Kat had assumed the role of big sister attorney. It felt like a summons.

"We have some serious matters to discuss." She was taking papers out of her leather briefcase.

"So what's going on?" Kat didn't reply and continued to arrange them on the table set for four. "Can't this wait?" She wanted to get on with the day.

"I'm afraid not, Allie." Kat looked at her steadily. "The insurance company has reopened their accident investigation."

"What?"

"Apparently, they're not convinced it was an accident. That's why they haven't cut your check yet." The lines around Kat's mouth were tight.

Stunned, Allison looked through the doorway at her Cambria seascapes. Their innocence mocked her. "I'm sorry; I don't understand."

Kat put on a pair of half moon reading glasses,

picked up the top paper and scanned it. "According to this report that John Henry obtained, they think it's possible someone sabotaged Tom's truck, causing him to lose control."

"But the state police said it was an accident."

"I know." Kat took out a pack of cigarettes and offered one to Allison.

"No thanks."

Kat put the cigarettes down and picked up a second paper. "Anyway, they've hired a team of experts to re-examine the wreck even though fire destroyed most of it."

"You mean they think somebody deliberately tried to kill them?" Her mouth was so dry it took an effort to get the words out.

Kat reached across the table and took her hand. "That's their assumption."

"But everybody loved Tom." This was not possible.

Kat looked at her evenly. "Not according to the insurance company, and being the bureaucrats they are, their first suspect is always the person who benefits the most."

The room swirled around her. "Me?" Allison glanced at Tristan to be sure he was still there.

"Well, you are the beneficiary of a ten million dollar life insurance policy, not to mention inheriting the Windhorse and Tom's share of the business."

"You're kidding, right?"

"Calm down, Allie."

"Calm down?" Allison stood up angrily, knocking her chair over backwards. "They think I killed them, the most important people in the world to me?"

"Suspect, Allison, there's a big difference."

"Mommy!" Tristan yelled. Alarmed, Dotty Girl gave a low growl. Mackay barked.

Kat quickly came around the table, righting the chair. "Sorry, Allie, I didn't put that very well."

The kitchen was hot and close. Tears streamed down her face as she reached out to reassure Tristan and the dogs. "It's okay, guys, nobody's mad at you."

"Oh, Allie, I love you. I'm so sorry to have to bring this up, but you need to know what's going on."

"I can't believe this is happening." She fell into Kat's open arms.

"It's going to be alright; we'll get through this, we will."

Tristan pulled on her pant leg. "Mommy," he announced loudly, "I want to go outside."

She wiped away her tears. The devastating news meant nothing to him. "That's a good idea, honey. You and the dogs can go find Afracela."

While she put on Tristan's winter coat and ushered the trio out the door, Kat methodically turned her pack of cigarettes over and over on the table. Allison brought her a cracked saucer to use as an ashtray.

Again Kat offered her a cigarette as she lit her own.

"No thanks, I feel sick. I don't want to hear any more of this."

"I understand, but you need to know why they consider you a suspect." Kat picked up the report again, removed her reading glasses, and wiped her eyes.

Allison waited with dread. Suspect. The word hung over her like a guillotine. She glanced at her painting of Tom and the twins, smiling, happy. Murdered? Inconceivable.

"This report contains several interviews done by the company's private investigator, and it was on that basis they decided to reopen the investigation."

She watched a thin stream of smoke from Kat's cigarette slowly make its way toward the ceiling and wished she could drift away with it. "Who did they talk to?"

"Lyn for one."

"Lyn? When?" *I don't ever want to see or hear from you again. I understand, Allison, please forgive me. Only days ago.*

"Shortly after Tom died." Kat tapped the paper with her forefinger. "Apparently they did a computer search on you and Lyn's old arrest record came up. They found him living in the San Fernando Valley. He claimed you two have always been lovers, and now that Tom's gone, you'd promised to marry him."

She clung to the back of her chair. Spiders swarmed across her face. Webs clouding her eyes, clogging her ears.   Panicked, she tried to rip them away, thrashing her arms. "Go away; get off me."

Alarmed, Kat stood up. "Allison, what's wrong?"

There aren't any spiders, Allie. Calm down.

"Nothing. Everything.   This is simply too much."   She hurried to the kitchen window, trying to calm herself.   Tristan, the dogs and Afracela stood at the corral rail, petting Happy and Eagle's Light.   Would they be the final storybook painting of her life at the Windhorse?

"I'm sorry, Allie, I know this is terribly upsetting, but we have to deal with it.   Look, once they read Jim's report about the motel incident, Lyn's credibility will be less than zero.   Why don't you come back over here and sit down with me?"

Allison turned to face her. "I'd rather stand."   This was her kitchen.   She and Tom and Afracela planned and built it together.   She and Betty had made thousands of cookies here for their families and school bake sales.   Tom loved oatmeal cookies, especially hot from the oven.

Kat put out her cigarette, adjusted her glasses and continued.   "Ben Howard was also interviewed.   He told them Tom had bad luck with women, his first wife had gone crazy and left him, and, according to him, you're a young gold digger who caught Tom on the rebound and are running his ranch into the ground.   He said it was common knowledge that you were sleeping with the man who wrecked The Three Bears Motel."

Maybe you should make some cookies, honey. It's been a long time.

"Too long." Not since the accident. Red checked table cloth spread out on the grass, lemonade in tall frosty glasses, piles of rich brown cookies in ochre Indian baskets. A happy gathering of friends, horses looking on, birds circling. She went to the cupboard to find Betty's recipe.

"Allison, are you with me? What are you doing?"

"Looking for something. Go on; I'm listening." She pulled down the little oak recipe box off the top shelf her mother had given her and began thumbing through it. There was nothing as satisfying as making cookies on a cold fall afternoon, feeling the warmth of the oven, savoring the smell of fresh dough. *Tom and the twins will like them.*

Kat paused, looking over at her to make sure she still had her attention, then continued. "The final interview was conducted a few days ago by telephone with Reverend Snook who claimed you had promoted the hiring of a teacher, a personal friend you knew to be a homosexual, and that you'd lived with this man when you were a teenager in California."

The cookie recipe was on a distinctive pink card, "From the Kitchen of Betty Christian with Love." Raisins, chocolate chips, baking soda, salt, all purpose flour, butter and oatmeal.

"Reverend Snook also told them you were mentally unstable and cited as proof the pistol you brought to the school board meeting. You forgot to tell me about the pistol, Allie."

Tears running down her face, she looked up from the pantry where she was checking on what she had in stock and calculating how many cookies it would make. "I didn't want to upset you. It was a dumb thing to do." She got down on her knees to search for the bag of flour. Kat would see it as another example of her emotional instability.

"Next time upset me, okay? Not only can they charge you with a misdemeanor or even a felony, they've got a photo to prove it."

"What do you mean?" There was Afracela and Carlos, Tristan, Dave, the Christians and now Billy. They all could be counted on to eat their share. Oddly enough, she couldn't remember if Kat liked cookies.

Kat held out a newspaper clipping, `Gun Toting Teacher Defends Darwin in Small Town Shootout over Intelligent Design.' "There was a wire service reporter there, undoubtedly invited by your friend Reverend Snook."

Allison looked up and saw a grainy image of herself, hands on hips, the pistol clearly visible. "That's not good." Did they have a photo of Lyn too?

"No, it isn't. And it isn't good for the insurance investigation either. What in the world are you doing

221

down there on your hands and knees?"

She got to her feet and closed the pantry door. "Do you like cookies, Kat? I can't remember. I make them for Tom and the boys all the time." If the weather was bad, she could move the cookie feast inside, spreading the table cloth out on the kitchen floor.

"Yes, I still like cookies, Allie, but that's not important now. Have you been following any of this?"

"Yes, sort of. As best I can."

"And?"

She took a deep breath. "I just can't comprehend why they'd say such ugly things about me, or why the insurance company would believe them. I can't face it, Kat."

"Listen, Allie, we need to consider this report in the light of what it is---a desperate attempt by the company to avoid paying you what they rightfully owe you."

"By accusing me of murder?" Standing at the edge of the abyss again.

"Nobody's accusing you of anything, Allie. This report is nothing but a bunch of wild accusations. They're just stalling around. Come on, sit down."

She reluctantly abandoned the cookies. "I don't want to deal with it, Kat; I just can't."

"We don't have a choice."

She felt light-headed and disoriented. "What have I ever done to deserve this?"

"Absolutely nothing. You've put too much faith in

the basic decency of people, that's all." Kat paused. "You're incredibly naïve about human nature, kiddo. You always have been."

"You think so?"

"I know so. Let's face it, Reverend Snook would stone Dave to death in the town square if he thought he could get away with it and half the town knows damn well his boys painted your horses."

"And they got away with it."

"So far, but the point is none of these people have your best interest at heart. Take Ben for instance, I've never liked that man. Actually, it's a lot more than that. It seems to me he's one strange piece of work."

"I agree." The dead bull elk, eyes glassy with shock. Would Red Coyote be next?

Kat folded her hands. "And as you recall, I told Mom and Dad years ago they should have prosecuted Lyn."

"I know."

"So now you and Jim let him off the hook again, Allie, no charges filed only Jim's report. And look what he did to you."

"I felt sorry for him. I thought he was sincere. I had no idea he'd tell these lies about me."

"You and I live in different worlds, kiddo. I see people for what they are and most of it isn't good. You're a romantic optimist. You look for the best in everybody---and everything."

"I'm an artist, Kat," Allison protested. "That

doesn't mean I don't know there aren't bad things in the world---and bad people---it's just that I don't want to go there."

Kat sighed. "That's what I love about you, Allie---and admiré. But you can't assume everyone is a nice person."

"It doesn't look like it."

"I've seen a lot of baseless charges made against innocent people like you and sometimes, believe it or not, they stick. This report is full of holes, but we can't afford to take any chances. I'm going to have John Henry make sure this thing never goes anywhere but a shredder."

"I'm grateful for your help, Kat, but the truth is I just want to be left alone." She stared at her painting of Tom on Keith, overwhelmed by loneliness and longing. It was the only way to bring him back.

Take care of our son, Allie. I'm counting on you.

"I will."

"You will what?" Kat looked at her questioningly. "Look, Allie, we need to make the insurance company pay you what they owe you."

"I want to be able to dream my dreams in peace. I don't think that's too much to ask, do you?"

"No, God knows you deserve some peace. But Tom's not here, kiddo. You're going to have handle this yourself."

The kitchen door burst open and Mackay rushed in

barking a greeting, followed by a rosy-faced Tristan with Dotty Girl limping behind.

Kat shook her head and smiled. "I'll tell you what, why don't you go out for a ride with Billy; he'd love to see the rest of the ranch. Get some fresh air. It will give you a better perspective on things. We can talk about this later."

Allison hesitated. Take care of our son, Allie. "No, you go ahead; I'll stay here with Tristan."

But Tristan took her hand and pulled. "Mommy, I want to go riding with you; you promised." Mackay barked enthusiastically.

"Please go, Allie, take Tristan. You'll be doing me a big favor. I really haven't got time; I have to finish my Rodriguez brief."

"Are you sure?"

"Yes, I'm sure. I have a lot of work to do. And I'd like you to get to know Billy a little better and tell me what you think."

"About what?"

"I don't trust my judgment about men. I need a second opinion."

Allison went over to her. "Okay." The irony of the request did not escape her after Kat's comment about being naïve. "If you really trust my judgment," she said with a smile.

"In this case, I do." Kat put both hands on her shoulders and turned her toward the door. "Now go.

When you get back, we can all make your cookies together."

DREAMS OF APPALOOSAS
Chapter Nineteen: Return of the Warrior

The full pale yellow moon was low on the horizon as they rode across the frozen creek just as she had in her dream. Tom called it a Comanche Moon, a good time to steal your neighbor's horses. Allison had his drover coat buttoned up tight against the cold; emotional turmoil whirled around her. Unfaithful gold digger. She promised to marry me. Assaults, violations. Lying bastards. Murderer.

She rode Moon Woman with Tristan tucked in front of her, bundled up in his blue snowsuit and red down mittens. Billy was on Keith. Thin ice crackled and popped in the morning stillness as horses broke through; steam rose off open leads where hot springs bubbled to the surface of the shallow stream.

Dotty Girl couldn't handle deep snow and stayed with Kat, howling in anguish until they were out of sight. Mackay trailed them, leaping through belly high drifts with boundless energy.

Keeping one arm firmly around Tristan, she spurred Moon Woman up the opposite bank into a meadow glistening like a white satin sheet in the piercing sunlight that beat down out of a cloudless blue sky. Ten degrees above zero, but her face was hot with suppressed anger. *You've got to realize not everyone has your best interests at heart, Allie.* Would it ever end?

"Go faster," Tristan cried with delight. "Go faster."

"Alright, hang on tight." The damning statements clung to her as they loped across the meadow, powder snow flying behind.

Kat knew her too well. *She was incredibly naive.* Accusations by Reverend Snook might be expected, even from Lyn, but Ben was family and he had betrayed her.

Oh, Tom, what are we going to do?

Pay attention, Allie. That's my son you've got there.

Don't worry, she's a good horse.

What'd I tell you about horses?

Never trust a horse; be ready for the next surprise. Allison pulled Tristan against her. Surprises like the confidential insurance report.

"Mommy, you're hurting me," he complained.

Quit dwelling on things you can't control. It's a beautiful day, relax, enjoy it.

"Sorry." She loosened her grip on Tristan and slowed Moon Woman to a walk as Billy pulled alongside. "You're right, it is a beautiful day."

"Pardon?" Billy adjusted his black flat brimmed Navajo hat, leaning across the gap between them.

"I was just saying it's a beautiful day. We might as

well slow down and enjoy it." Keith kept pace with Moon Woman on a loose rein, his wild eyes alert but uncharacteristically calm and watchful.

"Good idea." He reached over and patted Tristan on the head. "You warm in there? You look like a little fat blue snow bunny."

"Bunny!" Tristan waved his arms and giggled.

Billy wore a faded orange Patagonia parka, his jet black hair, tied in a pony tail, hung over the collar. He sat relaxed in the saddle, knees high like Tom, but with a straighter back.

Allison was surprised by how easily he managed Keith. "Thanks for riding him, Billy. He needs the exercise but he's more than I can handle."

Billy patted his mount on the neck with a gloved hand. "We get along pretty good, don't we, old man?" Keith turned his head and nickered.

"I haven't seen him like this since Tom rode him."

"Like what?"

"So calm, almost mellow."

Billy smiled and rubbed the horse's neck again. "Well, we're old friends. I knew him before Tom bought him from Uncle Billy."

"Do you think he remembers you?"

"Horses never forget."

Mackay, finally able to catch up, circled Keith, barking enthusiastically. The horse lowered his head and put his ears back, warning him off.

Billy took the lead as they started up the hill. The horses slowed, picking their way through high ridges of drifted snow. Tristan slumped against her. Eyes closed, not a care in the world.

"We're so fortunate," she murmured.

Yes, we are.

As they climbed higher, she heard the raucous caw of a raven overhead and stopped. Shading her eyes, she found him silhouetted over Horse Heaven Hill, a dark smudge, a light brush stroke on the winter blue canvas of sky.

Billy stopped too, following her look. "He's watching us, isn't he? I wonder where his mate is; they're usually in pairs."

He was a handsome man with a wonderful smile. He seemed open and caring with a gentle disposition, comfortable in his copper skin. She hoped for Kat's sake she was right, prayed that her cynical sister would not judge whatever flaws he might have too harshly.

They went on, searching the sky for raven's mate. She was relieved when Billy pointed out a second bird swooping down to join the first. This was not a good place to be alone.

When the trail started to switchback, Billy dismounted. "This could be slippery; let's walk. I'll carry the boy."

Allison carefully handed Tristan to Billy. He murmured but kept his eyes closed, cherub face rosy with cold. Mackay, who had lagged behind, caught up, eager and panting. Tristan and Mackay, every day was a happy day.

They walked the rest of the way in silence. A Stairway to Heaven, Allison thought breathlessly as she followed. A man, a boy, a woman, horses and a dog surrounded by spirits. A great painting, but she was too preoccupied to compose it. Maybe later.

I'm right with you, Allie.

"I know." She felt giddy in the altitude. "I love you." How could anyone doubt her love for Tom?

Billy heard her, glanced back for a moment and smiled.

They stopped on the untracked summit of Horse Heaven Hill, breathing hard from the steep climb in cold thin air. Snow blew in a steady haze along the ground. Gone were the flowers of spring and rich green grass. Gone were songbirds and the hum of insects and smell of sage. The horses turned their backs to the wind, tails flying over their rumps like fans. Billy held Tristan protectively, feet spread wide, not moving, looking down at the bare tepee poles on the Big Hole Battlefield.

Allison started to speak but thought better of it. Snow piled around her feet. She pulled Tom's coat closer, ducking her head behind the high stiff collar. Feeling alone and sad, she looked around for her friend Red Coyote. No sign of him, only drifting blowing snow. Billy continued to stand with his back to her. She wanted to tell him about Tom.

Go ahead, honey, he'll understand.

"Tom and I used to come here."

He nodded, still looking down at the silent, deserted battlefield.

Go on, Allie.

She stepped up beside Billy. "I had a dream recently about being on this hill. Tom was with me. He saw Eagle from the Light, over on that ridge." She pointed to the bare spine of rock that rose above the dark green timberline across the Big Hole River.

"Looks like a good place to keep an eye on things." Billy held the brim of his hat as a blast of cold wind swept across the hill.

"I saw Tom riding by on Keith in a snowstorm the other night. Don't you think that's strange?"

"No," he replied easily. "I don't."

Encouraged, she added, "I have a painting to commemorate it."

Billy looked at her. "I'd like to see it sometime." The wind whipped his pony tail to the side.

"Did Kat warn you about me?"

"No, why? Katherine said you were a talented artist. A creative, sensitive, brave woman struggling to cope with the tragic loss of your family. She's very proud of you."

"I don't know what I'd do without her. She's always been there for me, but I don't think she understands when I include Tom in my conversations. I talk to him all the time now." Coyotes too.

Clouds appeared on the horizon, long sweeping mare's tails moving fast from north to south.

"And how is Tom?"

"Good. It's comforting to have him around. I'd be totally lost without him."

"I know what you mean; I see my dad sometimes." He gripped his hat brim again as the wind gusted around them.

"Here?"

"No, he was a salmon fisherman on the coast. He died years ago."

"I'm sorry, what happened?"

"He disappeared. They found his troller, but he wasn't on it. He fell overboard, I guess. He was fishing alone. I was away at college." He shrugged. "When I visit my mom and go out fishing, I sometimes see Dad ghosting along in the fog right next to me, telling me where the fish are biting. He's usually right too." The wind shrieked around them now. "Come on; let's get out of this."

They found a spot over the crest of the hill in a rounded depression which seemed familiar. It was here that she and Tom made love. She was sure of it, but everything looked different in the snow. They were in another world, isolated, harsh, elemental---and incredibly beautiful. Pure. Basic. Lonely.

Billy sat down across from her still holding a sleeping Tristan.   He remained that way for sometime not speaking.

"Are you okay?" Allison finally asked.   "You're very quiet."

"I was thinking."   He took off his hat, shook the snow off, and replaced it.   "My father's people were originally from the Wallowa Valley, Chief Joseph's band. They were here---down there---on that day---the morning it happened."

"I didn't know that.   This place is special to you then."   As it is to me.   The wind moaned above them, streaming snow over the lip of the hollow.

"I haven't been here in years."   He shifted Tristan's curled body.

"You want me to take him?"

"No, he's fine. It feels good to hold a child."

"Yes, I know what you mean."   Especially one conceived on this spot. But at the bottom of the hill by the river, babies, as precious to their mothers and fathers as Tristan was to them, were murdered in their sleep by General Howard and his soldiers. No excuse for killing a child. None.

The horses crowded in to get out of the wind, bracketing them on either side in a V, shuffling their feet.   A good windbreak. Mackay spun around and around, finally rolling into a tight ball at her feet. Secure. A Nez Perce winter camp. All they needed was a fire. People and animals huddling close for warmth: a war chief, a little boy, a cowgirl, Appaloosas, a dog, a coyote, a raven and an eagle, the Circle of Life.

"We never lived on the reservation. My dad left there before he got out of high school and went fishing in Alaska. He made so much money he never went back. Mom's got Navajo blood, but she met Dad in Anacortes, Washington where she was an elementary school teacher. Still is, as a matter of fact."

He rubbed his chin. "My sister and I went to school in Anacortes, but every summer Dad sent us to live with my namesake, Uncle Billy, on the reservation in Lapwai, the guy Tom bought Keith from. My dad called it 'learning-to-live-like-an-Indian'. He said it would be good for us. Mom thought it was a waste of time. She wanted us to stay home and go to summer school so we could both get into a good college."

The wind whistled through the low pines that backed up to the hollow. "So your dad won?" I want to know what you think about him, Allie.

Billy Blackmere smiled. "Actually they both won. Mom got us into good colleges but Uncle Billy taught us a lot about life, you know, where we came from and who we are. I remember the first thing he told us was that Lapwai meant "Land of the Butterflies.""

"What a beautiful name, a great image."

Lapwai Man. *Billy in his Navajo hat---tall, erect, proud, surrounded by swarms of colorful butterflies.*

"My uncle is also one hell of a horse breeder. Years ago, he told me Appaloosas were an important part of our heritage and I should pay attention and learn everything I could about them."

"He's been a big influence on your life then."

Billy nodded. "Absolutely, he inspired me to become a vet. He also brought my sister and I over here to the memorial every summer. He made us tour the whole place---told us who stayed in what tepee, who gave the alarm, who helped the women and children escape, which braves drove the soldiers off and captured their mountain howitzer. Uncle Billy knew it all; it was very impressive. Unfortunately, I was too young to appreciate it."

"I think history is a hard subject to get involved with when you're young, and I come from a family of historians."

"Well, it sure took with my sister. She went on to teach American Indian Studies at Arizona State. We're very proud of her, especially Mom."

"That's wonderful, Billy, you both became teachers."

"Yeah, we did, and although I know a lot about horses, I sometimes wish I had a deeper connection to my Nez Perce roots. I never got involved like my sister, and the fight down there wasn't that long ago."

"No, it wasn't, but to most people around here, it's like it never happened."

"But you're not most people, are you, Allison?"

"And neither are you."

Tristan was awake. "Mommy, I'm hungry." His blue eyes sparkled and danced like Tom's, clear, far-seeing.

"I know, honey, so am I. We'll go in a minute." Snowflakes were drifting down. Allison reached out and took him from Billy. The horses stirred restlessly. Mackay jumped up, wagging his tail, ready to go.

"We should probably pack it up," Billy commented, getting to his feet. "The weather's closing in. I'll carry him down to where we can ride."

Tristan protested, clinging to Allison. "It's okay, honey, I'll be right with you. The snow's too deep for you to walk." She looked around one last time for Red Coyote.

"Forget something?" he asked.

"I was looking for a friend of mine, Red Coyote. I expected to see him here."

"Really? Now that's interesting." Billy picked up Tristan who kept his eyes on his mother. "That was Eagle from the Light's other name. Red Coyote was his Wyakin. You know what that means?"

"A spirit guide." Instantly recognized by Carlos and the underlying force that first drew her to Eagle of the Light and inspired her painting.

"Exactly. Uncle Billy said Red Coyote made Eagle sly and careful and even warned him that he would die if he came back here after the battle. Very powerful stuff.

Do you have dreams about Red Coyote?"

A shiver ran up her spine. "All the time. He warns me of danger. Carlos and I actually saw him after the horses were painted, sitting on a hill above the corral. Red Coyote told him more danger was coming."

Billy bowed his head. "You'd better be careful then. You don't want to ignore his warnings like Eagle did." He pulled Tristan's wool hat down over his ears to protect him from the cold and looked at her. "You're very fortunate, Allison. I've never experienced anything like that."

"You haven't?"

"No, I guess I'm not close enough to the land and my heritage. You think more like an Indian than I do. You really have to meet my uncle. He'd love your idea of establishing a herd of free roaming Appaloosas right next to the memorial, and he might actually help."

"You think he'd be interested?"

Billy checked the saddle cinches, one arm securely around Tristan. "I'm sure he would. He's the one who bred Eagle's Light for me."

"That's a great idea; I'd love to meet him."

"And you could talk me into it too." He looked at her intently, his face a mask of seriousness. "Maybe we could involve some kids from the reservation in the summer; let them work with the horses. It could be something very positive for them, Allison, and God knows they need it."

"That would be wonderful." He was so much like Tom. Full of good ideas and enthusiasm, ready to commit himself. Her report to Kat would be a good one.

Billy rubbed Keith's nose. "That way we'd get to see a little more of each other wouldn't we, old boy?"

Allison had to look away before she could reply. "We'd all like that, Billy."

"But right now we'd better get moving before we get snowed in. I don't like the looks of that sky."

She followed him down the switchbacks, considering the possibilities. They could rehabilitate the old bunk house, give some of the horses they raised to selected kids, Billy and his uncle could guide their breeding program. "Isn't this wonderful, Tom."

Yes, but watch your step, Allie.

She was glad Billy was carrying Tristan. Allison glanced back to make sure Mackay was still with them.

They were on the last switchback when she heard the sharp crack of a rifle and the angry buzz of a bullet. Mackay barked, hair standing on end. Another crashing shot and Red Coyote flashed by at a dead run, ears back.

Keith reared; Billy let go of the reins and held Tristan. "Hold your goddamn fire!" he shouted.

Keith bucked wildly in circles, stirrups flying. Moon Woman held her ground as Ben Howard emerged from the trees on foot in camouflage fatigues, carrying a rifle.

Mackay growled ominously; Allison grabbed him.

"What the hell do you think you're doing?" Billy challenged him angrily.

Ben stopped in front of them, looking from Allison to Billy. His rough beard was coated with ice. "Tryin' to shoot that calf killin' coyote. What's it look like? Been after his ass since last spring."

Billy quickly handed Tristan to Allison and advanced on Ben. "You goddamn near shot us, you idiot. We've got a child here."

Ben eyed him coldly, resting the rifle butt on his boot, standing his ground. "You better watch your mouth with me, Chief."

"I told you never to shoot on my land, Ben." Her voice shook with suppressed fury. "I thought I made that very clear."

He shrugged his massive shoulders. "No varmint's gonna get away with killin' my stock. I got a right to protect my animals. You don't understand how it is out here."

She heard Billy's ragged breathing beside her, felt his tension, tight as a bow string. There was a wild primitive look on his face. "I understand very well, Ben." Tristan squirmed against her. "I also know what you told the insurance investigator about me. You're a coward who tells lies behind my back."

He gave her a knowing smirk. "I call um like I see um, lady, and you don't know shit about ranchin' and that's a fact."

"Don't talk to her that way."

Billy started forward but she stepped in front of him. "Get off my land and stay off, Ben. I never want to see you here again."

He looked at her with his unblinking grey eyes.

"You can't do that. I been handlin' the business on this place all my life. We got an arrangement, you and me. You need to take my offer and clear out; then we won't have to have these stupid conversations anymore."

He put the rifle under his arm. "All over a worthless fuckin' coyote. I told um you were crazy. I warned um," he added ominously.

Allison hugged Tristan, fighting back tears she would not give Ben the satisfaction of seeing. "If I ever catch you shooting at my Red Coyote again, you'll see just how crazy I can get."

Allie!

As if he heard Tom, Billy took her arm. "This conversation is over."

"No, it ain't, Chief." Ben shook his head slowly and turned back into the trees with his distinctive cat-like walk.

Erect and still, Billy watched him go, and when he had disappeared, rounded up Keith and her horse. "Here, let me take the boy while you mount up."

"Thank you." Shaken and angry, Allison swung into the saddle and reached for Tristan.

241

Billy looked at her, eyes dark and burning.   She knew where she had seen that look before---Eagle from the Light.

"You need to be very careful around that man, Allison."

"He's Tom's brother."

"I know."

DREAMS OF APPALOOSAS
Chapter Twenty: My Journal

November 16

My Dearest Tom,

I'm in my studio. It's a beautiful night, the stars are out, there's fresh snow on the ground and a warm fire in the Franklin stove. But after hours of struggling with a painting of Tristan, Carlos and our new colt, I finally gave up and decided to write you in the hope that it will pull me out my depression.

In spite of the wonderful ride up Horse Heaven Hill with Tristan and Billy, it was a hard day, full of unpleasant surprises, starting with the reopening of the insurance investigation and ending with Ben trying to shoot my Red Coyote. Thank God you and Billy were there. If he'd killed him, I don't know what I would have done. Fortunately, I left your pistol at home.

I'm sorry, but I've come to hate the very sight of your brother. Maybe he thinks that if he makes life miserable enough for me, I'll take his buyout offer. The check is still on your desk, sitting there like a time bomb. I honestly don't know why I haven't torn it up. Possibly because somewhere in the back of my mind I am tempted to sell, take the easy way out, and leave all this behind?

Of course, I can't do that and I won't. It would mean abandoning our dream and I know in my heart that if our roles were reversed, you would be right here carrying on for the sake of Tristan and our horses. Fortunately, we are not alone. Not only do we have the powerful presence of Afracela and Carlos, dare I say magical presence (yes, I do!), but I'm sure it was providence that brought your friend Billy and Eagle's Light to us precisely at the moment we need them the most.

Not only has Billy volunteered to step in and guide our breeding program, but he's got some wonderful ideas on how to involve Nez Perce youth with the horses. Billy and Eagle are just what we need to get going, aren't they? I also gave Billy a big vote of confidence with Kat. She may think I'm naïve about people, but after I met you, I know a good man when I see one!

Carlos introduced our new colt to Happy the other day and now puts them in the pasture together when the sun is out and it's warm enough. What a wonderful picture---Eagle's Light following my Happy Horse around like a little brother. Eagle has no idea Happy is blind; he just knows he has a friend to show him the ropes.

244

Sitting here with you in these quiet, still hours before dawn, I feel my faith and courage slowly returning. As you know, I've been apprehensive about going to California for Thanksgiving. I'm not looking forward to facing my parents with their unspoken doubts and fears about my well being. And while you and the twins will be in our thoughts, I will greatly miss being home and our traditional Thanksgiving with the Christians and Garcias, surrounded by our dogs and horses.

Carlos, God bless him, realizing how difficult it will be for Tristan and me to be separated from Dotty Girl and Mackay, even for a few days, reassured us that he will have both of them sleep with him in the barn right next to Eagle's Light until we return.

So, no more excuses, I've decided to go ahead with our travel plans. The fact is, my parents love us, and that includes a special place in their hearts for you and the twins. They will be thrilled to see Dave and Tristan, of course. Kat and Billy will be there too, which will mean a lot to them as they are every bit as concerned about her happiness as they are about mine.

Also, Betty has urged me to stop in and see Priscilla as she will be alone in the convalescent center over the holidays. That gives me an added incentive to make the trip. I'm going to give her the painting I did of you and the boys fishing on the Big Hole.

Here it is, morning already. As the first light of day

tops the Beaverheads, transforming their snowy summits into glowing crystal palaces high above our darkened valley, I must admit I feel guilty about leaving and it scares me, because I'm afraid you might not be here when we return. I couldn't stand that.

You won't desert us, will you? I promise we will be back soon. Please keep the home fires burning and watch over all those dear to us at the Windhorse. And look for my Red Coyote on the hill.

All my love, forever,

Allie

DREAMS OF APPALOOSAS
Chapter Twenty-One: Priscilla

Sitting together on Horse Heaven Hill, side by side, on a warm summer day, surrounded by Prairie Smoke, Scarlet Gila, blue Lupine. The faint jingle of tack from horses grazing nearby, a cool breeze washing over them. Somewhere nearby a bluebird sings, an eagle soars overhead, a pair of ravens outlined against an orange sun. Oh Tom, I'll always love you. She leaned against him, secure in his arms.

A touch on her shoulder. "Fasten your seat belt please, the little boy too."

Allison straightened up and gently shook Tristan who was snuggled against her, warm and secure. "Time to wake up, honey, we're here."

They landed at the Long Beach airport in the middle of the afternoon, coming in low over the dazzling blue green Pacific dotted with sails and whitecaps, crossing freeways, palm lined streets crowded with houses, apartments and shopping malls, traffic circles and cul de sacs, turquoise swimming pools everywhere.

She once called this home. Convertibles, hot leather

seats, the smell of suntan oil, the taste of dripping double-decker chocolate-strawberry ice cream cones. The Eagles. California girls. Another time, another life.

"Is Daddy here?" he asked sleepily.

She squeezed his hand. "No, honey, he's in Montana. We're going to visit Grandma and Grandpa." I won't be long Tom.

Warm humid air laced with the familiar smell of salt water and acrid smog poured in through the aircraft door. Dave followed them down the open ramp with the carry-ons, squinting into the pale washed out costal sun. "Brings back a lot of memories, doesn't it?"

"Yes." Good and bad, triumphs and regrets, all in the past.

The shimmering white stucco terminal had been expanded and modernized but still retained the old fashioned Southern California look she remembered. Like Union Station in downtown Los Angeles. Not so romantic anymore.

Security announcements blared. Don't leave your vehicle unattended. Report all suspicious persons and packages. Was Lyn out there somewhere in one of those non-descript apartments? No forwarding address. No job. Lost in the maze.

She got the bags while Dave brought the rental car around, a shiny black Lincoln Navigator. "You think this is big enough?" he kidded, strapping Tristan into a child seat in the back.

"I like to be up off the road so I can see where we're going." It was as close to Tom's diesel pickup as she could get. "You okay back there?"

"Grandma and Grandpa!" He waved his green dinosaur, wide awake.

"Yes, Phyllis and Fred, you remember them?"

He dutifully repeated their names. No unsettling memories, no doubts or fears, only eager anticipation. "But first we have to make a quick stop."

She took out the directions Betty had given her to the Mira Mar Convalescent Center. "We want to go north on the Long Beach Freeway; I'll find the exit."

"Okay." He wheeled out of the parking lot and up the on-ramp. "So, are you glad to be back in the homeland?"

"It'll be good to see the folks, but I can do without the rest of it." A motorcycle flashed by with a roar, speeding down the lane divider, perilously close to cars on either side. "How about you?"

"Oh, I'll be glad to see them too, but except for them, there's nothing here for me anymore. Like you, my life's in Montana. It's got everything I need, fresh air, a lot of mountains and kids to teach." A big truck and trailer cut in front of them, he braked hard.

"Even after the vandalism and name calling and that horrible diatribe by Reverend Snook?"

"Minor league stuff compared to my life on the street before you guys took me in, sis."

What that life had been like she couldn't imagine and had never asked. A nameless, shapeless horror of sexual exploitation by subhuman people.

"You remember that high powered counselor your dad sent me to in Santa Monica, the Greek, Athena Lampropolis, the one who got me into climbing?"

"I do." They sped past Signal Hill where tall grasshopper oil well pumps still dotted the hillside, bobbing mechanically up and down as they had since she was a child, even though most of the oil was gone. The preying mantas shapes were very much like the old fashioned wooden "beaver slides" used to stack hay in the Big Hole Valley, but these were a study in black and rust.

"A great lady. I loved that woman; she really put it on the line. She said life for me was going to be like climbing an endless range of mountains, one challenge after another, so I might as well get used to it and learn to get something positive out of every climb, as painful and tiring as they might be."

"Good advice." Her parents didn't know about the return of Lyn or the pending insurance investigation. Unfortunately, the picture of her with the gun at the school board meeting had run in the LA Times. There would be some unavoidable discussion about that.

"She told me the important thing was to hang on and maintain a sense of self worth and no matter what, keep going---have faith that good things will happen."

"Words to live by." Faith and courage, Tom. I'm hanging on.

He laughed. "Sure are. You know, Athena's still around. I get a card from her every Christmas. Maybe you should go and see her."

"Maybe I should." She twisted in the seat to check on Tristan; he'd fallen asleep. They were getting close. "I think it's the next exit." What would Priscilla be like? Tom's first love, the homecoming queen, the prettiest girl in town.

He slowed and moved to the right. There were four police cars parked at the head of the off ramp, red lights flashing, officers handcuffing a suspect. What had he done? Beat up his girlfriend? Murdered his wife for the insurance money?

"So what's this place we're going to anyway?"

"It's a convalescent center. She was in a halfway house until the accident."

He stopped for a red light. "What happened?"

"She tried to commit suicide. Betty said she ended up in the county mental ward for awhile."

"That's awful. So Betty stays in touch?"

"Of course, they're old friends from high school, and you know Betty."

"I do. A good person to have as a friend. She really got those parents to say some nice things about me."

Allison grimaced. "I wish I'd been able to stay. I'm

afraid I did you more harm than good."

"You supported me, sis, one hundred and ten percent, like you always have; you were fantastic." The car behind them honked impatiently. The light was green. Dave looked in the rear view mirror and slowly pulled away. The driver swerved around them, tires screaming.

She stole a look at Tristan who was busy talking to his green T Rex, oblivious to the incident. "I lost my temper, just like that guy, only I had a gun. It was a stupid thing to do."

"Listen, I don't think it was stupid at all. You put that Bible pounder and his kids on notice big time and for that I will be forever grateful. You had the courage to stand up to them. You'll see it's all going to work out for the best."

"Do you think so."

"It will. You've got a lot of friends there."

"I haven't seen too many of them lately, except for Betty and Jim."

"And me. I'm your friend."

She leaned over and kissed him on the cheek. "And you, Dave. You're my best friend."

They drove on in silence past tawdry strip malls, pizza parlors, payroll check cashing, dog grooming, latte stands, and gas stations. No one should be left alone in a place like this, especially a girl from Wisdom, Montana.

"This is a good thing you're doing."

"I'm glad you're with me, Dave. I'm a little nervous."

Priscilla, Queen of the Wisdom Round-up, on a fine Palomino, silver studded saddle draped with pink roses, blond hair in a pony tail, waving mechanically, a smile on her innocent face. Supremely happy. Small children cheering. American flags.

"You'll do just fine. She'll like you."

Another traffic light. Brown faces like Afracela and Carlos, the new immigrants. Store fronts, Tienda Colorado, Casa Delores, Supermercado. Garish colors, fire engine red, glittering gold, tangerine orange, livid turquoise.

Afracela would be in the kitchen making bread, watching the Today Show. Carlos might be working Eagle's Light. The dogs would be with him. She vowed not to do this again. Wait for me, Tom. I'm coming home to stay.

The light changed. "So when did Priscilla leave Tom and the boys anyway?"

"I think they were about eight." She consulted her directions. "We're almost there."

"Hard on the kids."

"Hard on everyone. Tom finally decided the most important thing was raising the boys, so he sold the business and moved back to Montana to be a full time father."

"She never went back?"

"No, Tom looked for her everywhere and eventually

found her down here in Long Beach, broke and living in a shelter."

The pale pink convalescent center was sandwiched between a Laundromat and a Texaco station. They parked on the street and got out. A raw vitality filled the air, the smell of tortillas, music with a thudding beat but no melody, faint cheers from an unseen athletic field.

"Better lock the doors." She didn't belong here, she never had. A loud ping as he double clicked the automatic lock.

The faded pink Mira Mar was surrounded by a low cement block wall, an old "No Vacancy" sign advertising an ocean view hung next to the new one, "Mira Mar Convalescent Center, Loving Care for Your Loved One." Hard to see the ocean from here. She fingered her gold pendant as she went up the front walk. Oh, Tom, I miss you. I wish you were here.

Dave followed, holding Tristan's hand. The gate opened onto a rock garden studded with artificial green cactus and plastic daffodils. They announced themselves over an intercom and entered. A shabby lobby with a cloying hospital smell, but the Hispanic receptionist was friendly and cheerful. A smile like Afracela---with the addition of two gold teeth. It took great courage to be optimistic about life in a place like this.

Priscilla Howard was in the empty day room, sitting in a wheelchair at the end of a long table set for dinner with plastic utensils, starring listlessly through barred windows at overflowing garbage cans in the alley, graffiti on the crumbling walls---odd, swirling black and red patterns, threatening but making no sense.

She stepped forward. "Hello, I'm Allison. I hope they told you we were coming."

Priscilla turned her chair slowly. Despite the ravages of suffering and disappointment, she was still a beautiful woman. High cheek bones, almond shaped brown eyes with a faraway look. She was wearing a blue bathrobe with a gold crest over one pocket, her long hair prematurely white. "Who?" She asked in a raspy whisper.

"Allison. Tom's---wife."

"Oh, yes," Priscilla replied. "I'm sorry, I'm a little slow…." She waved a thin white arm. "What with all this stuff in me."

"I understand. I appreciate you seeing us." Allison glanced back at Dave. Tristan looked curiously at the slow turning ceiling fan. "May I sit down?"

"Of course. I'm afraid you're a little early for dinner." Priscilla gestured to the empty room.

Allison's heart went out to her. "It's okay; I came to see you."

"That's very nice." She spoke slowly, without emotion. "I don't get many---visitors---and you've come a long way."

"Oh, not so far really." She felt Priscilla's eyes on her and met them. There was a definite resemblance to the twins. "I'd like you to meet Dave and my son Tristan---our son."

Priscilla looked at her questioningly.

Allison motioned Tristan forward, realizing she had confused her. "This is Tom's son. Dave is a friend. We grew up together."

"Oh," Priscilla responded; her face lighting up. "Hello, little boy."

He gave her his best grin. "Hello, Grandma."

Priscilla smiled. "I could be a grandma but I'm not."

"This is Priscilla, honey. She's your---aunt, Aunt Priscilla. Isn't that a pretty name?"

"Yes," Tristan replied gravely.

"Blue eyes," Priscilla noted. "I know those eyes. I'm very pleased to meet you, Tristan---and your blue eyes." She reached out, touching his hand.

"I'm going to see if I can find a cup of coffee," Dave announced. "Can I get you ladies anything?" They both declined.

"I'm sorry if I'm not as quick as I should be," Priscilla apologized again. "It's embarrassing. I'll get over it once they back off the medication."

Priscilla put a long graceful hand on Tristan's head. "I know who you are---and your mother too. I'm so very glad to see you both."

"And we're happy to finally meet you. I've brought you something, a present."

She opened the tube she'd carried from Montana

and unrolled the painting of Tom and the twins fishing on the Big Hole. They were standing in the river, boys on either side of Tom, proudly showing off a string of trout. It captured what she loved about them, their enthusiasm for life. "I didn't have time to frame it, but I'll get someone to do that for you."

Priscilla leaned over the table, transfixed by the painting. "Oh my goodness, I know this spot. It's so beautiful---the twins are almost as tall as Tom---my boys. The last time I saw them was --- I don't know what to say; it's the nicest thing anyone has ever done for me." She began to sob in short, shallow gasps.

"I'm glad you like it." Allison put her hands on Priscilla's thin shoulders. "They never stopped loving you."

"Oh, I felt so badly for you, Allison, you know, when it happened, I knew how you felt."

"Thank you."

"I'm so sorry I couldn't be at the funeral. I wanted to be."

"I know you did."

Tristan pulled on her sleeve. "Mommy, I want to play."

She took a place setting off the table and put it on a chair. "Here, honey, feed your dinosaur some dinner; he's probably hungry."

"Tom would be glad about your visit, don't you think?" Priscilla asked, drying her eyes on crumpled tissues.

"I'm sure he would."

"He said you were a famous artist."

"Not so famous."

Priscilla smiled for the first time, and she saw the radiance that must have been there when Tom first met her. The twins had her beautiful smile.

"I have something for you too." Priscilla reached into her bathrobe pocket and not finding what she was looking for, switched to the other. "I know it's here somewhere." She finally produced a worn 4x6 photograph and handed it to Allison. "You didn't know him then."

An old black and white but there no mistaking Tom and the radiant Priscilla. What was surprising was the broad-shouldered John Wayne look alike, Ben, on the other side of her.

"You remember that old song, "Caught Between Two Lovers, Caught Between Two Friends?" Priscilla asked.

"I think so." Allison studied Ben. Taller than Tom. Self assured. A handsome man. What happened to him?

"They actually fought over me." Priscilla went on brightly. "Two men like that. I was what we used to call, sitting in the catbird's seat."

"I can see that." Allison heard the rattling of pots and pans in the kitchen. For the first time, she noticed the walls decorated for Thanksgiving---paper turkeys with tails that flared, secured with pins to pockmarked corkboard, faded pumpkins and ears of dried corn Scotch taped together, pious unsmiling pilgrims in tall black hats, facing stoic Indians in feathered war bonnets across the table.   A brief respite before the Christians got down to the business of killing them.

"I picked the wrong one, you know."

Priscilla's mood had reversed. The beauty queen was gone. Her face was tragic. "The wrong one?"

"I wasn't right for Tom; I was just a country girl. He was so driven and brilliant and created such a successful life. I couldn't cope."

Allison took her hand. "Tom loved you, Priscilla. He told me that many, many times."

"I left them when they needed me the most. I couldn't do it; I just couldn't."

"It's not your fault; you were sick. He knew that."

"I let him down; I let the boys down. And now….." She started to cry again.

"He forgave you and so did the twins."

"I should have married Ben. It would have been better for Tom. He could have married you and been happy."

"No, that's simply not true. Tom didn't even know me then. I was a little girl. He married you because he loved you."

"You think so?" Tears streamed down her cheeks.

"I know so." She felt a surge of inspiration. "And he doesn't want to see either of us crying like this. We still have his ranch and we're going to keep it."

"But it's not mine."

"You can come anytime and stay as long as you like. Tom and the twins are there."

"You mean buried...."

"No," Allison cut her off. "I mean all around us, every place we go, every time I look into Tristan's blue eyes. Look into his eyes and tell me what you see."

Priscilla became very still. "I see Tom."

"I want you to get better. I want you to come and visit us at the Windhorse. I sincerely mean that."

Priscilla looked at her cautiously. "I could---I suppose."

"I hope you will."

She brightened. "Is Ben still there?"

"He is."

"I wonder if he'd be glad to see me? I haven't seen him since Tom and I---well, for a long time."

A world of hope depended on her answer. "I'm sure he would." Allison squeezed Priscilla's hand. "Promise me you'll come." The crazy woman and the gold digger, that would serve Ben right.

"I promise." Priscilla turned to Tristan. "I'm so very pleased to meet you, young man. I hope we see each other again soon."

Dave was waiting for them in the lobby and they

walked out together into the hot filtered sun sinking over roof tops. Somewhere out there the Pacific Ocean was lost in the haze, the San Gabriel Mountains shrouded in smog.

"Pretty grim." He opened the back door of the Lincoln so she could put Tristan in his car seat.

"What part?" She clicked the safety straps in place and got in the front.

"All of it."

"You've got that right," Allison put on her seat belt.

A grey wash. Two mourning women silently passing each other, hazy, gauzy white on white, framed by a long arching tunnel fading to the blackest of blacks.

Across the street, a group of tattooed teenage Hispanics with shaved heads, low slung pants and tank tops stared at them. Kat's drug dealers?

"Lock the doors, will you, Dave?" She and Kat had biked down Pacific Avenue as girls going to the beach. Those days were over. So much had changed. I won't be long, Tom, I'll be home soon. Wait for me.

DREAMS OF APPALOOSAS
Chapter Twenty-Two: Memories of Padua Hills

The police helicopter woke her at 2 a.m., hovering over the house, a noisy penetrating clatter, flashing searchlights back and forth. Tristan slept through it, but she'd been half awake ever since, tossing and turning in the soft bed where she'd slept as a teenager, wondering who they were looking for. Lyn? Reliving the accident, over and over. Painted horses. Insurance investigators. Ben shooting at Red Coyote.

Trying to focus on the thrill of seeing the eagle over Horse Heaven Hill, the new colt and Red Coyote, but finding no escape from the past. Finally, when all else failed, the blessed relief of dawn crept over Padua Hills high above the Pomona Valley. Cooing doves, the smell of oleander, honeysuckle and lemon, the distant drone of morning freeway traffic, steady as a heartbeat, pumping life in and out of Los Angeles.

Familiar, but so far from the Windhorse, from the immense stillness, the sharp smell of sagebrush and wood smoke, the bright pure light of winter sun. The living presence of Tom's love.

Voices drifted up from the patio below through open windows, the scrape of iron chair legs on brick. Her mother and Dave, sitting at the round glass top table in wrought iron chairs with white cushions beside the pool where lemon-yellow leaves drifted across the surface like miniature sailboats.

Wearily, she sat up, lightheaded from lack of sleep. They'd stayed up late after putting Tristan to bed, talking and drinking wine in the Garnett's spacious living room. Adobe walls, old kilim rugs, polished tile floors and high windows open to the sky, hacienda style. Comfortable, sedate, old world.

Catching up, her mother called it, but she did most of the talking, and her opening gambit, based on the picture of Allison with the pistol in the Los Angeles Times, was their growing concern over her safety in Montana. "We really wonder what kind of a place it is, dear, where you have to carry a gun to defend Dave's right to teach evolution."

Her mother always included her father in these pronouncements with the inclusive "we". For his part, he'd listened but said very little, occasionally intervening as a mediator when it seemed like a good idea. Dave, from long practice, played the role of the engaged, but mostly silent observer.

"I know it's hard to believe, Mother, but a lot of people carry guns in Montana. That story got blown all out of all proportion." Fortunately, they didn't know the half of it, or what happened at the Three Bears after that.

Allison threw off the light blanket and put her warm bare feet on the cool tile floor. A nice feeling. Tristan stirred in his bed. She watched the steady rise and fall of his breathing. He was their only grandson and her poker playing mother's ace in the hole, a game at which Phyllis Garnett excelled.

Her mother had asked her why, now that Tom and the boys had so tragically passed, didn't they consider returning to Southern California, to friends and family, where their safety would be assured? Allison knew the euphemism "passed" was carefully chosen for her benefit.

Dave could get a good teaching job where he would be appreciated, she could resume her art career in a more receptive market where she was well known, and their grandson could get the fine education he deserved in the top notch private day school just down the road. In fact, they'd already reserved a place for him winter term, just in case.

A new voice came up from the patio. Kat. Reinforcements at last! Allison went to the window and waved. Kat, looking radiant in a stylish blue Nike running suit, waved back. Maybe they could go for a walk alone and talk privately, get away from the constant suggestions in the guise of questions from her mother who, wearing a spectacular scarlet, fushia and maroon kimono, motioned her to join them.

"As soon as we get dressed." The garden was still lush, green and colorful, just as she remembered it. And yellow leaves were sailing gracefully across the flat surface of the pool. Tom loved to swim here; her parents had installed the low board especially for him. They were impressed with his double summersaults, graceful jackknife dives and cannonballs that splashed Tristan and made him laugh, begging for more.

"And on the way down tell your father to turn off that game and join the party," her mother called up to her. "That man and his football on Thanksgiving no less!"

Something Betty might say. "I'll tell him, Mom." She would miss having the Christians and Garcias around the Thanksgiving table. At least Kat was here, and Billy was on his way.

She lingered at the window for a moment, looking out over high, thick adobe walls covered with purple bougainvillea and red passion flowers, to the valley below. Once an uninterrupted view of thousands of acres of green orange groves, now an ocean of flat white gravel roofs fading into the smog. The five acre pasture and loafing shed where Happy and Kat's Arabian mare, Tabriz, once lived, had been sold to developers.

Tristan was up, bouncing on his bed. "I want to see Grandpa and Grandma."

"First we have to get you dressed, young man." In

the blue shorts and sailor suit top her mother bought him for the Thanksgiving holidays. It wasn't something she would have chosen, but that didn't matter. Allison went over and kissed him on the cheek. "My, you smell good."

Bright-eyed, ready to take on the new day; he'd slept fine. She took the talisman Carlos made for him off the bed post and slipped it over his wrist. His new clothes were neatly stacked on the distressed cherry wood bureau where the photographs of Happy as a colt, and she and Kat in their high school basketball uniforms were still on display.

Tristan looked cute in his little sailor outfit, but he belonged in Oshkosh overalls. Her mother would be pleased, and it was only for a couple of days. Allison found a running suit in the closet she hadn't worn since high school. Musty, heavy and surprisingly loose on her. Betty was right; she had lost weight.

Her mother had also commented on this as the long evening drew to a close. "You need to take better care of yourself, dear. You look very tired and thin, if you don't mind my saying so."

She tried to shrug it off, even though it was true.

"Perhaps you're trying to do too much."

Her mother's seemingly ageless face assumed a mask of concern. How was it that her mother still looked so young and she didn't?

"We've always thought your idea, what you call your

dream of bringing Appaloosas back to the ranch, was a wonderful enterprise, but don't you think it might be too much for you to carry on alone---without Tom to help you?"

There it was out on the table. "In the first place, it's not my dream, Mother, it's our dream. And Tom is there to help me, every step of the way. We're not going to give it up." She'd fought back tears.

"I see."

An awkward silence finally broken by her father.

"We certainly don't want you to give anything up, Allison, and believe me, we understand the importance of this to you. It's just that at the same time we think you need to be a little more realistic."

"About what?

Another long silence. This time it was her mother. "The fact that you're still struggling through your grief. We know the loving memory of Tom will always be with you, but you need to move on at some point. There are excellent counselors who can help; we have one on the faculty and... "

She had interrupted her. "I don't need a counselor, Mother. I don't need to move on. What I need is some understanding and acceptance of who I am and what I'm trying to do."

That had clearly taken her parents aback and another silence ensued.

Allison pulled the drawstring tighter on her running

pants to keep them up and adjusted Tristan's sailor suit top so it sat squarely on his shoulders. "So, are we ready to go see Grandpa and Grandma?"

He nodded, picking up his green T Rex. She took a last look around her childhood room. It was a lonely and isolated world without Tom. Kat was right, it was impossible to feel the presence of spirits in Southern California. Allison clipped Tom's gold horse pendant around her neck. She'd left her feathered necklace at home and regretted it.

Her father had finally come to the rescue, once again. "We love you, Allison; we always will, and we respect your feelings. We only want to help you get through this."

"I know, Dad." He was such a quiet force. When her affair with Lyn was so suddenly and violently revealed and she was in the hospital, he had responded with unconditional love and unqualified support.

Her mother had been there for her too, but her reaction was to see that Lyn lost his job at Scripps and would never teach at any other prestigious college. Looking from one to the other, she had addressed them both. "The thing is Tom is not just a memory to me. His living spirit is with me on the ranch, and always will be. Do you understand what I mean?"

"I think so," her mother replied quietly. Her father nodded.

"I don't think death is the end and I don't think

there's a heaven you have to wait for. I believe that when you love somebody, like I love Tom and Tristan and the twins, like I love you and Kat and Dave, our spirits are joined together. Forever."

"That's a wonderful thought, dear."

She had taken them by surprise. "I waited for Tom all my life and I am not going to accept his death. I'm going to go on and make a future for both of us; it's as simple as that."

And that was where they left it. Her mother gave her a long lingering hug, saying nothing. Her father kissed her on both cheeks. "We're very proud of you, Allison." There were tears in his eyes.

She took Tristan's hand. "Let's go see what Grandpa's up to."

They found her father comfortably ensconced in his Lazy Boy, watching football on a big screen TV in his chaotic study crowded with piles of books, papers, golf clubs, and fly fishing gear. Because of the Big Hole River, he'd always been more interested in visiting the Windhorse than her mother, especially during fishing season. Seeing them, he shut off the sound and sprang enthusiastically to his feet.

"Grandpa!" Tristan cried, running to him.

Her father picked him up and twirled him around the way Tom did. "My, you're getting to be quite a load," he remarked, putting Tristan down and embracing Allison.

Although his face looked older and his close cropped

hair whiter, his lean 6'5" body was the same. "Who's playing, Dad?"

"Oh, the Cowboys and the Redskins," he replied, squinting to check the score. "It's not a very good game."

"Where's Grandma?" Tristan took his hand.

"She's probably wondering where we are. Let's go find her, shall we?"

Allison followed them out to the patio. She'd never understood why her father, an economics professor and decidedly not athletic, a gentle man, was such a football fan, but he was and that was one of many reasons he missed Tom's company. They both loved the game, and her mother, quite uncharacteristically, left them alone to enjoy it. This total acceptance of Tom was a high compliment, considering he was a divorcee with children and fifteen years older than she was.

Tristan rushed into her mother's arms; her father went to kiss Kat. "So how are the bad guys, honey?"

"Bader than ever, Dad."

"Here's my favorite little boy in the world." Phyllis gushed. "Say, what is this neat little bracelet you have on?"

"It's a good luck charm, Mom. Carlos made it for him. It's made out of some of Happy's tail hairs." She and Kat smiled at each other across the table. She was glad to see her.

"Wasn't that nice of him. Very interesting. Sit

down, Allison," Phyllis urged. "Have some coffee and a piece of this marvelous coffee cake."

"So how's the game, Fred?" Dave inquired politely. Unlike Tom, he was not a football fan.

"Oh, not as good as seeing all of you," her father replied. "This is great." He put his arm around Kat.

"So, Katherine," her mother interjected, giving Allison a knowing look as she bounced Tristan on her knee, "when can we expect to have the pleasure of meeting this Billy Blackmere we've been hearing so much about?"

"Like I told you, Mom, he'll be here when he gets here. He had to change planes in Portland and it was late. He's renting a car in LA."

"This is not an easy place to find, Katherine, especially for someone from a small town."

"He'll have a map, Mom. Don't worry, he'll find us."

"I want to ride like the cowboys, Grandma."

Her mother bounced Tristan higher, holding him protectively under the arms. "I only know the one about the farmers, dear, but I suppose it's the same thing."

Taking a long walk through the neighborhood before Thanksgiving dinner was a Garnett family tradition, but it was Kat who suggested they go alone, leaving Tristan with their parents. Did they mind?

"Mind? Of course not." Her mother gave Allison a victory smile. "Your dad and I would love to take care of him all the time, wouldn't we, Fred?"

"Sure thing," he agreed. "Us men will go watch the game while Grandma makes us some breakfast, won't we, Tristan?"

"And we'll introduce ourselves to your friend if you're not back in time, Katherine," Phyllis added.

"Do you think Billy likes football?" her father asked Kat hopefully.

"I don't know, Dad. You can ask him."

They went through the tropical garden resplendent with Agapanthus, Bird of Paradise and Allison's favorite Jacaranda tree in full bloom then out the tall grape stake front gates. Dried palm fronds and pepper seed pods crunched under foot as they walked down the curving lane. The ground was frozen solid at the Windhorse, trees stripped bare by the advancing winter.

"So how are you holding up?" Kat asked.

"Not bad, all things considered. I managed to weather Mom's big pitch about coming home to stay, but it wasn't easy."

"I'll bet."

"She also suggested I see a counselor. She doesn't think I've come to terms with my loss."

"Is that right."

"I tried to explain it to her, to both of them, about Tom and me." She glanced over at Kat.

"That must have been quite a conversation."

They stopped in front of the community security gate. Kat punched in the code.

It was a conversation she'd been dwelling on. "Do you think I need to see a counselor?" Was she really so sure of herself?

"I don't know," Kat answered thoughtfully. "I've never lost anyone I really loved except our grandparents, and that was different." They walked onto the two lane road leading toward Claremont. "I don't know what you're going through or how I would react under the circumstances, I honestly don't."

"Should I take that for a maybe?"

"Take it in the spirit it's intended. You're fully capable of making that decision yourself, kiddo. Come on, let's jog a little."

She matched Kat's pace but felt the strain in her legs almost immediately. Heat rose off the blacktop. A trickle of sweat ran down her back. She was over dressed.

"The folks seem in good spirits," Kat remarked easily. "They're really pleased you came."

"Yes," Allison replied breathlessly. "Mom is thrilled to see Tristan."

"Who can blame her? I'm thrilled to see Tristan; we all are. He's a great kid."

"Yes, he is."

Knots of people in shorts and T shirts gathered around smoking grills, talking and drinking, others inside watching TV, probably the same game her father was enjoying with Tristan and Dave. California. Endless summer.

Hot and sweaty, she unzipped her jacket. Not something you'd do in Montana at this time of year. The smog hurt her lungs, setting off a spasm of coughing.

"You okay? Let's walk awhile."

"I thought you'd never ask. You know, you're in great shape considering you smoke like a chimney."

"Thanks. I work at it, along with everything else. You know I play basketball in the Women's Police League. The competition's pretty good. That little guard from Santa Barbara who almost beat us at State is on our team. Do you remember her?"

"No, but I'm impressed you still play."

Kat pushed the crosswalk button and they waited for the light to change on Foothill Boulevard; four lanes of traffic rushed past in either direction. The heady smell of exhaust, the sound of speed. She used to ride Happy across this road.

"I wonder where they're all going?" A numbing assault on the senses, making it difficult to maintain her bearings and think straight. Could you paint a scream of desperation? Yes, if you were good enough. Edvard Meunch did.

Kat shrugged as the light changed and they started across. "Thanksgiving dinner, I suppose. Watch yourself. " She held Allison back as a car hurtled through the intersection against the light.

"Thanks."

"You have to assume they're not going to stop, kiddo. It's different now."

"It sure is."

The Ralph's Market she remembered was surrounded by a new shopping mall. Cars circled; people pushed carts piled high with merchandise as they talked on cell phones. Home Depot, Toys R Us, Petco, Pier One, Starbucks, Pizza Hut, Bed Bath and Beyond. "When did all this happen?"

"When did all what happen?"

"All these new stores and people rushing around buying stuff." No franchises in Wisdom except the Sinclair Station.

A middle-aged, overweight couple in florid shorts, dark glasses, and sandals, posed with an overflowing shopping cart in front of Ralph's, blotting out all but a thin strip of Halloween orange sky. A ghostly Mission Indian wrapped in a blanket behind them.

The First Californians. Once there were thousands of Indians in this valley. Now there were none. Slaughtered by Spaniards and settlers, devastated by disease. Plowed under. Paved over. Gone forever.

She would not raise Tristan here.

"I guess you missed the consumer revolution while you were out riding in Montana," Kat joked as they exited the parking lot. "This is nothing. Wait until the day after Christmas. Two thirds plus of our Gross National Product. We make the world go around."

275

"Not my world."

"You looked shell shocked, kiddo."

"Do I?" They walked into old Claremont where they had lived before moving to Padua Hills. It was still quiet here.

"You do."

"I think it's ugly and tasteless."

"The place or the people?"

"Both." But as they moved further into the familiar neighborhood of stately old homes on wide tree-lined streets, her tension eased. These were the sidewalks where she drew hopscotch grids with colored chalk as a little girl. They'd lived only a block away.

They strolled past the Claremont Inn, a weathered New England style two story historic landmark from a bygone era. There were still red and yellow roses along the front walk. Tom had picked a red one for her. She was holding it when they met her parents on the veranda for breakfast and she had introduced him as her future husband. They had Eggs Benedict and, at her father's insistence, champagne.

She was wearing the engagement ring Tom had surprised her with by tying it around Happy's neck on a silver cord. "What's this?"

"The ring is for you and the silver cord will keep our hearts connected when we're apart."

"Is this a proposal?"

"I know it's not very romantic, but we're a perfect

match, and I love you."

"I love you too, and I think it's very romantic. The answer is yes." Tom had hung the silver cord over the rear view mirror on his truck every time he left on a trip without her. Consumed by flames but still connecting their hearts.

"Allie, I had a long conversation with John Henry yesterday," Kat said quietly as they left the Inn behind. "He wanted to talk to you personally, but I told him I'd rather do it myself. I hope that was alright."

"Sure, I'd much rather talk to you." But she'd rather not talk about it at all.

"Good. Besides, I didn't want to spoil our holiday. Basically, he put the insurance company on notice they could either wrap up their investigation and cut you a check or we'd sue them."

"Sue them for what?"

"Defamation of character, willful violation of state and federal insurance laws and so forth---that really isn't important."

Kat stepped closer. "What's important is their investigation is over. It's technical, but as I understand it, in spite of a supposedly foolproof system on Tom's truck that locked all the brakes if the air compressor failed, they'd hoped to prove someone tampered with the rear lines. That would cause only the front brakes to lock and make the truck go into a skid and jackknife."

Allison clenched her teeth. "I don't want to hear

this, Kat."

"I know, but the point is there's nothing left of the brake lines and they never had any reason to suspect you of anything except those salacious statements from Ben, Lyn and Snook which they have agreed to expunge from their files."

"So where does that leave us?" She felt the sickening plunge of Tom's truck and trailer freefalling into the black abyss, twisting, turning, bursting into flame. Her stomach cramped.

"They've dropped it and called it an accident. You should have a check by registered mail by the time you get home."

They were standing across from Scripps College with its ivy covered stone walls. Nothing had changed.

"Do you want to cut across the quad on the way home?"

"God no!" Kissing and fondling. Making love on the broken down couch in Lyn's office. Disgusting. How could she have done it?

Kat took out a pack of cigarettes, shook one out and lit it with the sharp snap of her gold lighter. "I've upset you."

"No, I appreciate everything you've done, I do." She bit her lip. "I just feel lost here; I want to go home. I'm not a very brave person."

"But you are brave," Kat insisted, "you're the bravest person I know."

"I wish I felt that way." A black sedan drove slowly past them.

"Hell, you're the woman who stared them down with a pistol." Kat exhaled, watching the car as it turned the corner, signal flashing.

"I lost my head. I never should have done that. I should have stayed in my studio where I know what I'm doing and that's what I'm going to do from now on."

"That's bullshit. You can't hide out in your art forever. Sometimes you have to come out and fight back and that's exactly what you did. I'm proud of you. That took a lot of courage."

"You think so?"

"I know so."

"But I'm tired of fighting."

Kat dropped her cigarette on the sidewalk, stepped on it, and put the butt in her pant's pocket. "Listen to me carefully, Allie, don't retreat into your art and imagination too far. You can get lost in there."

"Is that what I'm doing?"

"Sometimes, not all the time. And I know why; I really do."

"I retreat so I won't fall to pieces. I need to create a world where I'm happy again. Do you understand what I mean?"

"Yes, I do."

"Maybe Mom's right about counseling."

"Maybe." Kat extended her hand and she held it.

"But right now, let's get out of here. The campus triggers bad memories, doesn't it?"

"Yes, for all the good things that happened while I was at Scripps, I'll always remember the bad."

They passed an older couple with a Jack Russell terrier and exchanged "good mornings." The little dog barked a greeting; she thought of Mackay and Dotty Girl.

"Lyn's not here anymore, kiddo. He's out of your life for good."

"Are you sure about that? I don't believe it." Could you ever get rid of the past? The black car passed them again. "Did you see that car?"

"The black one?"

"Yes."

"Don't worry about them; they're with me."

"Who are they?"

Kat laughed. "My faithful guard dogs from the county."

"Bodyguards? What are they doing out here?" The car made a U turn at the boulevard and came back towards them.

"Their job." Kat waved; the two men inside waved back. "You know the Manuel Rodriguez trial I was working on at your place? Well, my star witness never showed. They found him in a garbage bag last week in the Long Beach Harbor, or at least pieces of him."

"Jesus Christ, Kat." They stopped and waited for the light to turn on Foothill Boulevard.

Kat shrugged. "Manuel's brother is still on the loose. He said I was next."

She looked at the passing cars; any one of them could be an assassin. "You need to find another job and get away from here. What kind of people do things like that?"

"Business people, Allie, engaged in the world's most profitable enterprise---drugs. They can buy and sell all those stores in that mall back there with pocket change and they'll kill anybody who gets in their way, including county prosecutors like me."

Her legs cramped as they started across the highway. The black car passed them again. "Seriously, Kat, you need to make a change."

"That's what Billy says."

"Well, he's right."

"He might be."

The musical chimes of Kat's cell phone startled them. She pulled it off her belt clip and flipped it open. "Garnett here."

Allison watched the color drain from Kat's face as she listened and then handed her the phone. "It's Billy, brace yourself."

"I've got some bad news, Allison. The Sheriff just called me when he couldn't get you at your parent's house. Somebody beat the hell out of Carlos and slashed up Eagle's Light. They went after your dogs too."

Her heart jumped. "Slashed?"

"With a knife, somebody tried to kill them."

Dizzy, she reached out to Kat for support. Traffic sped by. Exhaust filled the air. "Will they be alright?"

"Dotty's okay. They managed to stitch up Carlos and Mackay, but I'm afraid the colt's been hurt pretty bad."

"Is he going to live?" A thousand miles away. Helpless to save him.

"I don't know but I just chartered a plane to fly me over there. I'll try to help your vet save him."

Bile rose in her throat. "He can't die; he can't." Dreams shattered.

"I'll do my best, Allison."

"Oh, Tom, please don't let this happen." She dropped the phone, doubled over and vomited as Kat steadied her.

DREAMS OF APPALOOSAS
Chapter Twenty-Three: Coming Home

_____

A dark hooded figure savagely clubbed Carlos and slashed at their panicked colt. Desperately, she tried to fend him off, but her arms were weak and heavy. Gunshots, one after the other, soldiers shouting, screams of dying horses. They were slaughtering the Appaloosas.

_____

"Stop!"

"Mommy."

"What is it?"

"You're yelling."

"Sorry." The Missoula bound flight bounced and swayed, flying blind through thick cumulus clouds. "I was having a bad dream---about our colt." She massaged her temples, trying to relieve a pounding headache.

"Will he be okay?"

"I hope so." Thank God for Billy. Arriving in the dark, his charter plane managed to land on the ranch road despite bad weather. She'd been up all night getting hourly reports from Betty, restlessly pacing her childhood room, stopping to rearrange Tristan's blankets, listening to the hum of the freeway, going over and over the horrible scene in her mind. Who hated them enough to do this?

The colt, still in shock, had lost a lot of blood and was clinging to life. Carlos, clubbed from behind by an unknown assailant, was in the Wisdom clinic, conscious and coherent, twenty-five stitches in his head. Another murderous assault on innocents in the long, bloody history of the Big Hole. Red Coyote had warned her, but like Eagle from the Light, she hadn't listened.

Allison gripped Tristan's hand, staring ahead into the gloom of the cabin. The little plane bumped and groaned in the turbulent air. Boisterous weather. That was what Tom called it when he flew her into the ranch for the first time. It seemed so long ago. Tiny buildings scattered at the base of wooded hills, those marvelous yellow haystacks everywhere, a wandering green-blue river, white thunderheads in a cobalt sky. Low clouds tinged with pink, trailing delicate grey fringes of rain over pastures dotted with horses and cattle.

"This is it, honey."

"Oh Tom, it's so beautiful!" His silver cord connected their hearts.

284

Only later did she learn about the evil that lurked beneath the beauty, the unmarked graves of mothers and children burned alive in tepees and blind old men bayoneted to death on their ranch. That curse of the Windhorse was with them still, and now Eagle's Light, their last hope for redemption, was dying.

"Please don't take Tristan back to that place," her mother begged. "At least not until they catch the awful people who did this."

"I have to go back, Mom. They need me, and I can't leave Tristan here." She had no time to explain. The plane left within the hour. She hoped Kat would come, but her trial started on Monday. They flew standby; Dave didn't get a seat. He'd be on the next available flight.

"Take good care of your mother," Dave gravely told Tristan as they parted, betraying his own misgivings.

With a wrenching groan, the man in front of them vomited into an air flight sickness bag. Allison hoped she wasn't next.

"What's he doing?" Tristan tugged at her hand.

"He's sick, honey."

"Why?"

She put her arm around her son. "Because all the bouncing bothers him." The stench filled the cabin. Her gut rebelled.

"I like to bounce," Tristan declared enthusiastically.

"You're a lucky boy; you have a strong stomach---

like your dad."

Claustrophobia. She suffered her first attack in a stalled elevator with Lyn at the Getty Museum. *Jesus, Allison, what the hell is wrong with you?*

Panic. Trapped. No way out. *You're what's wrong with me, Lyn.*

What's that supposed to mean?

It means this is over. But it wasn't. It would never end.

The stewardess came lurching down the aisle to get the bag, bracing herself against seats on either side. The man leaned over his seatback and apologized. A pale Goya face tinged with green. "No problem, I might be next." More forgiveness than she felt.

"Are we there yet, Mommy?"

"No, not yet, honey. Soon." *Hang on.* Prickling hot sweat.

"Will Daddy be there?"

"Yes, of course, he will. Remember what I told you? He's always with us." Allison took his hand and squeezed. "His love surrounds us." *For God's sake, be there for us, Tom.*

Tristan looked at her questioningly. "Will my big brothers be with him?"

"Their spirits will be there."

"Are we home yet?"

"Soon, you have to be patient."

"I don't want to be patient," he replied, scowling. "I

want to play a game. I want to play 'I'm thinking of something'."

She shook her aching head. "I have a better idea; let's pray for Carlos and Eagle, shall we?"

"What's praying?"

"It's when we ask God for help. Come on, we have to close our eyes." She'd never been able to pray like Tom, but it might help now.

Tristan closed his eyes, tilting his chin up, making a show out of it. She bowed her head and gripped Tom's pendant with her free hand. God, please save Carlos and Eagle. And get me out of this plane.

"I'm praying," Tristan proudly announced.

"Good. Keep going." While Allison desperately prayed, the dark hooded figure kept slashing at their panicked colt. "No! No!"

"Mommy, you're yelling again."

"Was I? Close your eyes, honey; we have to pray really, really hard. It's important." Get a hold of yourself. This will never do.

The plane dropped suddenly, turbo props howling, then rose on an updraft before falling back to level flight. Stomach churning, she reached for their silver cord, mechanically reciting the names of mountain ranges she could not visualize. Beartooths, Beaverheads, Pioneers, Anacondas---flowers whose colors had faded---Prairie Smoke, Scarlet Gilia, Bitterroot, Rock Penstemon, Lupine, Buttercup, Paintbrush---birds whose songs were silent---mountain bluebird, rosy-headed finch, red-winged blackbird, house wren, magpie, raven.

"I prayed for the dogs too, Mommy."

Tom's clouds---cirrus cumulus humilis, nimbostratus, alto cumulonimbus undulates. Tristan stirred restlessly. She opened her eyes and kissed him on his tousled head. "Good job. Mackay and Dotty will appreciate it."

"I miss them."

"So do I, but we'll see them soon." The silver cord floated on the wind, a detached fragile spider web strand drifting away from her outstretched hand.

"Tell me a story, Mommy," he said cheerfully. "Please."

"I don't know if I can think of one, honey." The dark faceless figure relentlessly attacking everything she loved. Who was it?

"I want to hear a story now!"

The ride smoothed. "Good news, folks," the pilot's voice crackled over the intercom. "I think we finally found some decent air. Better late than never."

Good Night Moon. Good night room. The Runaway Bunny. Magical illustrations. "Well, I know one about a little bunny just like you."

"I'm not a bunny," he protested. "I'm a little boy."

The plane went into a slow turn over Missoula, visible occasionally through breaks in thick gray clouds. Utter black despair. She shouldn't have come back. The

288

elaborate illusion of their brief happy life overwhelmed by ugly reality.

"Are we there yet, Mommy?"

"Just about, fasten your seatbelt." Sunlight flashed through the window as the plane began its decent, and in that brief moment, the memory of wind rippling across hay fields, the smell of sagebrush and dust and high spirited horses running free held her once again. In love with the man and place. Be there for us, Tom.

"Whee," Tristan joyfully cried as the plane landed hard and careened down the runway. "This is fun."

Out of the narrow, confining cabin, she stopped to breath in fresh, clean, cold Montana air. Betty was waiting for them, standing tall above the crowd in her long white wool riding coat and high polished boots.

"Aunt Betty." Tristan ran to her. She picked him up and pulled Allison into the same generous embrace.

"Oh God, Betty, thanks for coming. It's so awful."

"There, there, we'll get through this, you'll see."

"I want to get down," Tristan protested.

Allison sobbed, still clinging to her friend. "I promised myself I wouldn't do this."

"Never hurts to have a good cry," Betty reassured her, putting Tristan down. "But I've got some good news for you. I just talked to Jim and Billy. They released Carlos, and the colt's still hanging in there."

"Thank God." Carlos the Shaman, Guardian of the Windhorse, Master of Horses, High Priest in iridescent feathered robes---still more powerful than the forces of evil arrayed against them.

"I'll tell you that Carlos is one tough old bird, and Billy's quite the vet. Here, let me get that." Betty took the carry-on bag off her shoulder and set it on the ground. "God almighty, that's a heavy load, girl."

"Why are you crying, Mommy?" Tristan looked up at her curiously; departing passengers flowed around them.

Disconnected voices, strangers. Tom always met her at the airport. Where was he? "Because I'm happy that Carlos and Eagle are still with us."

"We prayed," Tristan proudly told Betty.

"Good for you." Betty handed her a wad of tissue and picked up the bag. "Come on, kids, let's get a move on."

"How's Afracela?" she asked as they walked toward the entrance.

"She's a brick. Don't worry, we've got you covered. My boys are there helping out and Jake's standing guard full time until Jim runs down the cowardly bastard who did this. Ben even called from Nevada. He's down there gambling his Thanksgiving away, said he'd come right back if we need him."

"Ben?" Her anger flared. "After what he said about me, I don't want his help."

Betty shrugged. "Maybe he's trying to make amends. It's hard to know with Ben."

They stepped through the automatic doors that

opened with a hiss into the fading afternoon sunlight. Ben's check was still on Tom's desk. She stopped at the curb, feeling off balance.

Betty took her arm. "You don't look so good, girl. Are you sick or just worn out?"

"Worn out and I've got a major headache. I don't think I'm strong enough to do this without Tom."

"Of course, you are. Take a load off, sit down," Betty ordered briskly, conducting her to a wooden bench.

Allison put her head in her hands and reached for Tom's gold horse. "Give me a minute." Carlos struck down. Eagle's Light slashed and disfigured, clinging to life. Their dogs attacked. She turned the pendant over and over in her hand. Finally, she looked up. "Who did this, Betty?"

"We don't know yet, but when Jim finds him, it's not going to be pretty. I've never seen that man so mad. As far as he's concerned, it's attempted murder, pure and simple. He's got everybody on it, including the state police."

Allison got wearily to her feet. "I hope he finds them this time. I don't understand why someone would do this." She looked down at Tristan waiting patiently at her side. The headache was unbearable.

Betty stepped closer, lowering her voice. "People do all kinds of bad things for all kinds of reasons, Allison, there's no telling the why of it sometimes. The important thing is to find them and stop them.

"Jim's taking a long hard look at Snook and his boys and all that ugliness with your horses and Dave. Then there's the guy from California who wrecked The Three Bears."

"Lyn? I can't see that."

Betty shook her head. "Well, I don't know the man, but the fact is somebody's got it in for you, and Jim's not counting anybody out." She bent down and picked up Allison's bag. "Come on, we better hit the road before the sun goes down. I've got some Advil in the truck."

Cars stopping and starting along the arrival and departure drive, announcements warning of security measures in effect, people waving goodbye or welcoming someone they loved. Kisses and hugs. Tom wasn't here. "I don't think I can go back."

"You mean to the Windhorse?" Betty took Tristan by the hand. "Of course, you can. It's your home. Jake's there 24/7 and I'll stay with you."

Allison hesitated. "I'm afraid for Tristan."

Betty patted Tristan with a gloved hand. "This boy's a Howard, Allison; he's not afraid, are you?"

"No."

"Well, come on then, guys, let's go home." Betty led them to the lot where her truck was parked. After strapping Tristan in the rear seat, she shook out several Advil and handed Allison a bottle of water. "Take these, sit back and relax."

The effect was almost immediate as if a pain switch had turned off in her head. As Betty pulled onto the highway, she closed her eyes. Soldiers closed in on the peaceful, sleeping Nez Perce camp, led by the hooded figure slashing at Eagle's Light. She sat up with a start.

"What's wrong?"

"Everything. I didn't know what I was getting us into, Betty, going up against Reverend Snook and his congregation." A foolish woman. Romantic, unrealistic dreams.

"You didn't get us into anything; we did the right thing. We stood up for Dave. You defended your horses and property," she replied emphatically.

Allison twisted in the seat to check on Tristan. Sound asleep, clutching his dinosaur. Traffic thinned as they left the city and headed for the mountains. "But what I don't understand is why they'd go after Carlos and our colt."

Betty shook her head. "Listen, there's nothing scarier in my book than a bunch of religious fanatics who think they're right and you're wrong. You're the historian, you should know that. Look at the Crusades. Hell, look at Ireland and the Middle East or that guy who killed the abortion doctor. Violent people, Allison, murderers, every one of them."

"It's hard to believe one of our neighbors would do this."

Betty slowed as they entered Darby, a collection of

twinkling lights at the bottom of Lost Trail Pass, the last outpost at the edge of darkness. They drove past the Mad Hatter where Tom bought his cowboy hat with the silver band and spray of raven feathers. She remembered how pleased he was with it and all the photos of famous clients on the wall, western movie stars, professional rodeo cowboys. A full size standup cardboard cutout of John Wayne guarding the door; the reverse crown hat Clint Eastwood wore in "Unforgiven". A great day.

And ahead, the crosses. She wrung her hands in silent agony. A hostile rain slick road. The hiss of failing airbrakes. Sabotage? A jackknifed trailer. Over the edge to the thundering river below. Fire. Screams.

She fought to stay awake, transporting herself to a better time and place. Family gathered around the swimming pool in California sunshine, yellow leaves on its aqua surface. Red hibiscus and purple clematis. Her father teaching Tristan to swim. Red, yellow, blue, green balloons, a pink angel food birthday cake. Phyllis in her kimono, Kat and Billy. Songbirds.

But dark scenes intruded. Snowdrifts piled higher than the ranch windows, cutting off the sun, wind shrieking in the eves. No lights, no power. Howard ghosts roaming the halls, blood on their hands. A hammering at the door. Tom's pistol too heavy to raise. Weak, powerless. The hooded figure was coming for her. Where was Tristan?

294

"Tristan!"

"What's going on?" Betty asked, touching her shoulder. "He's right here." They were climbing toward the pass.

Allison impulsively turned to check on him. Still sleeping. She fell back.

———————

Sealed caskets with charred remains lowered into stony ground on the bleak windswept hill. Tom's business partner cold and out of place in California clothes. Ben standing apart next to the General's headstone in a taupe military great coat at parade rest. Priscilla, a ghostly apparition, arms outstretched in agonized supplication, long blond hair swirling around her ravaged face.

———————

"Allison, wake up." Betty squinted into the last rays of sun falling behind steep hills.

Fear sent a shiver through her. "I don't belong here."

Betty pulled out to pass a slow moving farm truck but fell back in the glare of headlights from an oncoming car. "The hell you say."

"Seriously, Betty, I'm not up to this. I can't stand any more violence against people and animals I love, the destruction of beauty. I die every time a bluebird hits a

295

window and breaks its neck. You're a lot tougher than I am. You were castrating calves while I was playing hopscotch. Ben's right. I can't handle this. Tom was my buffer." Why have you left me?

Betty chuckled. "You don't think I care about bluebirds?"

"You know what I mean."

"Yeah, but to tell you the truth, I never liked cutting calves." Betty found the passing lane open and stomped on it, diesel engine roaring. "But just between us gals, I can think of a couple of men I wouldn't mind gelding."

Allison smiled. It was not possible to discourage Betty.

"And let me tell you something else, you don't need a man to break trail for you. You brought as much to your marriage as Tom did, maybe more, and neither of you were ever short on courage that I can recall."

They drove on in silence through snow covered pines, the dark mountain road pierced by their headlights on high beam, the curves becoming sharper.

Exhausted, she slumped against the door, heard the crackle of tires on ice.

Five crosses. Kat and Tristan walking down a lonely beach, carrying their shoes, leading Eagle's Light, footprints in the sand, washed away by a surging tide. A hooded figure following at a distance. "Kat!" Thundering surf drowned out her warning. Hands trembling, she raised Tom's pistol and pulled the trigger. Deafening! The figure staggered. She pulled the trigger again.

"Hey, girl!" Betty shook her arm.

"Yes?" Where were Kat's bodyguards?

"Get a hold of yourself; I'm right here with you."

"Sorry, it was Kat and Tristan. I can't get these frightening images out of my head. They just keep coming."

Betty reached over and patted her knee. "You're exhausted. You need some rest. Where are Dave and Katherine anyway? I thought they'd be with you guys."

They had stopped by the side of road. "Dave got bumped and he's on standby. Kat couldn't make it. Her big trial starts Monday."

"That's more important than what's going on over here?"

"She's the lead prosecutor, Betty." Wind buffeted the truck.

Betty nodded and pointed to the three crosses in the headlights. "You want to pay your respects?"

Only three, thank God. "I swore I wouldn't stop here again."

"Up to you. Hard to drive by like they aren't here. You want me to come with you?"

She glanced back at Tristan. "No, I'll go."

She stepped out of the truck into the cold night, forcing herself to kneel, hearing the roar of the river far below. Tom, come back to me. Sharp gravel dug into her knees. Wind ripped at her open coat, driving icy fingers into her chest. Their silver cord trailed away. Nothing to hold her. No reason to go on.

Allie. Allie.

She jumped to her feet.

Hang on to your faith and courage.

"I don't want to, Tom. I want to be with you." The wind swept her words away. No answer. She waited, then stumbled back to the truck, numb with cold, breathing in ragged gasps.

Betty reached across to pull the door shut behind her. "You alright?"

"I'm freezing."

Betty turned up the heat, took off her blanket coat and put it across Allison's shoulders. "Hells bells, girl, that's because it is freezing."

Slowly the warmth penetrated her core; her breathing slowed. Betty's coat smelled of apple pie, cinnamon, five boys and a husband waiting to welcome her home. "I heard Tom---calling me."

Betty looked at her skeptically. "People hear lots of things in the wind, including voices."

"No, it was Tom."

Betty took her hand. "It's probably the place."

"You're not listening to me; it was Tom." Was she

losing her mind? She desperately wanted Betty to believe her. "He told me to hang on."

"Well, that's good advice, sounds like Tom, couldn't have said it better myself."

Allison looked out the window at the crosses. "Do you think that's crazy?"

Betty put the truck in gear and checked the rear view mirror. "Well, it's different, but we all cope with the hand we're dealt the best we can, so who's to say."

"My folks think I ought to see a counselor; that it might help me come to terms with things---you know---things the way they really are."

Betty pulled onto the deserted highway. "Probably wouldn't hurt and might help. What do you think?"

She sat back in the seat, grateful to be warm and safe. Small things. "I think I'm lucky to have a friend like you."

Hang on to your faith and courage. She closed her eyes, forcing herself to visualize goodness. Afracela, Tristan and the dogs in the garden with Red Coyote tipping his head, listening. The hum of bees and chirp of crickets on sunflowers. Magpies on the fence, quiet, alert, watching. Horses all around. The sweet hot smell of summer, the feel of loamy rich black soil underfoot, deposited by the river over centuries. Silence. A lone eagle looking down on them.

Beyond fatigue, she slipped in and out of consciousness as they crossed Chief Joseph Pass and started down into the Big Hole Valley. Thick, dizzying clusters of snowflakes flew into the headlights, moths to flame. They were calling her name, low guttural chants in the night---Eagle from the Light, White Bird, Yellow Wolf, Poker Joe. Hihiyahihiyahihi. The fallen warriors, faces painted red and black, in all their finery, feathered lances, riding Appaloosa war ponies decorated with yellow and crimson lightning bolts, welcoming her home.

Tristan stirred in his car seat. "Mommy, did you go away?" he asked sleepily.

She reached back and took his warm little hand in hers. "Only for a minute, honey, I'm here now. It's alright; go back to sleep. We'll be home soon."

"Was Daddy there?"

"Yes, he was." The silver cord was strong in her heart once again.

DREAMS OF APPALOOSAS
Chapter Twenty-Four: The Horse Colt

Snow lifted and the sky cleared as they turned onto the ranch road. The sweep of the Big Hole Valley bathed in hammered silver moonlight spread out before them. The sheer grandeur of it always surprised her. Bare tepee poles at the Nez Perce Memorial stood guard over the misty river; a luminous glow at the base of dark timbered hills marked the Windhorse beyond.

Welcome home, Allie.

"It's so beautiful."

Betty smiled and touched her knee. "Yes, it is."

Tom's presence grew stronger; the pull of the silver cord more certain. The road rose and fell, following gentle contours of the land until they topped the last rise and looked down on the ranch compound ablaze with light.

"Are we there yet, Mommy?"

"Just about, honey. See?"

Ground fog swirled around yearlings in the outlying corral. They stomped and bucked, crowding along the rails. Mercury vapor lights gave the chaotic scene a wavering, greenish cast. Thank God you are all alive and well.

"Horsies!" Tristan exclaimed.

Betty stopped and Allison got out. "I'll be right back," she promised. "Mommy wants to say hello to our horses." She needed to feel their power before facing Eagle.

She rushed to them, putting aside thoughts of death and danger, her constant companions. She ran bare hands along velvet noses, reveling in the sensuous feel, calling them by name---Yellow Bird, Five Crows, Thunder Chief and Bird Alighting. She scratched their heads and rubbed their furry necks thick with winter coats, reveling in the warmth. "You feel like teddy bears."

She put her mouth up to Rainbow's nose and breathed in the sweet, hot aroma of life, an old Nez Perce custom establishing an eternal bond between a man and his horse in a culture where all living things are sacred.

Like excited children, they crowded around her, vying for attention, having overcome their fear and panic from that horrible night when they'd been roped and painted. She walked the fence line, yearlings puffing and snorting, following in ragged formation. She climbed up on the lower rail, leaned into the corral and embraced them once again. These were the horses she rode in her dreams.

A magical kaleidoscope of ever changing colors and shapes. Their power and energy part of the sacred spirit that would sustain her in this life and carry her across to be reunited with Tom in the next.

Hang on to that feeling, Allie. Never let it go.

I won't.

"I'll be back, guys." She reluctantly turned away.

"I think they're glad to see you," Betty remarked.

"Not as glad as I am to see them. You were right, Betty."

"About what?"

"About everything. I can do this."

"Never doubted it for a minute, girl."

Jake got out of the green and white patrol car parked by the house. He was carrying a rifle. "Evenin', ladies." He touched three fingers to his fur trooper's hat in a salute. "Glad to see ya made it; we've been waiting for ya."

The kitchen door opened, flooding the snow covered yard with light and Mackay came charging out, barking enthusiastically. Allison got down on one knee to greet him and he jumped into her arms, wiggling and squirming. The side of his head and neck was shaved and stitched. "Oh, my poor brave little dog, what did they do to you?"

Dotty Girl followed, limping as fast as she could go and went directly to Tristan. "Dotty! Dotty!" he cried in delight as the old black dog licked his face.

"So where's Jim?" Betty asked the Deputy.

"Still out with the state police lookin' for that California guy who's been harassing Mrs. Howard."

"You think he did this, Jake?" Betty took Tristan's hand and started for the house, signaling Allison to come with her.

"Don't know, Mrs. Christian, hard to say; maybe him, maybe them Snook boys, maybe somebody else. But don't you worry none," he patted rifle, "We got this place locked down tight for ya."

Allison looked over at the barn with dread as she turned to follow. Eagle's Light was in there fighting for his life. If he died, everything would be lost. She was afraid to find out.

Afracela met them at the door in her red "I Am the Cook" apron. Without a word, she swept up Tristan. Clinging to her, he laid his head on her shoulder and smiled back at Allison as they went inside. His delicate pink skin glowed against Afracela's rich brown weathered neck---blond hair and jet black braids. Tristan's Guardian Angel.

Allison followed. "How's Carlos? I'm so sorry this happened; I should have been here." The kitchen smelled of chili and coffee.

"Carlos is out with the colt."

"He's hurt; he shouldn't be out there."

"That's what I say, Mrs., but there's no keeping him away."

Billy was hunched over in Tom's place at the kitchen table. He sat up with a start and slowly got to his feet, copper skin pale with fatigue.

"Thank you for being here." She went over and hugged him. "How's Eagle doing?" His white cowboy shirt was rumpled and smelled of sweat.

"He's one hell of a fighter; I think he might make it. Your vet and Carlos are out there now." He pulled out a chair for her. "Come on, sit down for a minute. You've probably been up all night too."

She put a hand on the chair to steady herself. "No, I want to see Eagle first." Her Cambria seascapes swayed and blurred. Another time, another place, gone. Their future was at stake. Please, God, don't let him die.

Betty put an arm around her. "You go ahead; Afracela and I will take care of things here."

They left Mackay inside. Billy didn't want him in the barn where he might upset the colt. The moon was high, the sky clear; the stars twisting skeins of glittering pinpoints---Ursa Major, Andromeda, Camelopardalis. Dry powder snow squeaked underfoot.

Oh, Tom, all your stars are out. Are you with me?
Right beside you, Allie.

Jake was leaning against the car as they walked past. "Sheriff just called in and said to tell ya not to worry. He'll be around to see ya soon as he can."

"Please thank him for me, will you, Jake?"

"We could do this later if you don't feel up to it,"

Billy said.

"No, I'll be alright." Stay with me, Tom.

Still here.

"Good."

Billy looked at her quizzically as he slid the barn door open on its well oiled track and stepped back to let her go first. The warmth and smell of hay embraced her, a secure, protected buffer against what was to come. There were soft lights at the far end. The rows of stalls, normally full of weanlings this time of year, were empty. She supposed Billy wanted it quiet for the colt.

"This looks really bad, but fortunately, a lot of the cuts aren't too deep, including those in the genital area. He won't ever be as pretty as he was, but he should still be a great stud if we can save him."

She nodded, trying to control her emotions.

"We can't stitch up all the damage; he'd just tear them out when he feels better. But we've got the critical wounds closed, and we're pumping him full of antibiotics and fluids and trying to keep him as immobile as possible."

"Couldn't you take him to Pullman where you've got better facilities?"

"He wouldn't survive the trip, and we've got Carlos here. He has a calming effect on Eagle which is exactly what we need right now."

"Tom thinks he's a great healer."

"Could be," he replied with a weary smile.

306

"You don't believe in healing energy?"

He shook his head. "I'm an Indian so I guess I should, but my experience tells me penicillin works better."

Their local vet was sitting in one of Tom's lawn chairs in front of Eagle's stall. He stood as they came in, a small red faced man with a pot belly and no discernible butt in his loose jeans. "Good to see ya, Mrs. Howard." He extended a hand. "We got us a tough little horse here."

"Thanks for helping, Jeff, we really appreciate it."

His hand was rough and calloused. She could see Eagle's Light now, partially suspended in a sling, head hanging motionless, IV tubes taped to his flanks, crisscrossed slashes oozing blood everywhere. Her stomach turned over. "Oh, my God." She burst into tears.

The vet pulled her into an awkward embrace. "Here, here," he said gruffly. "Come on." He led her to the stall, an arm around her shoulder.

She'd been dreading this moment; it was worse than she imagined. Deep cuts on his flanks and underbelly, tape on his penis sheath. "Oh, Tom." She clamped a hand over her mouth.

The vet held her steady. Eagle stood, supported by the sling, legs splayed, eyes closed, breathing in short, laborious wheezes as if each desperate heave might be his last. Carlos was inches from Eagle's lowered head, sitting crossed-legged, head and face hidden under the rough grey blanket he used to protect newborn colts. He was chanting in a low deep, barely audible voice.

She fell to her knees, sobbing. "Oh God, please help our colt."

Jeff gently helped her to her feet. "Come on, Mrs. Howard, you go back to the house with Billy. We'll take good care of this little guy tonight."

DREAMS OF APPALOOSAS
Chapter Twenty-Five: My Journal

November 26, 3 a.m.

My dearest Tom,

I wasn't prepared to see Eagle's Light in such agony. I can't get the picture of Carlos and our little colt out of my head. I am overwhelmed by grief and sorrow and so angry at whoever did this I could kill him.

You and Kat no longer have to worry about me getting lost in my work. I tried that tonight, and all I could do was sit in the studio, staring at my lifeless paintings. They mean absolutely nothing to me. I have no inspiration. My world has become flat and colorless. I am at your desk, trying to get my rampaging emotions under control and hang on through this nightmare. I must keep Tristan safe.

Small things help calm me. The old horse cabbie hoof pick you bought us in that little funny antique shop in London. I open and close it, trying to recapture that day, walking down cobblestone streets in the drizzling rain, secure in your embrace. And the bundle of delicate black and orange flicker feathers you gave me with great fanfare when you came home late and I was anxiously waiting. A present that meant more to me than diamonds and still does.

But as many times as I turn these comforting, familiar objects over and over in my hand, feeling their weight and texture and intimate connection to you, I cannot force the shock of seeing Carlos out of my mind, wrapped in his blanket, facing our colt, once so full of life, now immobile, head down, slashed, disfigured and covered with blood, clinging to life.

I pace our room, stopping to reassure myself by touching your boots and guns and books and clothes, not knowing whether it is best to run before something else terrible happens, or fight. Will they come after Tristan? I can't bear another loss, and I know I couldn't stand losing him. I should have left him with my folks. I should have listened to them.

Ben's check is still on your desk. Its presence reminds me, despite all my brave protestations to the contrary, of my indecision---and yes, constant fear. Where in God's name, dear Tom, is my faith and courage?

Fear that I will never be rid of Lyn, that he will haunt me at every turn for the rest of my life. Fear that I am increasingly surrounded by unseen enemies who come in the night. Fear that Dave and I will be hounded by the likes of Reverend Snook to the ends of the earth. Fear *that they will come after our son.*

But as Betty has reminded me so many times---Tristan is a Howard, the Windhorse is his heritage, and I must stand firm for his sake. With your help, despite my doubts and fears, I will remain steadfast and loyal to our hopes and dreams.

I have just now torn up Ben's check, and for some strange reason, this frees me to be closer to you. Please pray for Eagle and wake me in the morning like you always do.

All my love,

Allie.

DREAMS OF APPALOOSAS
Chapter Twenty-Six: The Miracle

Tom woke her with a gentle nudge.

Time to go.

"Where?" she murmured, turning over, reaching for him.

We need to check on our colt.

Another nudge, more insistent this time. She looked into the baleful yellow eyes of Mackay. "Did something happen? I told them to come get me if something happened."

Still dressed, she swung off the bed, full of foreboding, and went to the window. The dog followed. It was dark, snowing and blowing. Jake's patrol car was buried to the windows; the barn where Eagle clung to life lost in the storm.

She leaned against the window frame, trying to shake off the premonition that something terrible had happened while she slept. The stars and blaze of ranch lights that welcomed her home only hours ago were gone, replaced by a hostile, smothering white wall.

"We can't lose Eagle, Tom. That would be the end. Will you come with me?"

Of course.

Mackay looked up at her.

"You too," she assured him. "We'll all go."

Hurriedly, she threw a red wool blanket around her shoulders and went into the bathroom. "No, he's still alive," she said to her image in the mirror, quickly brushing her teeth. "He has to be."

The drawn face that looked back at her was not reassuring. Allison reached for her feathered necklace and horse pendant. An angry wind pounded on the windows. Cold drafts and wandering ghosts closed in. "Come on, Mackay, let's go do something useful."

Collecting her snow boots from the closet, she went to Tom's desk; his holstered pistol and granite paper weight sat side by side. She traced the engraved cross and Faith and Courage lettering, then reached for the pistol. Cold to the touch.

Her gold wedding band glowed in the subdued light. What would save Eagle, the sword or the cross? A policeman or a priest?

A shaman.

"You mean Carlos?"

Yes.

"Before we go, I need to check on Tristan."

She found him where she'd left him the night before, safe in his bed, surrounded by his herd of dinosaurs.

Afracela was beside him in a rocking chair, knitting. Dotty Girl looked up as they came in, then relaxed with a sigh and closed her eyes.

Allison leaned over to kiss him. A child protected by a circle of soft, cuddly prehistoric beasts, including his oversized favorite, the indomitable T Rex, and his Guardian Angel Afracela Garcia.

"You've been here all night; you should get some rest," she suggested, although the old woman looked as vibrant as ever. Stay close to Afracela; she will protect you.

Afracela smiled and pointed to the sweater she was knitting. "I am happy here." White with blue ribbing, it had a small brown burro on the front with a red ribbon around its neck. "For the little boy."

"It's lovely; thank you so much." She took Afracela's brown weathered hand, energy from this remarkable woman flooded into her. The woman who led Carlos out of the fire, across the river and into the light. From Vera Cruz to the Windhorse. Parrots, Magpies, Burros, Appaloosas. "If you're okay here, I'm going out to see how our colt's doing."

Afracela nodded and smiled. "Please take coffee and rolls to the policeman and Carlos. They are in the kitchen. I make some for you too."

"Thank you. Where's Billy?"

"Asleep. Very tired."

"Carlos should get some rest too." She glanced at

314

the crisscross of stitches along Mackay's head. Her circle of brave defenders.

Afracela shook her head, rocking slowly. "He is a strong man."

"I'll take him coffee then."

"Miss Kat called from Los Angeles," Afracela said as she was leaving. "She and Mr. Dave are coming today on the airplane."

Kat wasn't supposed to come at all. "In this weather?" Draining fear gripped her.

A faint smile crossed Afracela's lined radiant face. "I will put a big roast in the oven for dinner."

"Thank you, they'll like that. I'll be back soon."

She paused in the kitchen to examine her painting of Tom and Tristan with Keith, remembering the intense joy she felt when she painted it. Would she ever be able to find that passion and inspiration again?

There were two paper bags on the table, one labeled "Carlos", the other "Police" in Afracela's childlike block letters. There was also a note from Betty. "Gone to feed your horses. Stay warm. Lots of Love."

The original pioneer woman goes out to feed our horses in a blizzard. "What a great friend."

Mackay wagged his tail in agreement.

Yes, she is.

"Thanks for being here."

Always.

She stuffed the paper sacks into a red day pack, put

on his drover coat, ski hat and winter gloves, and stepped out into the storm with Mackay on her heel. The snow was knee high; sharp needles stung her face. "Stay close," she ordered him, ducking into the wind. "I don't want to lose you."

Jake's car was just beyond the gate. He saw her coming, turned on his headlights and stepped out to meet her, bracing against the door to hold it open. Shouting to be heard over the roar of the wind, she gave him his coffee and rolls and told him she was going to the barn.

"Want me to come with you?"

"No, we'll be fine."

The barn was only a hundred yards away but she couldn't see it. Tom told her his father had strung ropes from the house in the old days so he and Ben wouldn't get lost. When she turned to check on the dog, she tripped, falling to her hands and knees.

Get up, Allie.

Mackay crowded in, pushing, urging her to move.

"Alright, I heard you." She struggled to her feet, brushed herself off, and stared into the whiteout. No shadows, no shapes. Unrelenting white. "Where are we?" Unsure, she and Mackay plowed on, groping their way a step at a time through drifting snow.

She smelled exhaust and heard an engine. "Listen." Tom's red farm tractor appeared out of the storm, lurching along, an oversized hay bale hung on the bayonet loader. Betty, in a florescent pink snowmobile suit, was at the wheel.

"Hey, kids, what are you doing way out here on a day like this?" she shouted jovially, her face red with cold.

"Trying to find the barn," Allison shouted back.

"Right in front of you, girl, right where it's always been." She pointed to the barn doors, faintly visible through the falling snow.

"Thanks." Steady, undaunted Betty had saved her again.

"We'll see you later then, got a bunch of hungry ponies counting on me." And with a wave of her hand, she was off, bouncing and bumping through deep snow, as easily as if driving down a city street.

Allison stepped out of the storm into a sanctuary. Wind sang high overhead in the barn rafters, melodious, sonorous organ tones. Hay whispered under foot as they walked past darkened stalls, some occupied now, some not, toward a golden light.

Head bowed, Mackay at her side, she prepared herself for the sight of Eagle and Carlos, slashed and brutalized by unknown hands. "Please, God, heal them." Horses snorted and snickered at her in a rhythmic soothing chant as she passed by. She gripped the feathered necklace and gold horse, her crucifixes. The Church of the Horse. Quietly, respectfully, they proceeded toward the light.

Carlos, wrapped in a flowing white robe, a shotgun at the ready, stepped silently out of the shadows.

"Don't worry, it's only me."

He nodded, lowered the gun, and motioned her forward. One side of his head was shaved, bruised and swollen, crisscrossed with stitches like Mackay. The remaining white hair cascaded over his shoulder giving him a twisted, lopsided look.

Carlos dropped to his knees and gently embraced Mackay. "The brave dog," he intoned solemnly, giving a blessing.

Directly behind him, Eagle stood on his own in the stall, head up, eyes closed, breathing steadily, leaning against the formidable bulk of Happy. "My God," she said in wonder, stepping forward. The IV tubes were still connected to the colt's flanks but the slashes no longer oozed blood. A pulsing energy filled the barn, evidence of things not seen. Calmness settled over her.

Happy turned toward her, his lower lip quivered and head bobbed slowly in recognition. Hot tears burned down her cheeks. She put her arms around his neck and hugged him, in harmony with a boundless universe. "This is a miracle, Tom."

It is.

Carlos stood impassively behind her, watching with ancient, obsidian Mayan eyes. Mackay sat at his side, a stone statute.

Still crying, she turned to him. "How can Tom and I

318

ever thank you?"

He wrapped his white robe around him and bowed. "Your coyote told me what to do in my dream."

"Red Coyote?"

He nodded.

A harsh crash shattered the moment. The barn door rolled open. Carlos picked up the shotgun and stepped in front of her. She heard the sharp click as he released the safety.

Jim came striding toward them, white Stetson under his arm, snow on his black parka, unshaven, crow's feet deep and jagged around sunken eyes. "I'm glad I caught you, Allison."

"What's wrong?" Kat and Dave in a terrible plane crash. Flaming wreckage tangled in snow covered trees high on a mountain pass. Bodies burned beyond recognition.

"We found Lyn Barnett."

"Where?" Time stopped, nothing moved.

"Down at the Blue Anchor Bar in Twin Bridges. This time he really has a gun."

"What are you going to do?"

"Go down there and put a stop to this. I don't know if he tried to kill Carlos and the colt to send you some kind of sick message, but I sure as hell am going to find out." Jim ran his hand over his unshaven face and put on his hat.

"Do you want me to come with you?"

"No, stay in the house and lock the doors until you hear from me. I'm not making the same mistake twice. This guy's dangerous."

"Okay."

"You still have Tom's pistol handy?"

"Yes."

"Can you use it?

"If I have too."

DREAMS OF APPALOOSAS
Chapter Twenty-Seven: The Last Act

Allison and Mackay hesitated in the doorway of the old living room with its bloody history. Dusty dead animals, the General and his cold, killer eyes. Lights flickered. The relentless winter storm sent shudders and ominous groans along the high beamed ceiling, freezing air crept through chinks between ancient logs.

Her Eagle from the Light painting was still on the mantel; it would be a fitting present for Billy. Echoes of gunfire and screams of the dying blocked her way.

Faith and Courage, Allie.

She forced herself into the forbidding room, pistol secure in its shoulder holster under her left arm. "Come on, we can do this." Mackay assumed his place on her heel.

The old planked floor protested angrily underfoot as she approached the General in his arrogant pose of eternal defiance. The lights went out, living room doors crashed shut, Mackay growled.

"Lyn!" Fear crawled over her. Adrenalin pumping,

she ·struggled to pull the pistol from its holster. "Don't come near me!"

Take it easy, Allie, it's only the wind.

She yanked the pistol free, held it in two hands at the ready. The cold, dead, darkened room closed in around her, filled with ghosts from the past. In the distance, the generator started and seconds later the lights surged on. Heavy doors creaked back and forth behind her. "Who's there?" She swung Tom's pistol around the room, searching for the intruder until it came to rest pointing straight at the General's heart.

Put it away, Allie.

Holstering the pistol, she went to get her painting, looking at the warrior's fierce dark eyes, Billy's eyes, Carlos and Afracela. The first Americans.

The painting was heavy. Arms spread wide, she side-stepped out of the living room and down the hall, grateful to reach her studio with its bright lights and warm stove. She put Eagle from the Light in the place of honor next to the painting of Tom and her in their passionate swirl of red hearts.

Some of your best work, Allie. You should be proud of yourself.

Mackay curled up by the Franklin stove. "I don't think I'll ever be able to do anything this good again." Love and inspiration lost, buried under smothering layers of anger and fear.

What happened to your big idea, Dreams of

Appaloosas?

Redemption. Deliverance. Thousands of Appaloosas leading wandering spirits of the Nez Perce home, lifting the curse that haunted the Windhorse since 1877. "I can't see it anymore, Tom. That magical parade across the sky is gone."

Don't give it up, Allie; start with the sky.

"The sky?"

That Montana blue sky you're always working on. Once you get that right, everything will fall into place.

"Really? My God, Tom, sometimes you come up with the strangest ideas."

Trust me; it will be the beginning of something truly grand. Go find it.

She closed her eyes and once again smelled the sage, felt the sun on her back, the warmth of a horse. She put her foot in the stirrup and stepped up into a better world, a world of grace and endless possibilities where Tom, the twins and Red Coyote were waiting.

The harsh, insistent ring of the telephone startled her. Lyn? Or had something happened to Kat and Dave? They should have been here by now.

"Allison."

His gruff voice, unexpected and shocking. "Ben?" There was laughter and loud music in the background.

"I been callin' and callin' but you never call me back. Why the hell is that anyway?"

He sounded drunk. Her anger flared. "Because we

have nothing more to say to each other." She stared out the window, trying to find Jake's patrol car.

"Hell, maybe you forgot. We got us a deal, lady." His voice was muffled.

"What are you talking about? What deal? Where are you? I can barely hear you." There was a loud cheer in the background.

"I'm in Elko, Nevada, playin' cards, sister, an' I'm talkin' about my buyin' you out," he replied loudly. "Why the hell haven't you cashed my check?"

Tell him.

She reached for Tom's pendant. "I tore it up. We don't have a deal, Ben, I'm not selling and that's final."

A long pause. "Now why would you do a stupid fuckin' thing like that?"

"Because Tom and I are going to create a sanctuary for Appaloosas here. I know he talked to you about it and so have I.....*"

"Tom's dead," he interrupted harshly. "When you gonna get that through your head for Christ sake?"

"He's---not---dead."

Ben snorted. "Well, he sure as hell is to everybody else, lady. Dead and buried with those kids of his. Christ, you're as crazy as that two timin' Priscilla."

Ragged, thick, heavy, his breathing echoed over the phone.

Stand up to him, Allie.

"You have no right to talk about her like that, she's a

324

wonderful woman." The specter of a hollow-eyed Priscilla drifted across the room, longing to see her beloved Ben once again.

"The hell I don't; she's a bitch. You're 'nothin' but a couple of whores, lady. I warned Tom about the both of you, but he was too fuckin' smart for his own fuckin' good and now it's too damn late."

"I'm not going to listen to any more of this, we're done."

"We're not done 'til you get the hell off my ranch!"

Allison slammed the phone down, hands shaking, head buzzing with rage. "Tom? Tom?" It was getting dark; Kat and Dave were late. Something terrible had happened---a plane crash, a car wreck, the drug dealer. Enemies everywhere. Ben cursing and threatening. "Where's Tristan?"

Safe with Afracela, Allie. Get a grip on yourself.

The room swayed; Mackay barked and ran to the door. She put her hand on the pistol. This time she would be ready. I won't be a victim.

"Hey, kiddo." Kat and Dave were standing in the doorway.

"Kat, thank God you're okay. I was worried sick."

"Well, here we are alive and well," Kat announced, grandly.

She rushed to hug them both. "You'll never know how glad I am to see you guys. How'd you get through in this storm?"

Dave's blue parka was covered with melting snow. "It was rough coming over the pass but we made it."

"It was more than that, but we're here; that's the important part." Kat had a bottle of red wine in one hand and three glasses in the other, held upside down by the stems. "So where's Tristan?"

"Setting the table with Afracela. He loves to help out." Still on edge, she tried to control her jumpiness. Don't pace, don't keep looking at the door.

"I'll bet he's good at it." Kat set the glasses and bottle down on the drafting table. "I smelled Afracela's roast on the way in. It smells delicious. Let's have a drink."

Dave shook his head. "Maybe later. I'm going out to see Eagle if you don't mind. Billy says he's going to make it. That's really a piece of good news, sis."

"It's the best. He's very weak but like Billy says, he's a fighter." Good news pushed into the background by Ben and Lyn.

When Dave had gone, Kat opened the wine; Allison went over to join her. "I thought you weren't coming because of your trial."

"Being here is more important. I told them I had a family emergency and they'd just have to get along without me." She noticed the pistol. "What's going on?"

"Lyn's showed up again. He's in a bar in Twin Bridges and this time has a gun. Jim went down there a couple of hours ago."

"Christ, Allie, what happened?"

"I don't know yet. Jim thinks he might have slashed Carlos and the colt."

"Really? I guess it's possible. Come on, let's sit down."

She poured two glasses of wine, handing her one. "Is something else wrong? You look terrible."

"I just got off the phone with Ben. He threatened me."

"What do you mean?"

"He's furious that I didn't take his buyout. He was drunk and called me a whore."

"What an asshole! Who does he think he is?"

"He thinks it's his ranch. I hung up on him."

"Good for you. This has gone far enough."

Allison waited, unsure of what to say.

"We're going to get a restraining order to keep him off this place and away from you. But first, let's have a drink." Kat raised her glass. "Here's to us and to the Windhorse."

Allison smiled in spite of herself. She'd always been in awe of Kat's ability to take charge in a crisis.

"You know this stuff isn't half bad. I bought it at the airport on our way over."

Allison tried to steady her glass. "That never worked with Lyn."

"Like Betty says, this isn't California, kiddo. Jim's the law here." Kat shook out a cigarette and offered her one.

"Thanks. I see your point, but I don't want to make things worse than they already are."

Kat lit their cigarettes, keeping her eyes on her. "Listen to me, Allie. There's something very wrong with Ben Howard. It seems to me he has a pathological obsession with putting these ranches back together, wouldn't you say?"

The wine and cigarette rushed to her head. "I don't know. He's certainly very angry." She floated above it all, looking down on the cemetery where Ben stood apart from the others as he had on that stormy day. At parade rest, bareheaded in his taupe military great coat, staring off into the distance. An odd stance for a mourning brother. Why is that, Tom?

I'm not sure.

"The point is Ben's not entitled to a goddamn thing. We need to put a stop to this right now before it goes any further, just like we should have stopped Lyn. If we'd done that, we wouldn't be sitting here with the doors locked and you with a pistol under your arm like Annie Oakley."

"You're right."

"I know. With the exception of Tom, I don't trust most men when it comes right down to it."

Allison leaned back, relieved to have her big sister with her. "Well, you must trust Billy."

"We'll deal with Billy later. I came for you, Allie."

"You'll never know how glad I am to see you, Kat. I'm really losing it." She went over to build up the fire.

"What do you mean?"

She swung the heavy stove door open, put a fresh log on the grate and threw her cigarette in after it. "My mind is out of control. I don't know if I'm dreaming or awake anymore; everything's all mixed up."

The logs burst into flames. "I had a dream about that drug dealer trying to kill you, at least I think it was him, or it was the guy who slashed our colt and clubbed Carlos. I couldn't see his face. Anyway, he was following you and Tristan down the beach by your condo. I shot him with Tom's pistol. I think I killed him. It was all very real." The heat from the stove was so intense she had to back away.

"A world without those people would definitely be a better place, kiddo. Seems to me you're just unconsciously protecting those you love. I don't see anything bad about that."

"You don't?" Dreams as violent as reality.

Kat took a long drink, finishing her wine. "No. Frankly, I think you're under what to most people would be a crushing burden. What you're trying to do here is downright heroic."

She fought back tears. "I don't want to be heroic, Kat, I just want to hang onto the good things and move on."

"Look around this room, Allie. Look at these

beautiful paintings. These all represent good things, don't they?"

"Yes, they do." Tom and the twins, Tristan and the horses. The hills and sky. Transporting her to a better world full of hope and love. "But I've been so upset lately, I can't paint."

"Well then, you'd better force yourself to get back at it. You know, I probably gave you some bum advice about getting lost in your art. Now that I think about it, it's your salvation, no doubt about it."

"That's what Tom was saying just before you got here."

Kat nodded slowly. "He's right." She turned to the Eagle from the Light painting. "And speaking of art, where are you going to hang my favorite picture?"

"I'm not. I'm giving it to Billy for everything he's done for us."

"What a wonderful gift. He loves that painting."

The outside studio door rattled. She reached for the pistol.

Kat stepped in front of her. "It's only Jake; I'll get it."

He came in, breathing hard. "Sheriff just called in; there's been an incident."

"An incident? What does that mean?" Kat asked.

"That guy down at the Blue Anchor shot himself. He's dead."

Chapter Twenty-Eight: My Journal

December 4, 11 p.m.

Tom,

I can't believe Lyn shot himself.   It seems so completely unreal, so utterly senseless, but then very little makes much sense to me these days.   All I know is it weighs me down, agonizing over every last detail from the past.   I vacillate between relief that he's finally out of my life and feeling guilty that somehow I could have stopped him, although I don't know how.   And I still can't believe he slashed Carlos and Eagle.   Why?   To get back at me?

I guess we'll never know, and I'll have to live with another nagging uncertainty.   At least in the aftermath of all this, we did get a couple of things cleared up. When Jim brought the Snook boys in for questioning and they realized the gravity of the charge, they readily admitted to painting our horses and trashing Dave's trailer, but absolutely denied attacking Carlos and Eagle.

At Jim's suggestion, Reverend Snook brought them out to the ranch to apologize to Dave and me. They seemed genuinely contrite. Although Kat tells me I'm terribly naïve about people (which I am), I tend to believe them. I know they're bad kids sometimes, but I can't believe they're that bad and neither does Jim.

At any rate, in spite of their crime and assault on Henry, Jim recommended community service in lieu of jail time because it is a first offense and their parents are long time members of the community in good standing. I suppose that's all for the best.

That means, of course, that whoever did this, for whatever reason, is still out there somewhere, unless it was Lyn. Anyway Jim and the State Police are looking 24/7 but so far no leads. I'm frightened but determined not to let fear overwhelm me or stop us from pursuing our dream.

I haven't forgotten Red Coyote's warning about very real danger, however, and keep your pistol handy at all times to back up my brave words. I look for Red Coyote every day but haven't seen him since before Thanksgiving when Ben tried to shoot him. I hope nothing's happened.

When I told Kat about his abusive call from Nevada, she insisted we get a restraining order which Jim has promised to enforce to the letter. You'll have to forgive my paranoia, Tom, but sometimes I think your brother is largely responsible for the darkness that continues to hangs over this place.

Fortunately, we're into Christmas break at school so I can stay home close to Tristan and the horses where we have a lot of good people protecting us. Dave's been staying here during the break, and Betty comes out frequently and sometimes spends the night. Henry has been coming every day too, bright and early, despite the cast on his hand, to help us with the horses.

Eagle's Light is slowly but surely regaining his strength. He has such a big, big heart. Tristan and I walk him a little more each day. I'm not sure who benefits more, maybe we all do. All I know is that my strength and courage is renewed when I'm close to him and his indomitable spirit frees my mind from anxiety and fear. Tristan thinks it's all great.

I'm also very encouraged by how the community has rallied around us. People come out every day, including some members of the Church of the Divine Light, believe it or not, to extend their sympathies and ask how they can help. I've also received a big pile of cards and phone calls from kids at school, reminding me why I still enjoy teaching. All in all these sincere expressions of support have gone a long way toward getting rid of that sense of isolation I've sometimes felt here.

Kat and Billy have been with us continually since the attack, of course, and only left yesterday when Billy felt Eagle had finally stabilized. I gave Billy my Eagle from the Light painting and I could tell he was very moved.

Rather than go back to Los Angeles right away, Kat went up to Pullman with him, for how long she didn't say, and I didn't ask. All I know is he makes her happy. And she makes him happy. I can see it in their faces, the way they look at each other, the same happiness we share.

While he was here, Billy was busy planning a Nez Perce children's program with the Appaloosas. He also promised to start searching for some new mares to replace the ones we lost in the accident. Although at the moment all I can do is put one foot in front of the other, I assured him I was still very enthusiastic and promised to become actively involved as soon as I can.

Kat had a hard time leaving. I could see the worry in her eyes when she searched my face but I tried to assure her I would be okay. I'm sure she thinks I'm losing myself in a world of dreams, fantasy and imagination. To ease her mind, I even promised I would see a counselor if that would make her happy.

I hope and pray I can sleep tonight. Sometimes, when I'm alone like this, exhaustion overtakes me and I feel stripped of all emotion. Running on empty. I know I must find a way through this long gray tunnel and reach Tristan, Happy, and the horses and dogs who are waiting for me at the other end.

What happened to our silver cord that binds us together, Tom? I know it's still here, but to find it I have to get back to my art, my only salvation and lasting bridge to you. So I must force myself to pick up my paint brush once again and work. I can't stand living in a flat, colorless world any longer; I need light and far horizons.

Isn't it ironic that when I don't feel capable of painting a thing, all those Montana ranch pieces I sent to the gallery in Cambria are selling like hot cakes? Somehow I have to recapture the inspiration that drove me to paint them.

Actually Betty, that paragon of common sense, had a great idea to get me going again. She suggested doing a coloring book about life on the ranch and have Tristan do the coloring. So that's exactly what I'm going to do first thing in the morning.

At long last I feel sleepy. I love you Tom. I'll get through this, I will, so please keep loving me.

Always and forever,

Allie.

DREAMS OF APPALOOSAS

Chapter Twenty-Nine: Happy the Very Brave Horse

Allison sat cross-legged on the floor beside Tristan at his little art table while he colored in the animals she had outlined for him. Dotty and Mackay slept on either side of them.   Moonlight flooded through the windows, reflecting off snow that rose and fell in drifts along the sills like soft ocean waves. Silent snow that would mask hoof beats if Tom was riding by, forging through the feathery chest high powder on Keith. But there was no sign of him.

Instead, vivid images of Lyn lying face down in a widening pool of blood on the dirty linoleum floor of the Blue Anchor Inn in Twin Bridges, Montana. After all he had done for her. High above Palm Springs, a carpet of lights across the desert floor; a barbeque, live music, champagne, important people calling her by name. So this is the young artist…..

Who turned on him. Her teacher, her mentor, her

lover. Reduced to a shell of a man. Alone in the world except for a few late night cowboys who didn't give a damn and Jim Christian who tried to stop him. I'm sorry, Allison, but he took one look at me, put the gun in his mouth and pulled the trigger. What would that look like? Jim hadn't told her.

Pay attention, Allie. You need to help Tristan.

"Tom, you're here. I'm so thankful."

Tristan, head down in concentration, colored furiously, filling in Allison's drawings of horses, dogs, coyotes, eagles, ravens, magpies, antelope, moose, elk, deer, beaver, badgers--- hills, mountains, rivers and clouds.

He had left a one line note on the bar: "Allison, I did my best. I'm sorry it wasn't good enough for you."

"My God in heaven, why?"

That doesn't matter, Allie, it's over. Forgive yourself and move on.

"I don't know if I can." Lyn's corpse on the floor of The Blue Anchor. A vague shapeless form. Was the wound so massive he died instantly or did he linger in pain and agony, regretting what he had done? Jim offered no details.

Tristan look up at her questioningly, a pink crayon poised in one fist, a green one in the other.

"It's all right, honey, Mommy's just---don't worry. Those are wonderful colors. You're doing a great job, keep going."

Happy the Very Brave Horse was to be their book. Tristan was coloring in the title page. A healthy Eagle's Light leaned against Happy. Red Coyote looked on. Betty's idea was a great success.

Irrepressible, optimistic Betty deserved her own painting, something heroic in the mold of those pioneer women who pushed across the country in covered wagons and poke bonnets, sometimes burying a husband or child along the way, but never losing their faith and courage.

A pioneer woman in her pink florescent snowsuit! "Faith and courage," she said to Tristan. "That's what will get us through."

He stopped coloring. "Is that good?" he asked with blue-eyed innocence.

"Yes, it is."

Did you notice he's making Happy pink?

A door closed somewhere in the old wing of the house with a loud hollow boom. "Tom?"

He's coloring Happy pink. I've never seen a pink horse.

"Yes, I see that. What was that noise?"

And Eagle is green.

"Well, it's his book, Tom." The loud ticking of the grandfather clock penetrated the studio walls. "He can make them any color he wants." She faltered, listening.

Still....

A chill washed over her. The low fire in the Franklin

stove burst into angry orange red flames. "Did you hear that?"

Hear what?

Another booming sounded deep in the bowels of the house. She got to her feet. Dotty stood up; Mackay went to the door.

"Who are you talking to, Mommy?" Tristan dropped his crayons.

"Daddy. I'm talking to Daddy." She picked up Tom's pistol off the drafting table.

Be careful, Allie!

"Is he out there?" Tristan pointed to the window.

She put the pistol down. "No, he's right here with us."

Tom liked to sit in the studio at night while she painted, quietly doing his paper work, occasionally getting up and coming over to kiss her on the back of the neck.

"Tom?"

"Mommy!"

She was startled to find Afracela standing silently in the doorway in her Coat of Many Colors. "Oh, I didn't see you. Did someone come in? I heard a door slam."

Afracela nodded. "The wind I think, Mrs. Carlos has gone to look. I will take the boy to bed and stay with him."

"Oh, that's not necessary; we're finished here. I'll take him. You get some rest, please."

"No, not tonight," Afracela replied firmly, picking up Tristan. Dotty Girl joined them while Mackay looked on.

Let her take him, Allie.

"But why?"

Tristan will be safe with her.

Afracela waited patiently while she kissed him goodnight. "I love you, honey. Daddy loves you too. We'll be up soon."

Alone in the studio, she stood for a moment at the edge of the moonlight, listening, watching. Jake and his truck were gone but there were lights on in the barn. Overhead, she heard the squeak of stairs and muffled footsteps as Afracela carried Tristan into his bedroom.

"What do I do now, Tom?" She looked around the empty room, hoping to catch sight of him. A glimpse, a touch would be enough.

Carry on. See it through.

"For God's sake," she replied, exasperated. "See what through? This?" She sat down at her drafting table and surveyed the wreckage. Stacks of false starts, unfinished renderings, far short of the grand concept that once inspired her.

Alarmed, Mackay came over to sit beside her.

Get back to your art. Get on with your work.

"Dreams of Appaloosas?"

Quit feeling sorry for yourself. Get started.

"But how?"

Start with Happy who brought us together and

inspired our dream. Do what you always do, make it up, create something new and wonderful.

She stopped pacing and went to Tristan's work table. Mackay followed. There it was, waiting for her to give it life. Happy would be the lead horse in that grand vision she had of Appaloosas charging across her Montana sky, the vision that had collapsed into a pile of static, lifeless paper. The phone began to ring. She ignored it.

You're inspired, aren't you?

"Maybe, let me think." It had to be monumental, spiritual. True. Everlasting. The phone stopped ringing but now Mackay was barking furiously. The house shuddered around her. Something was terribly wrong.

There's a fire! Get Tristan!

A river of smoke crept across the floor. Screams of horses and men in the night. Naked brown children in burning tepees. Women throwing themselves into the flames to save them. Soldiers shooting. The deadly whine of bullets.

She grabbed the pistol and ran for the door, flying into the hall, blinded by smoke. Afracela in her Coat of Many Colors was coming down the stairs carrying Tristan in her arms. "Sheriff Jim called you. He said Mr. Ben wasn't in Nevada when your horse was stabbed. He was here all the time."

Afracela ran toward the door with Tristan. Allison followed but stopped when she saw Ben standing in the old living room in his taupe military great coat, wreathed in smoke, hair wild, feet apart, hands behind his back. Snarling, Mackay charged, but the big man kicked him aside.

"Ben!" she screamed. "What are you doing?"

"Claiming my birthright," he replied in a toneless voice, fixing her with cold grey hypnotic eyes. "Taking my ranch back." Behind him, flames shot up the old dry walls, licking at the portrait of General Zachery Howard in his heroic Indian fighter pose; glass-eyed animal heads burst into flame.

"It's not yours," she protested hoarsely.

"It's always been mine, whore." Ben and the General watched impassively as the flames grew higher and troopers methodically clubbed women and children to death.

"Stop!" Allison raised the pistol.

"You're not up to it, lady," he sneered. "And neither was Tom."

The General's portrait, ringed with fire, sagged and fell off the wall with a crash of breaking glass. Reverend Snook and his congregation in black stood at the edge of the flaming river, singing "Onward Christian Soldiers" while Nez Perce tepees burned.

"You and that bastard son of yours were supposed to go on that trip too."

Paralyzed, she watched as Tom's silver Kenworth skidded over the edge in slow motion, trailer first, carrying all her hopes and dreams. "You sabotaged their truck, you murdered them, you slashed our colt!" She pulled the trigger.

It misfired with an impotent click. "Goddamn you, Ben Howard!"

Spreading his arms wide, he advanced, welcoming her into a deadly embrace just as a massive fireball engulfed him with an unearthly roar.

Intense heat sucked the breath out of her. She fell into the abyss. "Tom!"

I've got you, Allie.

He carried her out into the cold clear night, cradled in his arms. Tristan waited with Afracela in the snow. Carlos, a dazzling vision in iridescent feathers and gold, wrapped his cape around her. Mackay and Dotty Girl crowded close as the rumbling tornado of flame spiraled skyward and disappeared into the stars.

On a hill overlooking the valley, silhouetted in the moonlight, Red Coyote watched over them with a mournful howl.

DREAMS OF APPALOOSAS
Chapter Thirty: Dreams of Appaloosas

The incandescent lemon sun was high in the robin's egg blue sky as the Nez Perce passed through the camp along the meandering frosty gold Big Hole River, trailing a curtain of rust red dust that wavered in the summer heat over knee high verdant grass, heading west toward Chief Joseph Pass, going home to their beloved Wallowa Valley.

Dogs darted in and out of the slow moving parade of men, women, children, and babies on cradle boards. All dressed in their finest deerskins painted in rich earth tones, decorated with glass beads, cowrie shells, porcupine quills, and white ermine. Some mounted, some walking, the elderly and sick on travois. A few stepped out of line to tie feathered charms---blue-black raven, orange flicker and eagle feathers---to tepee poles in remembrance of their suffering and sorrow.

Leading the procession was Eagle from the Light riding Happy painted with yellow lightening bolts, blue and green Windhorse prayer flags draped around his neck. The old warrior sat straight and proud on his prancing mount, bare-legged, head shaved, face a mask of ochre and black, wearing his blood red blanket coat, a war club swinging rhythmically from his wrist.

Ahead, steep, craggy purple mountains, snow streaming off rugged summits. Soaring eagles followed in their wake, riding updrafts, circling ever higher into an eternal blue vault of sky that framed the shimmering sun.

And on either side of this exodus, stretching the length and width of the valley, Appaloosas, thousands of them, some forging ahead, others dropping behind to graze. Trotting, wheeling, turning, splashing across streams in a continuous rainbow of white, black, grey, brown, dun, buckskin, and strawberry roan. Allison watched silently from the top of Horse Heaven Hill on Moon Woman, Red Coyote and Mackay at her side.

She stretched in the saddle, bracing herself with one hand on Moon Woman's rump.

Well, you finally got the sky right, Allie.

"Thank you, Tom." Red Coyote looked up at her and tipped his head.

It's quite a sight, isn't it? Nobody will ever see anything like this again. You did good, honey.

She held his gold horse between thumb and forefinger. A warm breeze passed over them. "I've never worked harder." She felt his embrace.

It's your best work.

"That's what Kat says too. But I was so sad when I finished, I sat down and cried and cried, I couldn't stop. I felt like it was the end of everything."

The flowers covered the hilltop around them in a pool of brilliant waving colors. Prairie Smoke, Scarlet Gilia, Bitterroot, Rock Penstemon, Lupine, Yarrow and Paintbrush.

It's not the end; it's only the beginning.

She smelled vanilla aftershave and the Black Label on his breath as he pressed warm lips to her neck. That old familiar quiver of anticipation ran through her.

"Were you talking to Dad, Mom?"

She turned to Tristan who'd ridden up on Eagle's Light. Silhouetted against the sun, he looked like his father. "Yes, I was."

These conversations no longer surprised him. "Is there something going on down there?" He pointed to the Nez Perce Memorial. Eagle's nostrils flared; he pawed the ground. Tristan patted his scarred neck to calm him.

She smiled. The stallion saw what she saw. "Oh, we were remembering what it looked like on that wonderful day when their spirits were finally set free and they returned to the land of their ancestors."

Tristan stood up in the stirrups and looked down at the deserted memorial. "Like in your painting, the big one that's in sections? The one I had to carry around for you all the time before you sent it to that art museum in Cody?"

She laughed. "Yes, like in that painting." Tristan turned his horse to face her. He was as handsome as

Tom; the light of her life. Learning to train horses with Carlos and helping Billy and Kat with the Nez Perce summer camps, and with Dave's encouragement, becoming an accomplished rock climber. She was very proud of him.

"You know, Mom, I always wondered why you put that guy out front on our old blind horse."

"Happy?"

"Yeah."

Still, that wide blue-eyed innocence. Tristan didn't remember her painting of Eagle from the Light or the part of the old house that burned to the ground with the General and Ben Howard in it. It was just as well.

"I put him on Happy because he was brave and noble like your horse." She reached over and patted the stallion affectionately.

"I get it. That's cool," he replied seriously.

"Well, I'm glad you approve, so does your father."

"But you should have made him pink, Mom. Happy, I mean."

Allison looked at her son. "You remember that?"

"Sure. And I bet Dad does too. You should ask him."

"I'll do that."

What a kid. You did good, honey. The twins and I are proud of you. I love you.

"I love you too, Tom."

Faith and Courage, Allie. Faith and Courage.

Dennis Higman and his wife, Lee, an artist, live in the remote high mountain desert of southwest Idaho with their horses and dogs. Surrounded by wild animals and birds with a relentless will to survive, amidst pottery shards and magnificent arrowheads of the Shoshone Indians who once hunted here, it is a place where imagination thrives and spirits ride the wind.

This is the world that inspired **Dreams of Appaloosas, A Love Story,** where reality is not necessarily what we see but what we feel, believe and create. A world where those we love, family, friends, and animals are a constant presence, a love that never dies. A place of incredible beauty but haunted by a violent past with unmarked graves of the first Americans whose wandering spirits cry out for redemption.

Dennis is the author of two previous novels, **Pranks** and **Laura Jordon** and, with Lee, wrote, **Dot's Story**, a children's book about their shelter dog.